Hinterland

L. M. Brown

Fomite

Burlington, VT

ISBN: 978-1-947917-58-3
Library of Congress Control Number: 2020940970
Fomite
58 Peru Street
Burlington, VT 05401
www.fomitepress.com

For Gloria and Davor
With all my love and gratitude

Each of us has a secret frontier within him, and it is the most difficult frontier to cross because each of us hopes to find himself alone there, but finds only that he is more than ever in the company of others.

— Carlos Fuentes

CHAPTER ONE

APART FROM FUNERALS, NICHOLAS hadn't been inside a church in years, yet he made the sign of the cross whenever he passed St. Joseph's, and thought of his daughter. He'd never considered the world such a scary place until Kate was born. It was shocking how much a person could worry. To leave her every night to drive the taxi was terrible. When he first went back to work, it had been a physical pain to shut the front door behind him and he'd never managed a full shift without checking on her. Within a few hours of work, he'd invariably go back to Summer Street and the house he'd known all his life. His parents had lived there before him and now his family, if that's what he'd call it, did too. In the depth of night, the houses would be quiet, and he'd close the car door gently. He never liked making much noise when he came back to check on Kate. He liked to step inside, listen to the silence, and imagine he heard his daughter's breathing. He thought the silence had changed since her birth to a softer quiet that had the ability to envelop him. Sometimes, he thought he could hear Kathleen too. She slept with her lips parted and omitted a gentle breezy breath, but her presence would make him stiffen. It would take several seconds before he walked to the bedroom in the back of the house, where his mother used to sleep, to look in on his daughter with the streams of hall light barely reaching her. He'd feel the house tick around him, before retreating to his taxi and driving to Davis Square in time to meet the customers from the Burren, where Irish music drifted out in strands, or from the sports bar across the road. On quiet nights, he'd make the trek to Logan Airport, hoping to get a longer fare, but he was always back by 7 a.m. to wake Kate.

Early February, the street lights were still on and people were starting to wake. He parked in front of his house. From across the street, he heard the Jacob's dog yapping. Nicholas could time his day around Mr. Jacob's coming and going. 7:05 on the dot, the insurance broker would leave for work. He was small with thin shoulders and as quiet as a mouse. His wife was a wide woman, whose voice carried for miles. Every morning, she stood at the door in her dressing gown to wave goodbye to her husband and Nicholas preferred to be in the house at that stage. Most of the time, Nicholas wished he didn't have neighbors, or at least neighbors who had known him since he was a boy. When his mother died, he thought he'd sell the house. He'd called the real estate agent, but she had only started wandering through the rooms when he decided he couldn't go through with the sale.

For the last few mornings, he'd finished work early, so he had time to go to the house to the right of theirs. The house was painted blue with potted plants on the porch and skirting around the sides were flowers in their beds. He'd watered the plants yesterday and would do so again later. Once his daughter was at school, he'd open the blinds and let some air in. Now, he only had time to stroll around to the back door, where he'd found his elderly neighbor, Tilly, three days ago. She'd been on her way to feed the birds when she slipped on some ice. Tilly had been unconscious when he'd found her, and days later, it was still shocking to think of her lying in the cold and what might have happened if he hadn't noticed the blinds weren't up and there was no light in her house. She was an early bird, up before anyone on the street, a creature of habit, she liked to say, so the change had concerned him. He'd gone to the front door and rung the bell, before running around to the back to find her by the door with her leg badly twisted. He'd covered her up and called an ambulance. At the hospital, he learned she'd suffered a broken hip. Kathleen was upset he didn't let her know where he was. Kate didn't make it to school that morning.

His reflection caught on the back door window showing sandy hair reaching for his narrow shoulders. He wasn't much different from when he was a lanky teenager running to this very door — apart from the eyes which were more watchful, and the laughter lines around his mouth that would have been due to Kate. Inside the back door, he found the birdseed and brought a bowl full to the birdfeeder. The air burned his cheeks and he could feel his breath move upwards. He liked these few minutes of the day when he could think of nothing, but the food and the birds that might appear. During the night, there were the passengers and the traffic and his daughter, and once he went into his house there would be the business of getting breakfast ready for Kate and taking her to school, but now, in the back garden of his neighbor's house, there was stillness and silence and his breathing and nothing else. Maybe it was the familiarity, but also the foreignness of his neighbor's place all at once. He knew the house so well, yet he didn't belong to it and he enjoyed the sense of detachment.

With the birdseed in place and the back door re-locked, he thought he might get a birdfeeder for his own garden. Once Tilly's daughter was home and able to take care of the house, he'd put one in his back garden where as a child he'd dug up the soil looking for insects, but he didn't think taking care of the bird-house with Kathleen's attention would bring the same ease as here.

It had been late in the afternoon by the time he'd phoned Tilly's daughter to let her know about the fall. Years had gone by since he'd heard her voice, and still his heart stopped when she said hello. Ina was due to arrive from California any day now and the thought unsettled Nicholas. Each morning, coming home, he found himself looking for signs of arrival, and at night too, he had to admit that he looked for lights in the house.

At home, he heard Kate's voice the moment he stepped inside, but he didn't go straight to her room. In the bathroom, he let Kathleen's yellow and blue pills fall into his hand. He grabbed some water before walking to Kathleen's door. She was curled up in bed. A gap in the curtains let in grey light. Kathleen could never sleep in the dark. He was aware of the blue house beside them, and how he used to stand at that window as a boy, waiting for the girl who used to live there. Since the phone call, the house loomed large.

He said Kathleen's name and she murmured something, but didn't move until he sat beside her and put a hand on her side. "Kathleen," he said again, and she stretched and sat up. She hardly opened her eyes before taking the pills from him and then the water.

"You have an appointment at 10:30," he said, and immediately wished he hadn't reminded her when he saw the effect. Kate's voice was a soft murmur from the back of the house, a car alarm started somewhere, and he said, "You can't miss another one."

She said, "Okay, I know." He'd seen her pause and flash of fear and knew it was not okay, but he said nothing about it. She said, "Go on and get Kate."

He glanced at the pills in her hand. She said, "I'm not a child."

He could have said that if she wasn't a child, she could get the pills herself. He could have said they all knew what happened when the responsibility was left to her, but instead he stood under her amused and slightly distant gaze — a gaze that suggested she knew exactly what he was thinking, and that somehow she'd won his acquiescence, though the amusement faltered when he said, "No, you're not." She might have wondered why he sounded so resigned.

In Kate's bedroom, Kate had her teddies lined up on the floor in front of her. She was reading to them, and she glanced at her father and put a finger to her lips. This was her classroom. He was used to this, though he missed how she used to cuddle and listen to him read. In the last few weeks, she'd grown too independent, and wanted to pretend to read the books she'd memorized. She had red hair like her mother, tossed now at the back, and was sitting cross-legged in her pajamas. He sat against the wall by the door.

"The very hungry caterpillar then ate one green leaf. He started to feel better," she said, and leaned forward towards the oldest of the teddies, a brown one with a torn nose she called Minty, and told him to hush and listen.

"Now the caterpillar wasn't small, he was so big. He was a big fat caterpillar." Her voice had risen by the last words and she nodded to herself and turned the page.

"He built a small house called a coco, and he nibbled a small hole in the coco and pushed his way through."

"A cocoon," Nicholas said.

She looked at him and then back at the book. For a moment she was silent and he had an urge to apologize. Later in the car, she might ask him what that word was again, but not in front of her teddies. She turned the page and smiled and said, "And then what did he become?"

After listening for a second, she clapped and said, "Yes, a big beautiful butterfly."

She closed the book. "That's all for now." Nicholas smiled, hearing her say words she'd heard from him.

"Are you hungry?"

She asked for pancakes and he said no, not today. Pancakes were for weekends, partly because, more often than not, she needed a bath to get the maple syrup out of her hair. Kathleen was still in her room when they had their cereal. Kate didn't ask for her, and it had been a long time since Nicholas came home to Kate sitting outside her mother's door. If she woke early, she'd wait in her room and read to her teddies or play with her toys until Nicholas finished work.

When she was leaving for school, she would run to her mother's door and knock and enter the room to give her mother a kiss, and her mother would sit up in bed and take her in her arms with red strands of hair blended into one another and their pale skin bright in the dim light. They looked so alike, daughter and mother.

Then Kate would slide down and Kathleen

would remain sitting on the bed and she'd look a little lost without her daughter, and Nicholas would think of Kathleen in the hospital or pulling at the skin on her stomach, and he'd wonder who the woman in his house was, as if she had drifted aimlessly into his and Kate's world.

Kathleen was gone when he came back from dropping Kate to school. He stood at the bedroom door and stared at the tossed bed and cursed with the thought of having to make the phone call again. He'd hoped to bring Kathleen to her appointment and wait outside. Maybe he could have dozed in his car and avoided seeing Stein. He hated that Kathleen ran from her appointments and left him to pick up the pieces. He dialed the doctor's number and thought of the office with the sterile walls and the messy desk and hoped it was empty, but the receptionist put him through and in the next second Stein was on the phone. He said hello and asked if everything was all right.

"She won't be in today." There was a pause and Nicholas was tempted to hang up. He might have if the doctor didn't make him nervous. Stein asked if she was taking her medication.

Nicholas thought of her sitting in bed with the pills in her hand and the frown that came to her. A few days ago, she'd said you don't have to mind me and it was the first time he'd risen without watching her swallow them and he'd known that was just the start, but still he said yes, she's taking them.

Stein said, "Good, that's the most important thing. How are you and Kate?"

"Don't ask about Kate," Nicholas wanted to say, but he answered, "We're fine."

Stein said, "Okay, we can make another appointment. I'll get a letter sent to you with a new date, but she can't miss this one."

After he hung up, Nicholas tried calling Kathleen and for the fourth time her phone went straight to voicemail.

CHAPTER TWO

NICHOLAS MISSED INA'S ARRIVAL. He might have been in the shower or in the kitchen making tea when the taxi stopped in front of her house. He last saw her six years ago when she'd come for his mother's funeral. They'd stood in this house; Ina and he, when he was a different man before Kathleen and Kate, and even then, it had been hard to be in the same room as Ina.

By Kathleen's bedroom window, he saw the light was on in the living room next door and the window was open. It was that time of the day when everyone had already rushed to school and work. His eyes were starting to sting. He put his mug to his mouth and realized it was empty. He was about to make more tea when Ina came out of her house.

Her hair was down and lay on her shoulders; the dusky strands were as frizzy and wild as he remembered. She was wearing a bulky black jacket and a pair of jeans. She kept her head down, yet he stepped back from the window, suddenly conscious of his survey and the possibility of her glancing towards him. He noticed she was wearing trainers. Her hands were in her pockets. She turned left towards his house and Davis Square. Her face was pale, and she kept her gaze towards the ground, like she used to when they were at school. Then, it had been a sign of nervousness. He watched her disappear and stood by the empty frame of the window until his doorbell rang. He thought immediately of Tilly, and the worry propelled him forward. Through the living room window, he caught a glimpse of Ina's dark hair. She was leaning against the porch railing when he opened the door and the smile she gave him was shy and uncertain. Her "hi" was quiet. She hadn't changed much, but he saw a new tightness around her mouth and her russet eyes had lessened in intensity.

"Is Tilly okay?" he asked.

"I don't know," Ina told him. "She says she is but when I saw her this morning, she seemed in pain. She refuses to admit it."

Ina glanced at the house next door where she had grown up. "Well, at least I'm here to help." She didn't sound too happy about it. And she seemed a bit expectant of him, as if he were the one who'd gone to her. He wanted to go inside and close the door. Yet, he was watching her glance at his car and letting her ask, "How long have you been driving a taxi?"

He told her not long after the funeral. He'd moved back to the house and needed a new job, but he didn't bother to add this. She nodded and waited but he refused to ask her any questions and pretend this was a normal occurrence, when the last time he'd talked to her alone she'd sat on the other side of the glass and hadn't been able to look him in the eye.

Besides, he was conscious of Kathleen's presence as if she lay curled in the bed, and it made him feel guilty and off-balance. A horn blasted a street away, punctuating their silence.

Ina asked, "Can I come in?"

"Why?" he said, or maybe it had gone off like a blast in his head and all she heard was the rustle of the leaves on the sidewalk, because she said, "Nicholas, can I?" in a voice that sounded concerned. She was stepping away from the railing and he'd have to block her from entering. She was his sister-in-law, his childhood best friend, and the last person he wanted to let inside.

But he couldn't stop her. She was still his brother's wife. He stepped aside and let her enter. The door clicked behind them and in the shadows, Ina was like a girl wrapped in women's clothes, a girl who used to run into his house barefoot, screaming for him to come on. Still, she followed him to the kitchen as if it were her first time and she hadn't spent her childhood running around the rooms. The door of his boyhood bedroom was open. He heard her steps slow as she glanced inside. She would have seen the clothes tossed on the floor, and maybe the place smelled different with Kathleen. He'd noticed the flowery scent when she'd first moved in, but had gotten used to the change.

Ina stopped at the kitchen door while he went for the kettle. At home, he drank nothing but tea, thanks to his Irish mother. He offered her a cup, mindful that during her years away she might have lost her taste for the bitter drink.

"Sure, thanks," she said. She had not moved from the doorway. The kitchen was small, with a table against the wall to her left and the chairs tucked neatly underneath. The fridge was behind the door and ahead was the sink and the window. A round clock hung on the wall and ticked through each second, while Nicholas filled the kettle and put it on the stove. He took two mugs from the high cupboard and placed the tea bags inside, and she watched him as if she had a right to. There was recognition in her gaze. Violin strains filled the room.

"Your mom always listened to that station," she said. He agreed. He'd taken the habit from her.

"Mom still really misses her," she said.

"I know," he told her.

He leaned against the sink and caught her sad smile and her glance around the kitchen and living room. She asked where his daughter was. "Kate, isn't it?" she said.

He said yes, Kate. He could hear Adrial in the garden next door and turned to see her running after her son, Manuel. Once, a few years ago, the boy had run out the front door and Adrial had screamed for him to stop. The piercing screech of fear had shaken Nicholas.

"She's at school," Nicholas said, when he met Ina's gaze.

"Already. God, it doesn't seem that long ago."

His gesture towards the chairs freed Ina from her spot at the door. She took the seat facing the window. Her hands were on the table, pale and fragile. They reminded him of small birds. When the fingers entwined, he had to look away, and met her gaze. He was caught by her face and his inability to read it.

"What's going on?" he asked.

"Nothing," she said. "I thought I could say hello. Is that so crazy?"

"Like old friends," he said. The kettle was starting to whistle. He sensed her apprehension in the pause. But she said yes, and it was impossible not to feel irritated with the sight of her at the table, as if she had never left. He reminded her that they hadn't spoken in a long time.

She said, "I know. I'm sorry."

He wanted to laugh at the ridiculousness. I'm sorry, she'd said, when every one of his letters had gone unanswered, but that was nothing compared to the shock when Nicholas had come home to find her with Stefano. Within the year she'd moved across country with him.

"I thought of you often, but I didn't know what to do," she said.

He said, "And now what? Are we supposed to fill each other in on the last twelve years?"

She looked taken aback. Her hands dropped to her lap. He turned off the gas and poured water into mugs. Their silence was disturbed by the spoon hitting off the mug. He remembered she took milk and no sugar. The DJ was asking for sponsorship. Her voice was low and deep, while Ina's silence was infuriating. He put the mug in front of her.

"Okay, where should I begin?" Nicholas asked. "Let's see, I stayed in Malden for a while after I got out."

A ripple of unease made her shoulders straighten and he had to pause to hold the anger that shot through him. Too much time had passed for her to act this way.

"I drove a truck for a few months, but I didn't like the long hauls. There were other jobs that are hardly worth mentioning, other apartments too, but I won't bore you. After Mom died, I thought of selling the house, but I couldn't, so I moved back and started driving a taxi. Within a year I was a dad."

He took a sip of tea. "I'm sure Tilly's filled you in on the things I've missed."

He thought Ina would say something about Kathleen. He was sure Tilly had told her what had happened, the bits Tilly knew at least. Instead she said, "What is it like being a dad?"

And he felt the thaw immediately, a loosening of his shoulders with the thought of Kate. Maybe Ina still knew him. At least, she knew how to push through his defenses. He shrugged and took a sip of his tea. The smile was automatic. "It's great," he said. It was also scary and overwhelming and life-changing, but he kept that in. "She's an amazing little girl."

"I'd love to meet her," Ina said.

Nicholas shrugged, and thought he saw a flash of her hurt in her eyes, but he couldn't be enthusiastic about Ina coming into his life after so long. There was a distant sound of a car passing and the following silence was like being underwater. Ina was watching him, and he said, "Go on, your turn, fill me in."

She sighed and glanced down at her mug before looking back at him and he felt the stone in his gut. He knew something was coming because for a long time, he'd imagined her looking at him in that way.

"I'm not going back," she said.

He said, "I think you've missed a few years."

"Can you stop being such an asshole?" she said. "I'm trying to tell you we're getting divorced."

"Am I supposed to be happy about that?"

"No," she said. "You're not supposed to be happy."

"What do you want then?"

She told him, "I don't want you to do anything. I just want to talk to you."

He said, "Fuck sake, Ina, it's a bit late for that."

"You're acting like everything is my fault."

He couldn't believe this. It was still easy to remember the waiting, how it had dragged him down and made him feel old. But she didn't seem to notice his tension. She said that they would be living next door to each other again and she hoped they could learn to talk to each other. She said, "It's been twelve years. You have your family, a child…"

His chuckle stopped her and he hated her anxious gaze and the way she brought everything back to him. He was not the same boy she'd once known. He emptied his mug into the sink. The piano on the radio was making him sleepy. The room had darkened and he was conscious that Ina had not moved. She sat at his kitchen table and he felt the rigidness in his body from his urge to shout at her to leave, but he withheld this by asking about Stefano.

She said, "He's fine. How's Kathleen?" And the softness in her voice was worse than the anger. He wanted to close his eyes and open them to her gone.

"Fine, she's gone for a walk. She should be back soon."

Ina said oh, and he saw in her straightening back, her urge to look around, and her sudden unease.

The sink ledge was digging into his back and he had a sense of floating. It wasn't just the exhaustion, but the inability to know how to end this meeting and get Ina to leave so he might breathe.

Finally, he said, "I'm sorry about your marriage, Ina."

She said okay. Her voice was so low he had to strain to hear it. Her shoulders looked slack now, as if she was falling within herself. Gloom from the grey winter day gave him the added impression that she was disappearing before his eyes.

"Did you know already?" she asked. He shook his head, and said he hadn't talked to Stefano in a while.

She said. "I always wondered what you talked about.... I mean it surprised me when he started to phone you regularly." Nicholas straightened. Her attention was seemingly fixed on the mug in front of her, though he had no doubt she felt his annoyance.

"Why?" He said, his voice low and even. "We're brothers, after all."

Ina looked at him for a long time while the radio hummed in the background and the clock marked time between them. She hadn't changed at all. He could see her stubbornness in the dark eyes and small mouth, and felt it in her lingering presence. He wondered what she saw in him, if she'd thought he'd changed.

She said, "Nicholas." He pushed from the sink and was ready to run from whatever she was going to say.

"I'm tired Ina." His voice came out sterner than he'd planned, but he had to stop her before she said anything else. She was scaring him. "I worked a night shift," he added. She apologized and rose.

"I just wanted to thank you. I should have been here with her, that's what I kept thinking, I had no reason to be away, but I was afraid to tell her and then..." she paused and a cloud drifted by and brought a passing gloom through the room; Nicholas was struck by her face, how lovely it still was, and the sorrow he saw there from the thought of her mother in the cold. Ina didn't need to say Tilly could have frozen that morning, the fact stood between them, but she did. Nicholas told her there was no point in thinking like that.

He said, "Everything's okay."

She smiled, and said, "Is it, is everything okay?" And before he could react, she said, "I'm sorry, it's just weird being back. It's all changed. The Johnson's house is gone."

"Apartments," Nicholas said, to ease the tightness in his chest.

Ina glanced to where Adrial and her son had been moments ago. "The O'Keefe's are gone too. They said they'd never leave."

"So did you," Nicholas might have said, but he kept it in. He'd had years of practice. She waited a beat and he had no idea what Ina expected. His mother would have said everything happens for a reason, but he'd never believed that.

Finally, Ina said, "Mom is worse than I thought, the fall really scared her."

"I know," he said. "I'm sorry."

There was a pause where the two of them watched each other, only inches away, so close he could see the rise and fall of her chest. She thanked him for the tea.

He said, "I'm glad you enjoyed it," which made her glance at the full mug. Maybe she smiled; he sensed a movement of her lips and in that instant, he wanted her to stay. But he fought the urge. He heard her steps through the living room and the front door open and close. He sat on the chair in the kitchen and felt some of the tension drain from him, though it was impossible to relax with the knowledge that Ina was not leaving.

CHAPTER THREE

"AND THIS IS WHERE we are supposed to go, the fairy garden? No, I don't want to…" Kate's voice drifted to Nicholas while he slept. "Let's go here," she said.

Kate was playing on the floor beside her bed with her toys scattered and her voice drifted to him every now and again, a soft rise and fall that lulled him to sleep. She'd always been good at playing by herself. At two she could spend hours with her dolls.

The silence woke him and he jumped up to see Kathleen at the bedroom door. She must have told Kate to watch television because he heard it turn on with a burst of voices. Kathleen was still in her coat, a colorful patchwork of material that she'd been wearing the first night he'd met her when she got into his taxi.

Nicholas's eyes were burning, and his mouth was dry. His body felt like a heavy sack on the bed and he would have loved to pull the blankets over him.

"Why do you always sleep here?" Kathleen asked. She was leaning against the door. She hadn't changed much since he'd met her gaze in the rear-view mirror and was struck by her beauty, though there was some roundness to her cheeks now and less fire in her grey eyes.

"I wanted to stay with Kate."

"But it's not just when Kate's here. It's all the time. In the mornings after you bring her to school you come here."

He sat on the side of the bed and rubbed his face. They'd gone through this so many times before. A few months ago, he would have said, "For fuck sake, I work, take care of Kate and you, what more do you want?" But he was tired of hearing her say, "Don't ask stupid questions," and of the arguments that would ensue. Voices would rise while Kate pretended to watch television. Sometimes Adrial, from next door, would appear with her son to ask if Kate wanted to go to the park with them. Kathleen never answered the door. The bell would go and she'd stand rigid and let him deal with the visitor and she would not move while he got Kate ready, and told her to be good, and thanked Adrial, a chubby woman with black hair, who had a way of looking at him that made him feel ashamed. So, though he was grateful for her care of Kate, he'd grown to hate her arrival too.

Now, he said, "I'm tired Kathleen, okay? I don't need this."

She looked tired too. She would have walked for miles. It was something he'd loved about her from the first time they met — her ability to wander for no reason but to look and observe.

"Guess where I went today?" she asked, and he was surprised by her sudden enthusiasm. Her red cheeks added to the childish air. He said he didn't know.

"Guess," she said, and he felt a tightening in his chest from the frustration. He was so tired. There was laughter from the living room.

"The MFA," he said. She smiled and said no, she was not in the mood for the museum today.

"I don't know."

"Silver Street," she said, and he had a flash of her small dark apartment.

"This morning, I kept thinking of that apartment. When we weren't in bed, we were so cold. Do you remember how it was?" She didn't wait for an answer. "Sometimes, I think I imagined it. The place seems hardly real," Kathleen paused. "But so does this place sometimes."

Toys were spread on the floor and they didn't look entirely innocent with the way Kathleen was looking at him. He wasn't sure where she was going with this, but he didn't want to egg her on by making statements like 'this is real', or 'I have no idea what you're talking about' and see her get riled up.

"You're not listening then," she'd probably say and there would be a back and forth of words and grievances that he wouldn't be able to stop.

"You must be hungry," he said after what felt a long pause, though he'd seen no impatience on her face, and wondered if the slow passing of time was how he imagined it. The seconds dragged when all he wanted was to sleep.

She said "no, not really," though she should be, and he imagined her rush in the morning. She probably jumped out of bed the moment the front door closed behind him and Kate. Kathleen would have left before eating anything.

He remembered Stein. "You can't keep missing your appointments."

"I don't need to see him."

He said, "Fine, okay, then you phone and tell him that."

He'd risen and stepped around the toys, while ignoring his shoes at the end of the bed. He was so close to Kathleen he could see the blue dots in her grey eyes.

"You're always leaving. Every time I come into a fucking room you leave."

He had to take a breath. His tongue was a dry slab in his mouth. He couldn't say that that was exactly what he didn't do — he didn't leave, not when he found her on his bathroom floor and rushed her into hospital, nor when he'd discovered in Stein's office that she was pregnant. Before Kate was born, before his daughter became more important than his Catholic guilt, he wished he were a man like his father who didn't give a shit and left and never came back.

"I need to make dinner," he said.

There was nothing for a moment, but the voices from the television. He recognized Elmo's squeaky voice. Kate laughed and Kathleen turned towards her, and Nicholas forgot his discomfort. He forgot everything, but the girl on that couch. "Kate, turn that down," Kathleen said to her. "Kate!" The television went low. Nicholas didn't move. He was watching Kathleen. Her frown when she spoke to Kate made him nervous.

"It was different waiting for you there," Kathleen said, and for a moment he didn't know what she was talking about, then he knew she was talking about her old second floor apartment. He felt the twist in his stomach that was more anxiety than anger because he knew somehow in Kathleen's twisted way she thought that Kate had made them different.

Earlier, Kate had seen Ina bringing shopping in from the car and had gotten excited when she heard the woman was Tilly's daughter. "I want to go over to her, let me, please, please," Kate had said.

"Not now," Nicholas had said. He hadn't thought of Kate's curiosity until then. Tilly was like a grandmother to her and had often watched Kate in her house, though Kathleen was shy and unsure around Tilly. "I don't like the way she looks at me," she'd said once.

Nicholas told her not to be silly, but the truth was Tilly was uncomfortable with Kathleen and she was not a woman inclined to hide how she felt. Given time, and reason, Tilly would also be a woman who would reassess her ideas. Had Kathleen tried to change Tilly's mind, she would have been open, but instead there were days when Nicholas brought his daughter to Tilly when he was due at work and said, "Kathleen's not able, she's afraid of what might happen, and I have to get some hours in." Kathleen had always been nervous around Kate as a baby. Kathleen used to drift to the cot and study her daughter, but any movement would make her draw back.

"She's so tiny," Kathleen used to say, "Anything could happen."

As Kate got older, there were moments of softness when Kathleen would reach out and touch the child's head or sit on the floor with her daughter, watching her play, but her gestures were never relaxed. Kathleen watched her daughter, as if she were not entirely sure where the child came from.

Since Tilly went to hospital, it had been hard for Nicholas. Kate had cried a few times to see her, and now here was a younger version of Tilly, the same petite bodies, the wild hair, though Tilly's was kept back in a bun and had long been white. Of course, Kate would want to go over, and even now, sitting at the table there was no disguising her delight when she told Kathleen that Ina was home.

"When did she get home?" Kathleen asked. Nicholas said today. Night pressed against the window and towards the family sitting at the table, eating fish and mashed potatoes. Kathleen had her back to the door. She never liked being blind to the window. Kate was in the chair between her parents.

Nicholas drank some water and felt every inch of Kathleen's stare. She was shrewd and had a way of looking inside him and seeing everything, or at least that was how he felt. Whenever she was with him, he was exposed.

"Can I go see her?" Kate was kneeling in her chair, so tiny and independent. Her face was dotted with Parmesan cheese that she wanted to eat with everything, including potatoes.

"Why didn't you tell me?" Kathleen said. "Is Stefano coming?"

Nicholas said he didn't think so. Kathleen said she'd like to finally meet Stefano. She'd spoken to him numerous times on the phone. Stefano had spent years phoning their mother and now he dialed the home number and talked to Nicholas, as much habit as anything else. Nicholas shared little with him. Kathleen was the one who told him about her pregnancy, and she'd found Nicholas's reticence hard to accept. "You're having a child. He's going to be an uncle, why didn't you tell him?"

"I don't like him very much," Nicholas had said. Stefano had never met Kate.

"Did Ina tell you he's not coming?" She'd put her fork down and was sitting back in her seat. She'd hardly touched her food.

"Yes. She came over to say thanks for helping Tilly and that she was staying for a while."

"I want to see Tilly," Kate said. Nicholas said she could visit her tomorrow.

"Ina is her aunt," Kathleen said. "Didn't she want to meet Kate?"

"She just got back, give her a chance."

Nicholas got up from the table, under Kathleen's scrutiny. He scraped the last of his dinner into the bin and asked if Kathleen was done. She pushed the plate away and he brought it to the sink.

"I need to work in a few hours," he said. The water ran over his hand, cold to lukewarm.

"So?" Kathleen said.

"So, I'm tired. I need to sleep."

Kathleen rose. She was in jeans and a t-shirt. Her thick red hair fell around her face. For a second she didn't say anything, but he sensed her reflection bearing down on him before she turned to Kate. "Finish up," she said. "And I'll bring you over to your aunt." The plate clattered in the sink.

Nicholas said, "She's not her aunt."

Kathleen's hand was on Kate's arm. Nicholas couldn't believe it. First, Ina arrived as if the birth of a child could wipe the past clean, and then Kathleen was determined to go next door out of curiosity, and was using Kate to do it, holding her hand so she might have a right to knock on the door and get inside.

"She's married to your brother," Kathleen said.

"Not anymore, she isn't. They're getting divorced."

There was a second where Kathleen didn't move or say anything, and he knew she was wondering how he knew this or what else happened today while she was gone, and maybe she considered addressing it then. Maybe she thought of asking what the story was between him and Ina, but decided this could wait because that night she said she didn't care if they were getting divorced.

"Come on, Kate."

Nicholas didn't move. He heard their steps through the living room, and their murmuring as they got their shoes and coats on. The door opened and a blast of cold made it into the house. Nicholas was still standing in the kitchen. The ticking of the clock was loud in his ears. He took deep breaths. The lightness of his head scared him enough not to react to Kathleen, while the sudden quiet made him think of that room with the glass partition and the worn chairs that he and Ina had sat at years ago, staring across from each other.

He fell asleep sitting at the table with his head against the kitchen wall. When he woke, he thought it was morning and he was supposed to have Kate ready for school and then he saw the dishes and the night outside the window and heard Kate crying, which was a subdued sniffling sound.

"She didn't want to leave," Kathleen told him when he appeared at the kitchen door. She was on the couch with her legs curled up and she spoke without looking at him. He should have been worried with the way she held herself and the brashness of her tone and her walk to Silver Street earlier in the day that would have taken hours, but it was hard to keep a grasp of it when his daughter was crying in her room. She was curled on the bed. Her little body was so small and light, such a fragile thing. He sat beside her and asked what was wrong. She didn't answer and he said her name, Kate.

He saw chocolate around her mouth.

"Did you have a biscuit?" She nodded.

"With milk?" She nodded again.

"Was it nice?" Nothing came from her. The television went on. Voices rose in the living room. "Kate, was it okay?"

"Mom shouted."

Once Kate was asleep, Nicholas asked Kathleen what happened. She was lying on the couch. The television was on, but he had a sense that she wasn't watching it, and had been waiting for him to come to her. She sat up and told him it was awful. She resembled a large child with her wide eyes and legs pulled up.

"She's a bit of a bitch," Kathleen said. She seemed to be waiting for something, but it was impossible to agree, and finally Kathleen continued.

"When she answered the door, she was okay.

She said hello, you must be Kate or something like that and she gave her a hug and said she looked like you, and then she rose and said I know who you are." Kathleen mimicked her voice as a monotone of cruelty. Nicholas could imagine Ina doing something like that. Her tone would not have been as cutting as Kathleen's impression, though it wouldn't have been warm and tender either. Ina wasn't like that, she was too matter-of-fact. "Yes, I know who you are," had meant nothing more than I know who you are, but Kathleen was the wrong person to speak to like this. Each word would have stung.

"I've talked to Stefano a few times, but not once did she come to the phone to talk to me, and then she has the nerve to say I know who you are, and in that snobby way too." Kathleen brought her hair back from her face that was partly lit by the light springing from the television.

"We went inside and she gave Kate a biscuit and milk and talked to her about school. You'd think I was the fucking nanny or something because she hardly said a word to me, and there was this big drama when the biscuit got too soggy and dropped into the milk, with her getting a spoon and saying they could salvage some, and then deciding to give Kate another biscuit. She doesn't even ask if it's okay with me, but I tell her that one biscuit is enough and she actually argues with me. She says she's sure that another biscuit would do no harm. She's talking just like she did at the door in that snobby voice. Kate's starting to get upset now because she knows something's wrong, but there's nothing I can do. I can't let her tell me what to give my kid and I tell her as much and she gets all thick and the next minute she's grabbing the cups from the table and saying that she doesn't have to deal with our rudeness and we should go. Kate has no idea what is going on when the milk is grabbed from under her and she's more or less shoved out the door. We are never setting foot in that house ever again while she's there."

She looked hard at Nicholas. "I don't want you to see her either."

In the dead hours after 2 a.m., Nicholas was still riled over Kathleen.

"Please?" she'd said, "You can't go there. She's so mean." She'd followed him into the bedroom and said, "You have to promise."

"She lives next door, for Christ's sake."

But this had only made Kathleen angrier. "Why can't you promise? What's going on with you and her?"

He had to relent, though it cost him to do so, and a nauseous feeling in his belly lingered for a long time. It was a relief to get out and move freely.

He told Ted, the dispatcher, that he was going straight to the airport. Although Nicholas leased the car and didn't have to answer to anyone, Ted insisted that he call his location in and not be a fucking idiot after a taxi driver had been murdered in Charlestown.

"Are you picking up a fare?" Ted asked. He had the deep gravelly voice of a pack a day smoker. Nicholas said no, but he'd discovered the strange phenomenon that there were always people at the airport wanting to get home. Ted told him to fuck off.

At arrivals, huddled figures scuttled out through automatic doors. A thin elderly woman was ahead of the rest. In the white lights and shadows of the airport, she waved Nicholas down, and looked like a bird trying to fly. She reminded him of Tilly, who used to be as free in her movements, but the fall had drained her. The last time he saw her, she'd told him she would be going to a nursing home to recuperate after the operation. He hadn't thought of asking Ina what she thought of that. All queries had dissolved with her gaze.

The woman gave an address in Dorchester. He drove out of the airport and onto West 90. The sea was out there somewhere. Houses were dark outlines. There was nothing but grey space and beyond it, the neon lights for McDonald's, Cracker Jack, and the empty Stop & Shop car park. There were always trucks on this stretch. A constant rumble of noise went by Nicholas, but it was better than slowly negotiating the streets around Somerville. He needed some speed and to gain some distance from the houses, where Kathleen and Ina slept.

The snow melted as soon as it hit his windshield. Ted had given him some fares in Dorchester, and he'd waited a few hours before heading back on 93. There was roadwork. Flashing lights reflected off his window and rear-view mirror. Some nights, he'd get lost in the lights of the city and the music. Fares would drift in and out without thought. Now, Ina stayed with him. She'd always been able to sneak up on him. At the kitchen door, he could be struck with the memory of her washing dishes at his mother's funeral, the way her head tilted slightly to reveal her pale neck, or the way she went around the rooms helping Stefano pack his mother's things, as if she belonged there. It was no wonder he'd wanted to sell the house.

He took exit 20. His wipers groaned slightly; the snow was turning to rain. The surroundings had a washed out, dazed look. The lights of South Station were a clean white and a few people milled about in the early morning. A bus pulled out down the road and a woman was running into the main entrance. Nicholas stopped for a red light in view of the South Station clock.

It was on this street that he'd first seen Kathleen.

She'd shuffled into the back seat and he'd met her gaze in the rear-view mirror. Long hair had surrounded her small face. In the dark, illuminated by streetlights, he'd been able to make out the humor in her grey eyes. She'd made him smile because of her relaxed manner, and the self-deprecating grin that came to her face. "Silver Street," she'd said. Her voice was deep and found a place under his skin. "Do you know it?" she'd asked and he'd said of course.

He'd pulled away from the curb. She'd said she couldn't remember the last time she'd taken a taxi. She liked to walk no matter the weather, but when she saw him, she put her hand out on impulse. The street had spread out before them. Streetlights pierced the grey.

"What do you think of that?" she'd asked. He thought that's the way people did things, and told her so.

"Are you kidding?" she'd said. "People have to have a conference to decide what underwear to put on. They don't think of the higher purpose or reason."

He'd said, "A cold night, a taxi at the right time, that's reason enough."

"You really think so?" she'd said. "What if I tell you I came out for a walk?"

"I'd say you picked a strange time for walking."

She'd laughed and told him she'd worked overtime in the nursing home and had just finished her shift. She hadn't wanted to go home. "You think it's a coincidence?"

He'd said yeah, he did, though he couldn't help feel something when he glanced at her. She'd held his gaze. When he looked away, she'd said, "I make you nervous."

"No," he'd told her, but there was an element of truth to her statement. On Melcher Street, he'd realized it had stopped raining, and she'd told him about giving a homeless guy outside South Station some food. "I was walking away when he shouted, 'Where's my fork?' He was completely serious." Her face had been framed by the rear-view mirror. She'd been aware of every glance he gave her. The fare would be over soon and that had bothered him.

"Do you have any stories?" she'd asked.

He'd told her about the woman who'd done a runner after getting a ride to Charlestown. She came back seconds later because she had forgotten her handbag. "She was very apologetic before she ran off for the second time."

"You let her get away with it?" She'd asked.

"She made me laugh." Kathleen had made an 'oh' sound as if he'd revealed himself.

On Silver Street, he'd slowed down. She'd stopped smiling before she told him to stop.

She didn't move for a long time. Finally, he'd heard the click of the door and felt the cold air tumble between them. She'd closed the door and knocked on his window and gestured for him to wind it down. Her body had been hidden under the long colorful coat. Her cheeks were red. She'd looked shy and mischievous at once. "So you have a reason to come back," she'd said and left without paying. He did go back, and after a few weeks, he'd brought her to the house on Summer Street to cook for her. She'd loved the little house and he'd thought that she brightened the rooms up. For a while, they'd been happy, but now he thought of those months as an act of deceit.

Ina came out of the house the moment Nicholas pulled up in the morning. A drizzle fell, and silver drops caught on her hair. The car door closed behind him and she stood with her arms crossed. He saw the anger in her eyes before she said, "Kathleen better not come near me again." Nicholas felt as if she'd hit him in the stomach.

"I don't care what you told her, or what the fuck is going on, but the next time she comes to my house, I'll phone the cops."

"What happened?" he asked.

She shook her head as though she hadn't heard him and said, "I feel so bad for Kate."

It was impossible to ask her the same question

twice. He was scared to know, and her sympathy was infuriating. He took care of Kate. She had him. He made sure she was doing okay, and Ina couldn't come waltzing back and determine how his daughter was, or that she needed anyone's pity.

"I have to go," he said.

He saw Ina looking towards him before he took the steps up the porch. She might have still been there when he closed the front door and she might have been aware that Kathleen was watching them from her bedroom window.

CHAPTER FOUR

THAT TERRIBLE MORNING IN March, Nicholas ran to Ina, not Adrial, with her sympathetic eyes, whose gaze shamed Nicholas, though he knew it wasn't fair to pull Ina in again as he had years ago. He grabbed Kate from her bed and ran out the door into the cold and down to Ina's unlit house. His daughter snuggled into him. He prayed she didn't realize what had happened and then he thought of Kathleen on the ground with her blazing eyes and he was close to getting sick. He gagged. A horrid sensation in his stomach and throat silenced him as Ina appeared. Were it not for Kate in his arms and his bloodless hands, he would have been brought back years when Ina opened the door in her robe with her hair a crumpled mess around her face. Inside Ina's house, he didn't know what to do. He'd run from his home with the thought of getting Kate out of there, but he didn't want to let her go now.

"What's going on? What's happened?"

"There's been an accident," he said, because it was the first thing that came to his head. "I need you to keep Kate. Please, just for a while."

Ina looked frightened and for a minute he thought she would step back and say no, but she came forward and reached out for Kate. She'd seen Kate during the last few weeks when Nicholas had brought her to visit Tilly in the nursing home, but never in Ina's home. To visit Ina would have been impossible with Kathleen keeping a vigil on the house next door.

"Come here, Kate."

She went to Ina without a fight and her subdued sublimation worried Nicholas. He wanted her to look at him, but she kept her head down and seemed sleepy.

Ina ran her hand through Kate's hair and was trying to look at her face.

Kate resisted this. She was straining to lie forward. Her father said her name and she turned to look at Nicholas, but said nothing. Ina's eyes held all her questions but Nicholas answered none of them. He said he'd be back as soon as he could.

The police were the first to arrive. Their flashing lights and navy cars pulled neighbors outside. The day was overcast and had a piercing chill. Ina wrapped a blanket around Kate to bring her to the bird feeder when she saw the ambulance. Kate nodded when Ina asked if she wanted to feed the birds, but she didn't move from her chair, until Ina held her hand and helped her. Even then, she seemed dazed and was nothing like the little girl who liked to crawl on the bed beside Tilly and talk about the garden the students took care of in school. When they came inside, the ambulance was still there. Kate didn't want to eat and Ina brought her to the couch in the living room, under the window, where Tilly used to let her lie down with a blanket. Ina saw Kathleen being brought out on the stretcher. Her red hair fell towards the ground.

Kate was watching television by the time the knock came and Ina opened the door to a man with soft brown eyes and a need of a shave. He showed his badge and introduced himself as Detective Stevens and said he needed to talk to her and Kate about what happened today.

Ina stiffened and glanced at Kate on the couch and the detective told her it would be okay; he wouldn't ask Kate too much.

"Where's Nicholas?" she asked. She was told he was at the station. He needed to answer some questions. She was sure Nicholas didn't know anyone was coming to talk to Kate, but there was no way to get in touch with him now, and besides, Kate had hardly said a word since she'd gotten to Ina's house. To Ina's questions Kate had given shrugs and nods and Ina thought there was something stuck deep inside Kate that was keeping her so quiet and Stevens would know the right questions to ask.

"Kate, we need to talk to you for a minute."

The child looked with cloudy blue eyes at Ina. She didn't seem too nervous, more uncertain, as if she wasn't sure what was happening. Ina turned down the television and Stevens took a seat beside Kate. He introduced himself and asked what Kate was watching and if she went to school. Her voice was low when she said Rugrats and yes, she went to school.

"But not today," Stevens said.

She nodded. Ina sat on the armchair near her and she had a sense that Kate wanted to glance towards her, but would not take her gaze from the man beside her. "Can you tell me why?"

This time Kate looked to Ina, a quick scared glance. Ina said it's okay, you can tell him and after a long moment, Kate said, "Dad was shouting. He was mad."

Stevens smiled at her. "Did something happen to upset him?" She shrugged.

He leaned forward and asked, "Did his shouting wake you?"

She shrugged again. Her head had fallen, and she was plucking at her pajamas, lifting Winnie the Pooh's face and letting it fall.

"Do you remember waking?" Stevens said.

"I couldn't open my eyes."

Stevens sat straighter. "Was it hard to breathe?"

Ina stood quickly. The effect of the words on Kate's face made her want to throw Stevens out. "That's enough," she said.

She could have whacked the hand that came out to quieten her, but the tension in the air deflated Ina and kept her still, while Stevens told Kate it was okay. "What was it like when you woke up?"

Kate said, "It was dark."

"Were you scared?" She didn't say anything.

Ina said, "Kate, were you scared?" The girl nodded.

Stevens sighed and seemed to take in the girl's statement and the girl herself, balled up and cagey. She'd hardly looked at him. Now, she asked if she could watch some more television. Ina felt heavy as if Kate's voice had gotten lodged inside her. Later she would cry at the thought of how scared Kate had looked, but at that moment, as she turned up the television volume and led the detective into the kitchen, she felt a numbing disbelief.

Stevens declined her offer of coffee. The kitchen was narrow and had a table and two stools tucked against the wall that were rarely used. Ina leaned against the draining board with her back to the window and the clearing day. The detective stayed just inside the door. His broad back blocked Kate from Ina. She had an urge to make him move, so she could see Kate, until he said, "Mrs. Giovanni, you made a statement against Kathleen Lehanne a few weeks ago."

Ina felt her blood drain from her face. She hadn't told Nicholas or Tilly. She didn't want Tilly to worry and she didn't want to talk to Nicholas about it because when she'd complained about Kathleen's first visit, he'd shown nothing but irritation.

"I didn't press charges."

"Can you tell me about the complaint?" All of a sudden, she felt exhausted. She nodded. From down the street, a dog barked and afterwards, the house seemed impossibly quiet.

She said she'd felt like Kathleen was stalking her. At first, she had a sense of always being watched. "Whenever I went outside, she was there, either at the side window of her house staring out or at the front porch. She'd sit on the steps and it was very unnerving, but I didn't do anything until I saw her in my back garden. It was mid-morning and she was standing at the back door staring in. I thought I'd better put it on record just in case."

"In case what?" Stevens said. Kate shuffled on the couch and Ina felt her heartbeat quicken with the question. She thought of the ambulance outside Nicholas's house and the limp girl in his hands. Ina said, "In case she came inside." Her gaze fell on her hands and the thin line of pale skin that had been hidden for twelve years under her wedding ring.

"Did she ever threaten you?"

Ina said, "No, the only time she spoke to me was my first night home."

"Can you tell me about that?"

He had a notebook and pen, but he wrote nothing down when she told him that she knew something was wrong when she opened the door. Kathleen didn't smile or say anything and when Ina tried to hug Kate, Kathleen kept a firm grip on her hand and wouldn't let her go.

"It looked as if she were hurting Kate." He asked why she thought that.

"Kate looked uncomfortable."

"Did they come inside?"

"Yes, Kathleen hovered around while I got Kate milk and a biscuit. She refused a drink and refused to sit. Then she started with a barrage of questions. When was Tilly coming home? When did I see Nicholas? Why did I go to her house when he was alone? Kate was getting distressed and so was I. I didn't know what to do. She was manic and I was about to tell her to leave when Kate's biscuit dropped in the milk and she started to cry. It wasn't because of the biscuit. I knew her mother's behavior was distressing her. Still, I went to give her another biscuit and Kathleen lost it, saying I had no right to give her any more. She yanked Kate from the chair."

Ina took a breath. Her cheeks were red thinking of the encounter and she was trembling with the thought of what might have happened next door.

"Did you think then that Kate could be in danger?"

"Why are you asking me this?"

"Please answer the question."

She thought of the stretcher coming out of the house, and the red hair that had seemed too bright in the dull light, and Kate's quietness, and Ina couldn't say no, though she hadn't considered anything like that until now. He was looking at her kindly, though it was still hard to meet his gaze when she nodded.

When Nicholas left Kate safe with Ina, he phoned the police and reported what had happened in his house. His voice was brisk and full of business. His chest took the weight of his words, so by the end of the conversation, he had to take a deep breath. He had to phone Stein next. He felt cold with the thought of talking to the doctor, though he'd known since before Kate was born that this phone call would be made.

"Kathleen can't do this alone," Stein had said years ago. "There's a lot at risk here." It had been Nicholas's first time in Stein's office, over twenty-four hours after Kathleen had been involuntarily admitted. When he'd found her on the bathroom floor and rushed her to hospital, it had seemed he was losing control, though that was nothing compared to the fear when he'd learned Kathleen was pregnant. From the first moment, Nicholas had known he couldn't walk away from the baby. "But what if she leaves when the child is born?" he'd asked.

"The law can terminate her right to take care of her child if she cannot meet its needs. I am of the firm belief that she can't."

Stein's gaze had been steady.

"It's as simple as that." If Stein had heard disgust in Nicholas's voice, he'd hidden it well.

"In this case, yes, it is as simple as that," Stein had said.

But nothing had been simple.

Stein answered the phone with a clipped hello. "It's Nicholas Giovanni. You need to get here."

The doctor didn't sound surprised. He said, "Tell me what happened."

When Nicholas started to talk to Stein about what had happened, he thought for a moment that he might fall.

Nicholas waited outside for the police to come. His hands were cold, and there was a vile taste in his mouth, but he could not step into the cocoon of darkness where he supposed the air would still be thick with his scream and he would relive what had happened. The police took a statement in the cold while Nicholas's eyes watered, and his hands were in his pockets to stop them from shaking. Every now and again, he'd glance over at Ina's house and think of his child there. Her limpness when he held her still scared him.

Stein arrived at some stage, though afterwards Nicholas couldn't remember if it was before or after the ambulance. The details became hazy in memory in the same way his mother's funeral was because of the shock and exhaustion, though he knew that Stein had issued a section 12 for Kathleen to be transferred to hospital to be evaluated so she wouldn't have to be detained by police. Kathleen had not resisted, and Stein had followed him to the police station to give a statement. Stein told the police that Kathleen had for the last three months continually missed her appointments, and a week previous Nicholas had called to ask the doctor if he could come to the house since she was not doing well.

They were in the station, sitting at a cluttered desk under the cacophony of ringing phones. The detective, a chubby man with receding dark hair and sweat marks under his arms, asked how Kathleen was when Stein saw her.

Stein said he found Kathleen to be agitated and easily upset. He was worried about his patient because he was sure she wasn't taking her medication.

"Was she?" The man's eyes were small and black and made Nicholas think of an insect.

Nicholas said he didn't know because for weeks she refused to swallow them with him present.

The detective's eyebrows went up in a gesture of impatience. "But if you had to guess."

"I wouldn't have left her alone with my daughter if I thought something was wrong."

"If you were so worried, why didn't you do something?" This question was directed at Stein. Nicholas had started to sweat thinking of Kathleen and her pills. He was too tired to keep everything straight. He hadn't slept all night and it was after 1 p.m. He'd gone over what had happened when the police arrived in the house and twice since he'd arrived at the station. The noise and heat of the station made his teeth clench and he had to force himself to sit still, while Stein said that there was nothing he could do. He explained that 41 states had laws requiring outpatients to stay on their treatment plans. If they refused, they could be involuntarily hospitalized.

"Unfortunately, Massachusetts has no such law. This makes it impossible to treat patients like Kathleen."

"So, you have to wait until they do something or something happens to them?" the detective said.

"Yes," Stein said.

Nicholas was exhausted by the time he returned to Ina's house. His eyes watered from the daylight. He didn't want to speak about what had happened, not to Ina or anyone, and he hoped Kate would forget about what Kathleen had done, though the moment he saw her, his hope disintegrated. A sorrow seemed to cling to her and diminished the gleam in her eyes. She looked as if she might cry any minute.

"She was asking for you," Ina said. Nicholas stopped outside the door. There was a smell of baking. "And Kathleen," she said. It was strange to hear Ina utter Kathleen's name. All he could do was nod.

"She didn't eat much, just a few bites of a sandwich."

It was hard to read Ina's face. He thought she looked worried, but withdrawn too and distant, and he felt unbalanced standing at her door. A knot had

formed in his stomach. He didn't want to talk about
what happened, but to speak about anything else
was impossible. Ina made no move to ask him in.
She reached out to touch Kate's back, but stopped,
and he was thrown back years by the gesture. He
had a flash of her touching his face, and for a while
it seemed as if nothing moved. All sounds on the
street had stopped. All he could say was, "The
arraignment is in a couple of days."

She looked at him and he thought she would
have asked what Kathleen was charged with, if
Kate wasn't there.

"Do you need me to watch Kate?" Ina said.

A car pulled in to Mrs. Jacob's house across the
road, and it seemed improbable that life could keep
moving on as if nothing had happened. Nicholas
felt separated from it all. He said yes and thanked
Ina. Although the thought of seeing Kathleen frightened him, he knew he needed to be there. "It could
take hours," he said.

"That's okay," Ina said. "Will you be okay?"

He could have laughed at that question. His
daughter was loose in his hands, and he thought he
could feel her trembling, but he said yeah, sure.

Kate paused before going into the house and
Nicholas felt like his body had turned to stone. He

couldn't pull her in if she refused to go, but after a moment, she stepped forward. Her small hand pushed the door opened and he realized it had remained unlocked all day. The living room was shrouded in darkness. The curtains were drawn and Nicholas wanted to open them and all the windows to get rid of the stuffy cloying feeling in his chest, but Kate was moving forward towards her mother's room. She seemed to glide as though she were sleep-walking or pulled by a force greater than herself, and he wondered if she expected to see her mother in the bedroom, if she thought after everything, Kathleen might be a bundle in the bed and would rise and say hello. Nicholas expected his daughter to stop at the door, but she went in and following her, he saw that the drawers of the dressing table had been pulled out. Some clothes were on the floor and others were spilled over the drawer. The bed was unmade, the blankets tossed and falling off the end of the bed, and it lent urgency to the scene. Nicholas could imagine Kathleen jumping from the bed suddenly that morning, and he felt sick with the thought of her anxiousness.

The closet was open, and they stopped before Kathleen's summer dresses. Nicholas imagined Kathleen standing before them. Her fingers might have touched the fabric tentatively, as she did whenever the dresses arrived in the post. There was a childlike awe to her when she opened those parcels and took the garments out. She would ignore Kate's pleas to try them on straight away. Nicholas assumed she wanted to make sure they were fully hers before she put them on her skin. He assumed those dresses meant something to her until he saw them spaced evenly apart on their hangers. He imagined Kathleen positioning them like sentries. The policeman would have been behind her, maybe frowning with confusion.

He might have told her, "You won't need them where you're going." But Nicholas didn't think so. It was easier to imagine him behind Kathleen, watching as she slid the hangers away from each other. The sight of them must have been as unnerving to the young man as it was to Nicholas now.

Kate's grip on his hand had tightened. He glanced at her. Her eyes were narrow with confusion, a periwinkle blue that could break his heart. He stepped closer and started taking the dresses down. He laid each dress on the bed without letting go of Kate. He waited for her to start asking questions. All morning, he'd wondered what he would say when Kate asked where her mother was. He had only come up with 'gone'.

Such a small word, but big enough to take his breath away. 'Gone,' he would say. Then to her 'where,' he'd tell her, 'I don't know' and worry about the lie afterwards. But she didn't ask anything.

✳

They spent the day trying to ignore the absence that could not be ignored. After dinner and a few minutes of reading that he was sure Kate had not listened to, they wrapped up for a long walk to Highland Avenue, and their favorite café, the 3Figs. The café was their haven. Kathleen had never gone with them. They sat at a small table and Kate nibbled on her pastry. Nicholas tried to excite her with the promise of the movies, and he realized their delight in their private excursions would never be the same again. Their cheekiness in stealing from the house, in sharing secrets across the table and buying the extra sweet, had disappeared with Kathleen. There was no one waiting for them at home, no one to ask what did you do, what did you get? No reason to snigger and hide sugared hands. It was just the two of them, staring mutely across gnawed buns.

At home, he wished there were a way to broach the question of what Kate remembered. While she sat in the bath, she might look at him with clearer eyes and he'd be able to tell her that he'd come home in time to save her. "Everything is okay now," he wanted to say, but his daughter played with her toys and he hadn't the heart to ask.

Chapter Five

The car park at Somerville District Court was nearly full at 10 a.m. He'd tried to get there earlier, but Kate had been teary-eyed and had clung to him when he'd brought her to Ina's house. He'd had to stay until she got settled, and it felt as if his body were alive with nerves with the thought of Kathleen in the dock.

Now in the parking lot, there was a moment when he didn't know if it were possible to go through the door and walk into the room where he'd been arraigned when he was eighteen. He could almost smell it already — the ripe bitter scent of bodies cramped together for hours, and the sweat that had clung to his skin, like groping hands, sweat so rank it had shamed him. His mother had sat with Ina and Stefano in the crowd. They'd waited through the morning and the afternoon for his name to be read aloud and he'd wanted to beg them to leave. His mother had cried when he pleaded guilty to Grievous Bodily Harm.

What would his mother think today? Would she need to question him about what happened in his house? Would she accept his innocence? It was a grey day, but not too cold, and he wore jeans and a sweater. He'd hardly slept and his eyes were stinging. He suffered from a persistent bad taste in his mouth and a low drumming headache. The courtroom was full of crying mothers and silent fathers, fidgeting kids who were told to be quiet. A group of teenagers waited stiffly beside lawyers with suitcases, policemen, and some reporters sitting with notebooks in their hand. The defendants were on the benches to the left of the door. There were nine in all, among them a pale-skinned junkie slumped beside a man with tattoos snaking up his neck. There was a woman with short hair and a top that just covered her breasts, and a young man with glasses who kept glancing towards the public, but the only person Nicholas saw in the room was Kathleen. He'd seen her the moment he entered. She was sitting on the far side of the bench from the door. She didn't look at the door when Nicholas entered. Her head was down, and her shoulders slumped.

He kept his gaze on her throughout the morning of cases and he was sure she felt his presence, but not once did she meet his gaze. Nicholas had only seen her once since the morning she was taken away. Stein had been against the visit and he had been right; Kathleen hadn't been ready to see Nicholas. She'd been agitated when she sat opposite him and her gaze kept straying from his face and wandering around the room. He'd wanted to know if she remembered what had happened and he'd grabbed her hand lying on the table.

"Look at me," he'd said, but she'd pulled from him and said that she didn't want to listen. She was sick of listening. Her body jerked back and forth with such force that the chair scratched against the floor. He'd been so shocked he'd pulled back, and dry-mouthed and lost, he could only watch while she was led away.

The man with tattoos was charged with a felony for food stamp fraud. Another fat and indignant man was charged in a domestic violence case. The teenager, who'd operated a vehicle while impaired, got his license suspended. The judge was a small black man with a balding head and a voice that was deeper than expected. He was quick with all the cases, and conducted them with an air of irritation.

"I'm tired of seeing you in my court."

"Time served."

It was just before noon when Nicholas heard, "The People against Kathleen Lehanne, for the attempted murder of her daughter Kate Giovanni, March she as, 2004."

Kathleen didn't look up. The court officer was beside her and telling her to stand. A hand was on Kathleen's arm and Nicholas imagined the way the man pinched her skin. Kathleen rose, but she looked unsteady and half asleep.

The legal aid attorney, a woman of around thirty with short hair and sharp features, stood and made Kathleen's softness in the curve of her shoulders and the soft swell of her cheeks more pronounced. The Assistant DA had shoulder length hair and creases in his suit.

"Your Honor, my client has been in and out of psychiatric hospitals for the last fifteen years and showed signs of psychosis leading up to the event," the legal aid attorney said. "I move to find her incompetent to stand trial."

"Your Honor, she knew why she was arrested and brought to custody."

"Just because she was compliant does not mean she was aware of what she was saying. I have a record of her hospital admissions and a statement from her doctor, who believes she'd stopped taking her medication and is not competent to stand trial. We need time for a thorough psychological evaluation."

Nicholas had forgotten to breathe. It was so hard to stay silent. His body was like a coiled wire and he had to press himself onto the seat. The judge was sitting forward. A mumble had started in the room and he shouted for everyone to be quiet. Nicholas had hardly been aware of the shuffling in the seats, the murmurs and the clearing throats, until they stopped and the quiet was like a heated blanket on him.

"Ms. Lehanne, do you have anything to say?" the judge asked. After a pause, a murmur moved through the court. The judge hit the gavel, and shouted again for everyone to be quiet.

"Ms. Lehanne." She didn't move.

"Your Honor, if the defendant refuses to make a plea, a plea of not guilty must be entered by the court."

"You think you need to tell me what has to be entered?"

"Sorry, Your Honor."

The judge nodded and scribbled something down. He didn't look happy. "I cannot ignore a request for the competency issue to be examined. Ms. Lehanne will be held without bail in St. John's State psychiatric hospital until evaluation can be completed. Second competency will be set for May 5th. We will reconvene at 2:15."

Nicholas watched Kathleen being led out. She looked pale and drained, a different woman from the one he'd seen only a few days ago and he didn't trust it.

Nicholas had not gone back to work since Kathleen had been arrested. He knew he'd have to change shifts and work while Kate was at school, but he didn't want to think of it yet. He leased the car, so he had no one to answer to. He'd been frugal, saving as much as he could, and the house was paid for, so he could last a few weeks. The thought of leaving Kate with anyone was unbearable, and the sight of Kathleen in court had only made it worse. It was impossible to forget the limp way she stood, and the round defenselessness that had never been in her before. He couldn't help think she was acting, just like she'd acted after visiting with Ina, and it scared him to wonder what she might say.

Sometimes, when Kate seemed okay, like when he came back from the arraignment to find her baking and laughing with Ina, he would be able to forget about Kathleen, but that was a rare occurrence. Their days had a heavy, slow quality and by the end of the following week, he decided it was best if they got back into routine. Tilly's phone call helped solidify this decision. She asked about Kate and Nicholas said she was fine because he didn't want Tilly to know how upset Kate was. She still would not sleep without him beside her, and though she didn't complain while they got ready for school, she never wanted him to leave her once they arrived. Fortunately, she would ease when the teacher came over and said a few words. Still, Nicholas hated leaving her. He'd considered asking Adrial for help. Manuel was older than Kate, but Adrial homeschooled him and had offered to take Kate any morning he wanted. It would have been nice to keep Kate close by while she eased into activities, but Adrial had been distant with him lately. She'd nod and look away too quickly, and he wondered what she'd heard the morning Kathleen left. There'd been screams, and the thought of them made it impossible to approach her.

The nursing home was a large red brick building on a quiet street close to Summer Street. Steps led up to the front entrance. There was a ramp on either side, and he imagined Tilly being pushed in her wheelchair. Her back would have been straight and still her white hair would have been barely visible over the silver rails.

The reception area was welcoming with a carpeted floor and a smell of flowers. He went straight to the room on the ground floor, down a wide corridor with the same red carpet and landscape pictures on the wall. The receptionist's voice and a faint sound from the television followed him. He knocked before entering the stifling room. A scent of lemon clung to the air and he was struck by the sudden soundlessness when he closed the door behind him.

Tilly was sitting on a single bed with a pale blue duvet. The room was sparsely furnished with a bedside cabinet, a brown wardrobe whose doors didn't close fully, and an armchair by the window. The bare space made Tilly look small and fragile. On his approach, his steps were lost in the carpet. Tilly's hair was pulled in a bun, which made her look regal. Her eyes were the same deep chocolate as Ina's and there was a constant hint of worry in them now after her fall, though when she smiled, it was easy to forget this.

"You look awful," she said, after he'd hugged her and asked how she was and received a shrug. He chuckled and said thanks a lot. Her hand had remained on his arm after their embrace and she squeezed now, and asked if he'd lost weight. He said he probably had. His face was thinner now than it used to be and his eyes were more red than navy. He'd always been tall and sinewy, but lately, he'd become more aware of his body and limbs. Hours could be spent staring at his hands. After a moment, Tilly's hand dropped, but her scrutiny didn't lessen. He saw the worry and something else there — something hard that made Tilly look less fragile.

"How's Kate?" Tilly asked. Nicholas shrugged and said she was doing okay. He knew Ina had spoken to Tilly about what had happened, because on the phone Tilly had asked if everything was okay and there was toughness to her voice that suggested that she knew everything was not okay. She'd been like that when he was young too, tough and determined. Standing on his mother's porch the day he was released from prison, she'd warned him not to break his mother's heart again, this small woman who barely made it up to his shoulder.

She pointed to a bag on the bedside table and said she'd gotten a present for Kate. "How did you manage that?" Nicholas asked.

She touched her nose and said, "Now that's for me to know." Her laugh made her cringe from the pain.

A coloring book was in the bag and it saddened Nicholas, since at home, Kate had been too restless to color. This sorrow would come upon him often. Cooking or sitting at the table with Kate at dinner were always some of the worst times because of the silence that surrounded them, which was enhanced by the sounds of forks on plates — simple noises that he'd never noticed before.

"Nicholas?" He'd forgotten Tilly. "Is it that bad?"

He tried to smile, but his mouth felt tight. "She misses her mother."

"Is Kathleen coming back?"

"I don't think so."

She nodded, and his heart lurched at the prospect of more questions. He couldn't tell if he wanted them or not. Some days, his only wish was to move forward and forget, while other times, sitting in the kitchen after Kate finally went to sleep, he'd study his hands, the long fingers for opening and closing, and he'd want to tell the whole truth and find some release.

"What happened?" Tilly said. Her eyes were soft with concern, but it was the alarm in her voice that made Nicholas tell her that Kathleen put a pillow over Kate's face.

"If I hadn't come home early...." he said and finished because he didn't want to think of going home that morning. Tilly covered her mouth. He saw the anger in her eyes, and would have liked to walk away from her because he was sure there was blame there too and he had no defense against that. Finally, she asked why.

"I don't know," he said.

He thought he saw disbelief in her face. The door opened and he heard laughter from the hall before Ina said hello. Nicholas nodded and felt a surge of unease as he stepped back from the bed and watched Ina kiss her mother on the cheek. After they'd spoken softly, Ina asked how he was and how Kate was at school. He told her she was okay. He thought Ina wouldn't want to know if it had been otherwise. The day of the arraignment, Ina had asked Nicholas to explain exactly what had happened that final morning with Kathleen, but when he'd started to tell her she'd stopped him.

"I don't want to hear anymore," she'd said, and he'd been angry at her need to protect herself, just as she'd done years ago when she refused to answer his letters.

He'd said nothing to her, but his frustration would have been obvious with his abrupt departure, and now he was uncomfortable in the room and he sensed Ina was too. She asked Tilly how she was. Outside, clouds drifted. Nicholas glanced towards them while Tilly said there wasn't much change since yesterday.

Ina had taken the armchair beside the bed after giving Tilly a kiss. Nicholas thought Ina looked tired too, or sad, a little defeated maybe, and he wondered if she was regretting her decision not to go back to California.

"I asked Nicholas to come today," Tilly said. Ina said okay and waited. Tilly smiled at him, and Nicholas was surprised with the nervousness he saw in that smile.

"I'm sure you won't mind visiting me when Ina goes home," Tilly said.

Ina was glaring at her now, and it was obvious Tilly was unsettled. Her voice didn't hold as much authority when she said to Ina, "You need to get back to your life."

"This is my life. I told you already. I'm not going back."

To Nicholas, Tilly said, "Can you talk some sense into her?"

He didn't want to be a part of this. Still here he was, so he had to say something, and it was "That's impossible." Ina didn't seem to think it was funny.

"It's my fault," Tilly said. "A stupid old lady falling in the garden. It must have been a shock for you, but I'm fine now, better than fine actually. You know I've made some friends already and I like it. I've decided to stay."

Months ago, the thought of Tilly in a nursing home would have been absurd, yet here she was, frail and nervous. Still, that she would choose to stay was a shock and Ina immediately softened at the news.

"Oh no, Mom," she said, and for a moment Nicholas thought she would cry. She must have cried for her mother already, for the change that had happened and the loss of the vibrant woman who used to be seen puttering around the garden at all hours. Ina was standing close to the bed.

She said, "You can't stay here." Tilly smiled sadly. She said she had to. She didn't know how well she would get around now and she needed help.

"And I like it here Ina. I have fun with Linda."

"I want to take care of you," Ina said. Tilly nodded and said she knew that, but it didn't feel right. Ina had her own life to lead.

"I wouldn't stay here if I didn't want to," Tilly said. "I'm not that selfless."

Ina might have smiled. It was hard to see her downturned face. "I'm not going back to Stefano."

"I'm sure you can work it out," Tilly said.

Nicholas became conscious of the rattle of wheels from the hallway, and tried not to think of the pleading in Ina's voice when she said, "Don't do that. Don't tell me what to do. Not now."

"But he's your husband," Tilly said.

"He has a child." Ina's voice was low and breaking, but she was not crying when Nicholas looked at her. She and her mother were separated by inches and Ina seemed to want to get further from her. She'd pulled back and was stone-faced when she said, "He has a child with another woman. His name is Cooper and he's four."

The air had left the room. Tilly had paled while Nicholas was remembering phoning Stefano and telling him that he had a daughter. He'd cried on the phone, and all this time Stefano had a child and had never said.

"Four," Tilly said, and her voice came out like a whisper.

"Yes, Mom, he's four, I only found out recently. I saw them together." Ina took a breath. "You were wrong about him. He isn't one of the good ones."

Nicholas stiffened. He wanted to ask what Ina meant, though there was no way to get between the two women now and besides, he was afraid to ask. The numbness he'd felt towards Stefano was gone, and he felt sick and tired. Tilly deflated in the bed, while Ina was straight-backed and determined, like she used to be as a girl, and Nicholas remembered phoning the house when his letters went unanswered.

"Ina isn't here," Tilly had said each time.

Ina caught up with him in the hall outside. When she called his name, he stopped and glanced at the long grass in one of the landscape pictures on the wall and saw the outline of his face, which made him look away again.

"I'm sorry," she told him. "I didn't know if Stefano told you and I didn't know how to ask."

She must have thought his abrupt departure

from the room was because of Stefano and his child, when it was much more personal. She looked flustered and sad. Her brown eyes were pleading and he wanted more than anything to walk away and forget this niggling feeling that had started in him.

"He didn't tell me," he said.

Ina nodded and when she remained standing, as if waiting for him to say something more, as if he'd been the one to call for her, he felt a mixture of frustration and pity. He would have liked to touch her face or reach out for her hand, but it was impossible when he was experiencing that sinking feeling in his stomach and a sense of his blood draining away, similar to, but lesser than, the day he came home to find Ina gone.

"She won't change her mind about staying here, will she?" Ina asked. Nicholas couldn't help smile. They both knew there was no changing Tilly's mind when it was made up. Stubbornness ran in the family.

He said, "No, she won't."

Ina nodded and for a moment he was afraid she would reach for him, but she sighed and said that it would be strange to be in the house without her. Nicholas hadn't thought of what the house would be like. Tilly had been there since he could remember and to think of her gone and never coming back would have been shocking if not for what was going on in his head. As it was, it was hard to concentrate on anything. The sounds filtered in and out, voices from the hall, a slamming door, and he could feel Tilly's presence in the room beside him like a ball of heat. It was hard not to storm back and ask her what she'd done all those years ago to get Stefano and Ina together.

"Ina isn't here," she'd said with every phone call. He was beginning to suspect that that was only the start of it.

Ina was speaking about the house. It was small like Nicholas's, with Tilly's room behind the living room, and she said she didn't like going to that part of the house without Tilly. "The other day I had to get stuff from her room, and it was so weird to walk in and see everything as she'd left it when she wasn't there, and now she's not coming back."

Her voice trembled slightly and she had to look away to get her bearings. Nicholas was thrown back to years ago sitting across from her, and he had to get away from her. He felt claustrophobic standing in the hallway with her so close.

"It'll be okay," he said, and knew even as he spoke how lame it sounded. She looked puzzled, and then resigned. When she said she should get back to Tilly, her voice was flat. He watched her disappear behind her mother's door and it took a few moments before he was ready to move. It was starting to drizzle. His car was parked just outside the nursing home. It was conspicuous, but he could drive it down the street a little and then wait by the building for Ina to emerge. It could be another hour at least before she went home, but he didn't have to collect Kate for another three, and he hated the thought of going back to his house. It would be worse today with his rising suspicion regarding Tilly. His stomach was a mess, and he wished now that he still smoked, so he could do something to distract him. Behind him, a phone started from reception and propelled him forward onto the quiet tree-lined street. The cold air was a shock after the stifling warmth of the nursing home. The streets were quiet, and the trees stark in their bareness. By the time he reached he car, the anger he'd felt towards Tilly had started to turn, and it was hard to acknowledge the grief.

He turned the car around and took the first left to Laurel Street, a residential area that might get him a ticket, though he couldn't care about that. His body felt like a nest of nerves.

"*You're acting like everything is my fault,*" Ina had said in his kitchen, and he'd been shocked. Now he understood what she must have meant. His legs were shaky when he emerged from the car. The realization was like a slow beating. His body was taking on the full extent of it and it slowed his walk. He was aware that he might have missed Ina leaving, though he doubted she would have gone so soon. Ina would have walked to the nursing home. She didn't like to drive. He remembered her behind the steering wheel, looking so small with her hair wild on her head and her eyes anxious. *"This is a box, that's all it is."*

He stood by the side of the building. His hair was damp and he could feel the drops of rain run down his skin. He stood still and waited until Ina came out. When he saw her, he leaned against the wall and hid.

At Tilly's door, he knocked and waited for her to answer before opening. He was cold and wet, and knew he must have looked a sight before Tilly frowned and sat up on the bed. Now inside the room, he found it impossible to move any closer. Tilly had a book in her hand and she laid it on her knees. A burst of laughter came from the hall. Outside, the rain fell steadily. Tilly asked if everything was okay before Nicholas managed to say, "Looks like Ina's staying."

He saw it then. The frown and flash of unease made him feel like the air had been pushed out of him. She kept her gaze on him. The rain sent shadows across the room.

"That worries you, doesn't it?" he said.

There was a brief pause, hardly sufficient, before she said, "You nearly killed that boy."

He'd always regretted running to Ina's house afterwards. In the bathroom, she'd cried while she helped clean off the blood. "Do I scare you?" he asked.

He would have liked to sit down. The anger he'd felt throughout the last couple of hours was seeping out of him, though there was still a bitter taste of disgust in his mouth.

It was some relief to see the effort on her face. "I think you're unpredictable."

"For five years, I've done nothing but take care of my daughter and drive a taxi."

"What about Kathleen?"

"Don't do that."

He had not moved into the room properly. He'd stopped just inside the door and found it impossible to approach her now. Tilly seemed expectant and proud and he would have hated her for that if he wasn't so drained.

"Do what?" she said. "Talk about the woman you lived with for five years?"

For hours, he'd forgotten about Kathleen because he couldn't stop thinking of Ina when she'd visited him in prison. She'd looked so small and fragile. He'd hated seeing her there and he'd told her not to visit. He'd told her he'd write. The memory brought a low throbbing pain to his chest.

"Am I supposed to just forget about her?" Tilly asked.

"I took care of Kathleen."

Tilly was a frail woman, but there was nothing weak about her gaze. It was hard to withstand, and her tone was cutting when she said, "Then what happened to her?"

The question threw him and before he could answer she said, "Mrs. Jacob said an ambulance came."

He'd seen Mrs. Jacob outside the house that morning and he'd prayed she wouldn't come over. Now, he paused to let Tilly's statement sink in.

"What are you saying?" he asked, and was surprised by the calmness of his voice.

"You know what I am saying."

He did and wished he didn't know what she was talking about. He'd made one bad mistake years ago when he was a kid, but that was not who he was now. Voices came from the hall and highlighted his unease and strain.

"Kathleen needed an ambulance because she had a psychotic breakdown. It's not the first time she'd been involuntarily admitted, you know that."

Tilly might have nodded; the movement was so small he wondered if he'd imagined it. He would have loved to turn his back on the judgment in her face and the stony way she was viewing him.

He'd come back angry and upset, and now it

was hard to remember that anger, and feel anything other than the sinking sensation of resignation when Tilly said, "People don't change Nicholas."

She paused, but he would not argue his innocence with her. He'd never tried to.

"Should I tell Ina what Adrial told Mrs. Jacob? Do you want to know what it was?"

He stepped a little closer to her bed. He could feel the strain in his body and the tightness of his jaw and was relieved to feel the fury swell in him. Her expression had not changed, but he had the sense that she would have loved to draw back from him.

"Kathleen nearly killed Kate and I don't give a fuck what Adrial or Mrs. Jacob said."

Tilly's reaction was brief. The flash of surprise in her eyes dulled quickly.

After a long moment, Nicholas eased. He was starting to walk away. The room seemed too dark now and he had a sense of floating. It was hard to understand everything that had been said this morning. Tilly had always wanted to keep Ina from him, he knew that now, and it was shocking to him, as was the fact that Adrial and Mrs. Jacob seemed to find him guilty without knowing details. He wondered if Adrial had learned of his past from the neighbors and if the judgment in her eyes had as much to do with that as anything else.

The thought sickened him. All he wanted now

was to be alone. He didn't expect Tilly to say any-thing more.

But when he'd reached her door, she said, "If Kathleen suffers from mental illness, she couldn't be held responsible for her actions, could she?"

He stopped and it took all his effort to look at the woman on the bed, who'd been his mother's best friend, and who he'd loved for years.

"But that cannot be said for you, you need to take some responsibility for what happened." She was like a statue on the bed, except for her hands that clung to her book and he didn't know if the grip was from anger or fear.

"What do you think happened?" he asked, though he realized too late that he didn't want to hear the answer. He'd enough to deal with already.

There was a brief shake of her head and her voice was low and softer when she said, "I don't know what to believe, but I don't think you're inno-cent. Something happened in that house."

Nicholas parked the car outside his house. Across the road, Mrs. Jacob was probably preparing her lunch, and Adrial and Manuel might have been watching television. Sometimes, with all the win-dows open, he could hear the sounds of cartoons from their living room. The rain drummed against the windshield and he could feel the cold drifting into the car. He was exhausted and this helped quell his anger, as did the nausea that had risen in his stomach after Tilly's last words. He'd left without saying another word to her and had hardly felt the rain on his journey to the car. He should have sold the house and moved away. He should have known that people don't forget; after so many years he still made his neighbors nervous. He'd only been eighteen when he'd gotten angry with a boy from school. It wasn't his first fight. He'd grown up punching faces and thinking of his father, the man with quick hands and an even quicker temper. After his father left, Nicholas had gotten angrier. The abandonment was the worst cruelty. He still was not sure why the other boy had enraged him so much. He was younger, only fourteen, and maybe it was his ease that had gotten to Nicholas. This boy, who had a father at home, smiled at Nicholas the wrong way.

The rain gave a soothing rat-a-tat-tat and Nicholas felt incapable of getting out of the car. It had been a spring day when he'd stood outside Ina's house covered in blood. He hadn't cried then or when he'd stood back to see the bloody mess of the boy, or afterwards when the ambulance came, and the boy was taken to hospital and the witnesses came forward and he was charged. He didn't cry until he heard the boy was left with brain damage.

A flicker of the curtain next door made him aware of how he must look, sitting outside his house, and he started the engine and drove towards Somerville Avenue. A half hour later, he stood in Kate's school. He was early, but her teacher didn't seem surprised. She was a tall, dark-haired woman who had a habit of frowning. She looked worried when she said that Kate had been very quiet all day and seemed distracted.

"She might be coming down with something," she said.

Nicholas wished it were as simple as that.

Kate's nervousness stayed with her. He had never needed to distract her with the television before. When he showered, he used to take his time, knowing she would be in the same position on the floor, content with the coloring pencils and books he had given to her. But now, he would come out of the bathroom to find her waiting outside the door, her hands empty and eyes watering.

"Do you want to watch a video?" he'd started to ask.

She'd nod and climb on the couch, waiting for him to put on Sesame Street. He'd feel her gaze as he retreated and hear her nervous fidgeting. She didn't like being alone, but he hoped these few minutes each morning might ease her into it. He never expected her to leave the house.

There was a song on the television. He heard a squeaky female voice when he opened the bathroom door and called to Kate. His skin was still wet. He'd wrapped a towel around his waist. A sudden feeling of unease had ushered him out to the living room where the empty couch made him feel cold. There was a cacophony of voices. 'Let's do…." The rest of the sentence was broken off by the sight of his open front door.

A strange sound came from him. He nearly ran out in his towel but darted to his room for his sweatpants and t-shirt. Big Bird was talking as Nicholas ran through the living room. He was Kate's favorite character. She'd said she liked his size and color. She would have loved to walk to school with him some day. She'd told Nicholas this when he sat down with her a few mornings ago. She had held onto his hand, not wanting him to go. He should never have left her alone. A car passed the house. The driver kept her attention on the road. Nicholas was struck with the sight of the vehicle and was sick with fear.

He couldn't think of how Ina would react to his visit. He hadn't spoken to her since the nursing home. It was impossible to forget Tilly's harsh judgment and he couldn't speak to Ina with that on his mind. Ina had not sought him out either, and he knew it would have been hard for her to breach the distance twice. Now there was nothing on his mind, but his need to find his daughter. His body felt like a block of cement as he ran to Ina's house and up the porch steps. The door was unlocked and he knocked quickly before opening it. And there she was, his little Kate. Her red hair was messy on her head. Her little body was covered by Winnie the Pooh pajamas. Ina was before her crouching down, so they stood eye to eye. She was holding Kate's hands.

Nicholas's relief was immense. His urge to yell at Kate to never do that again was lost when Ina looked at him. For a second, she was startled by his presence, but her eyes softened. Maybe she saw his fear and worry and was telling him that it was okay. Kate had turned around. She looked sad to see him and he felt like an intruder on this scene.

"It's okay, she can stay for a while," Ina said. He didn't deserve to see Ina look so softly at the little girl, and to witness Kate's eyes widen with her desire to stay. "Please, Daddy?"

He would have liked to join them, to pat Kate on the shoulder and say something to Ina, but he nodded instead and walked away.

Nicholas heard Kate's voice. He was standing by

the door when she and Ina reached the porch. Kate's hair was tied back in a ponytail and he couldn't recall her going to school like that. Nicholas was happy if he managed to give her hair a few strokes of the brush.

"We had fun," Ina said. "We had a picnic inside."

"Yeah," Kate said. She was still holding Ina's hand and Nicholas recognized her reluctance to let go.

"Did you know crocodiles can't stick out their tongue?" Kate asked.

"I'm a fount of useless knowledge." Ina told him.

Adrial emerged from the house next door and was shouting for Manuel, who appeared flustered with his shoelaces undone. Adrial glanced at Nicholas and nodded. Kate waved to her and said, "Ina says I can go to her house tomorrow."

Adrial smiled, but Nicholas saw the surprise flash across her face. He imagined how it must look, the fights and arguments, and finally Kathleen being brought away in an ambulance weeks after Ina's return home.

CHAPTER SIX

IN THE MORNINGS, NICHOLAS would drop Kate at school, then return to the house where the stillness held too many sounds and made him jumpy and tense. It wasn't hard to imagine Kathleen rising from the empty bed in all her red-haired glory, her face pale and her bright eyes pleading, or to think of her sitting in the kitchen waiting. He started to look in every room to ensure that she was gone. And such was his turmoil that he didn't know if he wanted to find her or not. One morning, his brother phoned.

"How is everything?" Stefano said. He sounded nervous.

Nicholas had called him after he'd learned about Cooper. "I know you have a son."

"I'm sorry," Stefano had said. "I didn't know how to tell you."

"Yeah, I'm sure it was hard to tell Ina too. You're a bastard, you know that." Nicholas had hung up before Stefano had a chance to answer and he considered hanging up now, but he thought of being left with the house and its soft sounds.

Nicholas said, "We had a bit of a crisis here."

Crisis- where did he get that word from — Stein, his mother? It didn't matter because he could almost feel Stefano straighten on other side. "Tell me."

He told his brother about coming home and his scream and lunge towards Kathleen. He told him about seeing his child pale on the bed and about Kathleen being brought to hospital and her competency trial that was scheduled in a few months. Nicholas let it all out and felt a little better for the release. When his words trailed off, there was a suitable pause. Then Stefano said, "Jesus, that's insane."

For the first time in weeks, a chuckle erupted from Nicholas. "You could say that."

Stefano offered to come down for a few days, but it wouldn't be possible for at least another week. There was too much going on at work. Nicholas told him not to bother; he'd call if he needed anything. He didn't want Stefano to come and start digging with endless questions, and besides, the knowledge of his affair with another woman, and his child, left a bitter taste in Nicholas's mouth that he hadn't been able to deal with yet. Stefano asked how Ina was.

"She seems fine."

Nicholas didn't mention Kate's visits to Ina after school. A few afternoons ago, he'd phoned Ina and said Kate wanted to run to her house alone and he asked if Ina could keep watch at her door. There'd been a pause where Ina might have considered this a ruse in order not to see her, which it wasn't. Kate had voiced the idea while they ate a snack in the kitchen. It was the third week in March. A bright day was visible outside the window and the low hum of the fridge and tick of the clock was the only background noise.

"Please," Kate had said, and it was impossible to take away her excitement. Her eyes were lit up and her legs swung inches from the floor. Nicholas agreed and stood on the porch to watch her run across the grass and driveway towards Ina's house, with her red hair flowing behind her. He had to fight the urge to run after her.

"I'm sorry, Doctor Stein is not in his office. Do you want to leave a message?"

It had been over a week since Nicholas had

talked to Stein and he'd left three messages already. There was a pause where the woman's breathing drifted down the line before he said no. She was in the middle of wishing him a nice day when he hung up. She probably had not put the receiver down on the other side by the time he'd grabbed his jacket from the back of the kitchen chair.

St. John's Hospital was a 40-minute drive from Boston. He went north on 93, and after the exit, passed a farmers' market that was still closed. Although soon there would be the red, orange and white of tomatoes, carrots and cauliflower, now the dark mouth of the galvanized store yawned bare in the pale blue light. On either side of Nicholas were open spaces of green. His hands started to sweat. There was a feeling of isolation, of being stretched too far. It seemed an eternity before the hospital appeared on his left. The parking lot was in front of the building. At 10 a.m. it was three-quarters full. A man, his head lowering towards his knee, his hand up against his cheek, was sitting in a wheelchair before the front entrance. The front door was at the side of the main building. It was unassuming and flanked by large windows on either side. Nicholas thought the entrance looked innocent compared to the sprawling edifice, as if it had been put there to beguile. He had never liked the feel of the place. The gargantuan walls, the grounds that spread outwards, and the parking lot with the loose gravel seemed a mask to something less orderly.

Inside the main door, sunlight was squeezed out and discarded. The floors were red tiled and the walls were painted a light brown. To the right of the door was a counter and behind it, a man in a navy uniform. He had a mustache and lazy blue eyes and sat straighter when he saw Nicholas. A blonde, stocky woman with a yellow vest over her clothes came from the corridor that stretched in front of him. She ambled past and up the stairs to her left without glancing at Nicholas. A sign showed the cafeteria was down the corridor she had come from. From a directory on the wall, Nicholas had read years ago that administration and dentistry were on the same floor. He knew the visitors' room was upstairs and not far from Stein's office. He had the familiar sense of walking into an enclosed world when he told the security guard who he'd come to see.

After the phone call from the guard on duty, it took Stein nearly fifteen minutes to come down to the main desk. Stein was a tall, bespectacled man with receding dark hair. Dressed in a white shirt and dark pants, he didn't look happy to see Nicholas.

"She's still not ready to see anyone. It's going to take at least another week before the Clozaril starts to have an effect. You know what it's like."

"Has she said anything at all?"

Stein sighed before telling Nicholas to come up to his office. They were silent on their walk up the stairs and down the white walled corridor that smelled of coffee and air freshener. The floor tiles were well-worn. Nicholas could hear a woman's voice from behind a closed door and a ringing phone off in the distance. There was one window at the end of the hall, streaks of dirt on the white walls, and a slight chill to the air.

Stein's office was small with a large desk and two chairs opposite his. Two bookshelves took up the far wall and his academic achievements were framed behind him. There were no photos on his desk. Once Nicholas had taken his seat, he asked if Kathleen had spoken to Stein about what happened.

The doctor said, "No, and I wouldn't be able to tell you if she had."

"She hurt Kate. I need to know what she's said about it." Stein apologized in a way that made Nicholas feel he was not sorry, and said that he had to abide by patient confidentiality. Nicholas couldn't believe this. "You talked easily before."

The doctor may have smiled. It was there for a second and then gone, leaving his face blank and distant. "She gave me written consent that time. You needed to understand the full situation."

"Did she understand the full situation?"

From the hall, there was a scuffle of steps. Stein was watching Nicholas with a frown. "What are you talking about?"

"You deemed her an unfit mother."

Stein sat forward and his dark eyes showed a flare of anger. "I told you that if she tried to leave, you would have rights as a father, given her history. There is a difference."

Bullshit, Nicholas thought. Stein had been Kathleen's judge and jury without giving her a chance.

The table was a mess of paper, just as it had been the first time Nicholas sat in this office, when he'd discovered the extent of Kathleen's illness. Stein was regarding Nicholas the way he always did, but there was a hint of curiosity thrown in as if he wasn't sure what to make of him.

"Kathleen knew what she was doing when she hurt Kate," Nicholas said.

A hard glaze came over Stein's eyes and his lips tightened before he said, "You can't seriously believe that." The windows were rectangular and high on the walls. Nicholas saw patches of cloud-less sky. He said, "I saw her the last time she was brought in here. I know what happens when she stops taking her meds, but she wasn't like that."

"Do you know what you are saying?"

Nicholas nodded. There were hurried steps outside, a muffled yell. They were not far from the visitor's room where Nicholas had visited Kathleen before. "I would testify to it." Neither man looked at Stein's phone when it started to ring. The noise was shrill and wore on Nicholas's nerves.

"She's been hospitalized three times," Stein said. "The last time was after a suicide attempt." The ringing stopped.

"She took the pills when I was there for Christ's sake," Nicholas said.

"Are you saying she knew you'd save her? You need to be careful," Stein said.

"What's that supposed to mean?"

The phone started again and Stein lifted it up before cutting the caller off and leaving the receiver on the table. He looked agitated now. "You were in charge of administering her pills," Stein said. "Why did you stop?"

Nicholas sat forward. It had suddenly gotten hot, and he wished he'd taken off his jacket. "I didn't stop giving them to her."

"Are you sure?"

A cold spasm ran down Nicholas's back. "What has she said to you?"

"I can't tell you. You know that, but I will tell you that I saw the bruises."

"She nearly killed Kate," Nicholas had been shocked with the blame in Stein's tone, though he knew he shouldn't have been, since recently, whenever he'd phoned the doctor, he'd noticed a change in his tone. Stein had been abrupt, almost curt. Nicholas was sure Stein regretted what he'd done years ago. His patient was pregnant, and he'd made promises that he shouldn't have, and his hostility was defense more than anything else.

Stein shook his head and Nicholas was struck by the thinness of his face, the skin too tight on bone and wondered how he'd never noticed it before. "You want me to believe a woman I have seen on and off for fifteen years and who has been on Clozaril for ten was suddenly able to go off her medication and be aware of her actions?"

"She knew what she was doing." Nicholas repeated. "And that's exactly what I told the psychiatrist who phoned me."

Stein's jaw tightened. Outside had darkened, the bright March day dimmed by cloud. "There is no way I'm going to agree with that, and my colleagues won't either. She was off her meds and in her condition that is cause enough for psychosis." A low tone came from the disconnected phone and got to Nicholas. "I don't think you've thought clearly about this," Stein continued. "Why would you want your daughter to grow up knowing her mother meant to kill her?"

"You think her insanity will be any easier?"

Stein leaned forward, his gaze probing and alert.

"If this goes to trial, I'll have to give a court order for Kathleen's records. They will see everything that is on there."

"I'm not afraid of that," Nicholas said.

Stein said, 'Maybe you should be."

CHAPTER SEVEN

INA PULLED THE CURTAINS in her mother's room. The bed had been unmade when she'd come home from California, and Tilly's nightdress had been thrown on the bed. It had been a sad sight for Ina, given that her mother was so organized and tidy. Up until then, Ina had refused to think of her mother hurt or that Tilly' life had changed in any way, but the silence of the empty house and the simple unmade bed had made her finally admit the truth. She'd cried with a sense of release and exhaustion. She hadn't cried when she'd first heard of her mother's accident or in the weeks and months before Stefano stopped coming home.

Tilly's room held a double bed with a quilt Nicholas's mother, Maureen, had sewn years ago.

Beside the bed was a chest of drawers. A Mills and Boon romance had sat atop it, opened to the first pages. Ina had since brought it to her mother as well as a few more slim books with pictures of couples entwined on the cover, and she'd goaded her mother about being an eternal romantic. In Tilly's bedside drawers, there was an old photo of her and Maureen on Tilly's front porch, and one of the children in Maureen's back garden, as well as an old wedding photo of Tilly outside the church with her husband. A framed photo of the two cutting their wedding cake hung on the living room wall.

Ina had asked if Tilly wanted her to bring the photos to the nursing home and had been surprised when Tilly said no, she didn't want anything brought from the house yet. Once she was able to move around, she'd go and help Ina pack.

Ina didn't bother telling her how restless she was in the house. She was a self-employed accountant, and she still worked with some clients from California. Every morning, she unfolded the table in the living area to work on, but after a few hours it was impossible to concentrate and she'd find herself roaming around the house as if she had never been here before, and was looking for the first time at the pictures on the wall or the notes scrawled in her mother's writing that hung on the fridge. Ina had a feeling of loss, but also an idea that she'd gone back in time to when Nicholas first went away. She was hit with the same sense of aimlessness, so it was good to have something to do. She'd already gone through the drawers in the kitchen and sorted the takeout menus into a folder. The old bills she'd thrown away, along with the scattered shopping list. The morning after Stefano's phone call, she'd also organized every cupboard, and filled two plastic bags of food gone past the expiration date, to calm herself down.

"Hello, Ina," Stefano had said on the phone, and she had no idea why she didn't hang up. The surprise wouldn't have been enough. Maybe it was a morbid curiosity to see what he would say, though it was true that his voice brought his child to mind, a dark-haired boy, who had clung to his father when Ina stopped them on the street, and the memory made it difficult to speak. She might have known that there was another woman, but the fact of the child ripped a hole in her, which re-opened with the sound of Stefano's voice.

"Nicholas called and told me what happened." Ina said nothing.

"I didn't want to say anything to him, but he has a record, if there is any question...."

Ina hung up. Seconds later, the phone rang again. She felt as if she watched from a distance her hand reaching for the receiver. "Don't call here again," she said.

"Should I go to him?" Stefano said quickly.

"Why are you asking me?"

"Since you're there, and you know what happened."

"I have no idea what happened," she said, and regretted immediately the implication that there was more to know than what he'd heard from Nicholas. The pause was drawn out, and she remembered their silence on the street and the way Stefano had pulled the boy close to him. And she hung up. He didn't try calling again.

The living room held little to sort out. There was a cabinet with Tilly's good china that was dusted a few times a year. Ina used to be too nervous to hold the dishes, fearing that they would crumple in her hands. There were books and odds and ends on the bottom ledge of the coffee table. Ina had tidied them up before she'd wandered to her mother's room.

She'd already brought some clothes to Tilly, and she'd thought she might organize others now. There was a chill in the air, but Ina knew March days could be surprisingly warm, and it was around this time that she and her mother used to begin taking out the spring clothes.

Standing in front of her mother's wardrobe, she ignored her sense of guilt at the idea of invading her privacy. Her mother was fastidious. Everything had to be done a certain way, and it wasn't surprising that she wanted to pack her clothes herself, but there was also no knowing how long she'd be immobile. There'd been complications when a healthy portion of her hip had fractured during surgery and needed to be fixed with pins. It could be well into the spring before she could get back to the house for a visit, and even later before she was able to roam around, so she would have no choice but to let Ina take care of this for her.

There were pants hanging in the wardrobe, some blouses, a Boston University sweater that Tilly bought when Ina was in college and probably never wore, and some long cardigans that she wore during the winter when feeding the birds. On the floor of the wardrobe, there were a few pairs of shoes. Tilly had never understood the fascination with shoes; she had trainers, rubber boots for the rain, a few pairs of black dress shoes that she used to wear in the clothing store she'd managed, and winter boots she'd been wearing when she fell, and were now by her bed in the nursing home along with the slippers Ina had brought.

Ina sat on the end of the bed. Every now and again since coming home, she was hit by a grief that scared her. It was more a premonition than anything else because it brought with it the idea that her mother was gone. She had to move past it, otherwise she might cry again and she was tired of crying. She went quickly to the hall and the attic door she pulled down with the help of a string. It was up there that she and her mother stored their clothes when each season was finished.

In the attic, Ina was able to stand upright. The light was brighter than she remembered. The floor was wooden and the roof insulated, and there were more boxes than she recalled. There were the two large suitcases that contained the clothes they stored, always wrapped in plastic to prevent mold. An old single mattress had been put up there years ago and never moved, along with some schoolbooks of Ina's Tilly didn't want to throw out, a box of Halloween decorations and masks collected over the years, and Christmas decorations that were used every year. There were a couple of other boxes Ina didn't recognize. A plastic one with a lid held old Christmas cards and letters that Ina had sent, as well as her MCAS results and report cards. Beside this was a small trunk that opened on swimwear and towels. She recognized the child's swimsuit with a picture of Ariel and, in the same plastic sheet, some toddler shorts and tops. Ina sat on the floor beside the trunk and felt as if the air was being squeezed out of her. Her mother had never said anything about the clothes she had kept, and Ina wondered if she'd hidden them in her room until Ina left and then decided it was okay to move them up here out of her way. Ina had not set foot in this attic for years — a good place to hide the hope for a grandchild Tilly must have harbored right up until a few weeks ago. Below the shorts was a yellow summer dress with white frills. If Ina had ever worn it, it would have been only once or twice. She'd always hated dresses, but now the sight of it made her feel a shocking sense of loss. There would be no grandchild for the yellow dress, or the white one Ina had worn for her first holy communion. She remembered that dress, knee-high with short sleeves. There was a photo downstairs of her standing side by side with Nicholas, her in her white knee socks and him in a suit that made him look like an old man before his time with his long face. There were two more dresses below the Communion dress. Ina recognized the blue one as one she'd worn to her high school prom. Her mother must have taken it out of her wardrobe to keep in plastic and store when Ina left. It was hard for Ina to understand how she was feeling. She was sad, but there was unease too, a sense that something wasn't right, and by the time she reached the bottom of the trunk her stomach was turning.

A blanket Maureen had crocheted was there on the bottom. Something was under the blanket that raised it by an inch. Ina assumed it was paper or more plastic to protect the clothes until she pulled back the blanket from one corner and saw the stamp. Her voice moved up her throat. Her mouth opened and she felt a need to scream though no sound came out, because the cry had fallen back into her depths by the time she'd pulled the blanket off and saw her name and address written over and over again in Nicholas's hand.

Chapter Eight

Ina,

This is my first time ever writing a letter and it feels weird, like I'm pretending to be someone I'm not. I'm sorry for taking so long. I didn't realize that everything costs money here, and I'd have to buy the paper and the pen. I had to wait until Mom came up for a visit, and then I couldn't even ask her because she was so upset, and so I had to wait until her next visit. While I was waiting, I kept thinking of things I wanted to tell you and now that I've started writing, I can't think of any. It's 5:00 in the morning. I like this time because it's quiet. It's hardly ever quiet here. I always try to wake before the count, when everyone's asleep. I wish I had a window though. It's hard when you don't know what kind of day it is. Maybe you can tell me what it's been like at home.
Nicholas

Ina,

I dream about that kid a lot. He's always on the ground and I'm hitting him, but I don't want to, I want to stop, but I can't. It's hard to forget the dreams after.

Ina,

Sorry that letter was so short. I just needed to say that to someone, and you don't talk like that to the guys here. I don't talk much here but I'm lucky because my bunkie, (that's what you call a cellmate) is all right. He's been in for ten years and works in the library. He can speak fluent Spanish and is learning French. He said he could teach me and I told him I can hardly write a letter in English. He wasn't impressed with that, said I should use my time to better myself. Maybe he's right. It's hard to concentrate on anything though. I'm always keeping an eye on other stuff; a sound can make you jump in here like it wouldn't outside, and then you feel stupid for it. How's school?

Nicholas

Ina,

Are you still angry with me for not wanting you to visit? I know how stubborn you can be, but I hated seeing you here and I didn't want you to get used to seeing me in this place. I've started to read a little. Fred, my bunkie, got To Kill a Mockingbird *from the library for me. I know we were supposed to read it for school once, but I never did. I like reading it now because Scout reminds me of you.*

Nicholas

Ina,

Fred's asked who I'm writing to all the time. I didn't want to tell him. This was the one thing I had to myself. In this place, there isn't much privacy; we have to go to the toilet in front of each other for Christ's sake. When I didn't answer, he said maybe I should stop writing to him. He thought I was writing to the kid I hurt, since I keep writing and writing and never get an answer. I didn't tell Fred he was wrong, because I've thought of writing to him and his parents. (Only, what can I say to them?) And I didn't want to say your name in this place.

Nicholas

Ina,

I'm starting to get worried that you are not getting my letters. I wouldn't put it past the guards. I thought of asking Mom when she came to visit, but I couldn't. She worries enough. She's nervous in here and sad with everything, so mostly I just let her talk about what she's been doing so we can forget where

I am. I don't like when she stops talking and starts looking around, because you can see how much it gets to her, and it takes a little while before she can concentrate. It reminds me of when Dad left.

The opened letters were beside Ina. It was getting harder to read. A low throbbing pain had started in her head. Her mouth felt like sandpaper from crying and each word pulled at her heart and made her move between anger and sympathy. It was so easy to picture him at eighteen, tall and thin and quiet. He would have watched everything closely and he would have been careful and distant in his observations. She could read his fear off the page so clearly. *Sometimes, I don't know if I can do this.* Nicholas wrote in one letter, and Ina felt like her heart had become dislodged in her chest. He'd written little else, but that one sentence was enough.

Some letters weren't signed and read more like diary entries than correspondence.

Today was the same as usual, breakfast and then work in the laundry until 12, before going for lunch and back to work until 5. One of the guys forgot to sign his menu sheet so he has the vegetarian option all week. He wasn't too happy about it. I don't blame him. Food's bad enough as it is and the vegetarian dish usually looks like someone ate it already. I'm on my second Sydney Sheldon book. There's no surprise he's popular.

Then there were others that made her feel like he was beside her.

Ina,

We used to finish each other's sentences, or you used to finish mine, because I was never fast enough to finish yours. We'd leave the house at the exact same time and after a while we got so used to it that we didn't laugh about it anymore. I shouldn't have taken that for granted. I should have let you visit. I was wrong. Where did you go?

The knock came late. Nicholas had fallen asleep beside Kate in the sliver of space given in her small bed. Her little hand was in his, and he opened his eyes to her sleeping with her mouth open. She was frowning and he was sure she was dreaming. He wished he could clear her head and help her to sleep easily as she used to do. Another knock came before he considered sliding away from Kate. She still had a grip on his hand and he eased himself from her.

He could see Ina outside. The street lights gave shape to her form, but nothing could have prepared him for her reddened face and the opened letter she held in her hand. The long slim envelope brought back how he had felt every week sitting in his cell writing to her.

"I didn't get them," she said.

Her voice was low and he had no idea what to say. Ina was the first to move. Her arms wrapped around him. He felt the warmth of her body against his and the slight tremor left from her crying. He heard the rustle of the letter she held and then nothing, but their breathing

A passing car lit up their bodies, and he managed to lead her inside and close the door. The room was dimly lit by a lamp, and light spilling out from the kitchen. A low couch faced the window. Everything was draped in gloom and the air was thick with silence.

"They were in the attic," she said.

With her before him and her hair as wild as it had been when she was younger, he had a sense that they'd gone back in time, though they hadn't, and he only had to clench his fist to feel the present bearing down on him. He'd always thought she'd read those letters and put them back in their envelopes and walked away. It was impossible to envision her throwing them out or burning them while he was in prison, though later, when he'd come home to Ina with Stefano, he'd thought of it.

Now, she was the one looking lost when she said, "Mom hid them."

The house ticked around them. The street was so quiet. He had no idea what time it was.

"She was protecting you," he finally said, because she seemed to be waiting for something.

"How could you say that?" When he didn't answer, she said, "She had no right."

For a moment he thought she would start to cry. She looked drained already, and he thought she might go to the couch where she used to stand on her head to watch television. But she was stepping closer to him with the letter grasped in her hand. He wondered which one she brought and knew in the same instant that he didn't want to know. He didn't want to look at those letters and remember waiting every day for the mail. By his last months, he felt each letter he wrote diminished him, but to go the other way, to not take out his pen and paper would have made him close completely. He'd seen men like that, and he couldn't risk it.

"You wrote every week." She was so close he could see the tear-stains on her cheek and smell the coconut scent from her hair. Part of him wanted to pull away from her and gain a safe distance. A niggling voice in his head reminded him of Kathleen and the fact that a few weeks ago she was in this house, but to move away from Ina was impossible.

"I didn't know what to think. You looked so angry when I saw you there. You looked different. I didn't know...."

Suddenly, he knew what letter she held and he felt a mix of relief and sorrow. That letter was written so long ago, but he couldn't say that. She was starting to cry and his arms were around her. For a moment there was nothing but their still bodies, but all she had to do was pull back and look at him. His mouth was on hers, and he felt a rush of helplessness that he'd always known with Ina. They could have been teenagers again, with nothing but each other. He didn't register his daughter's voice the first or the second time she called.

"Daddy."

She was holding her teddy close to her chest and on the verge of tears.

"Kate," Ina said and then looked at Nicholas. He could feel her worry in her glance, but he was already going to his daughter. He was afraid she might step back from him. There was uncertainty on her face, and later he would try to tell himself that was only his guilt speaking, but he would never quite believe it, because it seemed all their problems began after this night.

Still, she let him pick her up and snuggled into him. "Let's get you to bed," he said.

There was no knowing what Ina saw in his

glance towards her, whether it was his guilt or help-lessness that made her say that she should go, but he was sure she paused at the front door to look at him walking towards the back bedroom with his daughter in his arms.

Later that night, when he'd finally gotten Kate to sleep and felt okay about leaving her, he found the letter that Ina had brought lying on the arm-chair by the door.

CHAPTER NINE

DISTRICT COURT JUDGE FRANK Carlin has ordered a mental competency evaluation in the case of a Somerville woman arrested for the attempted murder of her five-year-old daughter. Kathleen Lehanne (33) of 15 Summer Street was arrested March 2nd at 10 a.m. at her home. Records show Kathleen Lehanne has been in and out of psychiatric hospitals and has been treated for schizophrenia. The evaluation hearing will be held May 5th.

Ina read the article twice. She hadn't slept all night and her eyes stung from crying and exhaustion. Earlier, Ina had seen Nicholas bring his daughter to school. Hand in hand, they'd walked to the car, and he hadn't looked in her direction. Other people had spilled out of their houses to go to work or school, including Mr. Jacob, punctual as ever at 7:05. Then Mrs. Jacob walked her dog. The morning had flowed onwards with Ina by the window in the living room, at the kitchen sink, on the couch, at her mother's door, at the bottom of the attic stairs; she was in constant movement to try and stop thinking of the letters, but Nicholas's words kept coming back to her.

I'm so afraid of forgetting what it's like outside here.

Ina had seen Mrs. Jacob leave her house a second time. Mrs. Jacob, square shouldered and well-built, had walked towards Ina's house with the newspaper in her hand. Ina shouldn't have answered the door, but she did, and now she felt close to falling apart. She was reluctant to meet Mrs. Jacob's gaze. The two sat at the living room table. Mrs. Jacob had thin greying hair and a way of sitting that made her look soft as putty.

"I got a shock when I saw it too," Mrs. Jacob said.

Ina nodded. Her shoulders had folded inward and gone limp, and she felt like a sack on the chair. Ina slid the paper away and took a sip of her coffee. It tasted foul and clung to the inside of her mouth, but she wanted to do something with her hands. Mrs. Jacob's coffee was nearly all gone. Biscuit crumbs were on the table before her.

She said, "I'm sorry, I didn't mean to upset you."

Ina said it was okay, though she found it hard to believe Mrs. Jacob's concern. The phone pierced the silence. Mrs. Jacob glanced towards the couch and the small table that held the phone. There was a build-up of tension that Ina had neither the energy or will to ease. The ringing stopped and Mrs. Jacob seemed unsure where to look. She must have known Tilly was the caller, and that this had happened more than once in the last two days.

Mrs. Jacob smiled now as if willing Ina to speak. She'd hardly said anything after she'd asked Mrs. Jacob in and offered coffee, two things she had regretted immediately. She should have said she wasn't feeling well, which wasn't exactly a lie. Besides, Ina had always hated gossip and neighborly chats. She couldn't abide the notion that you had to be friendly with people just because they happened to live next door. Stubbornness kept her quiet. The phone rang again, and Mrs. Jacob frowned and asked if Ina wanted to get it.

She said, "Maybe it's your mother."

Ina said, "No, it's okay. I'll call her back later."

Tilly had left two messages yesterday, the first in the morning asking if Ina was coming in. In the evening, she'd sounded worried when she asked if everything was okay. Her voice had made Ina cringe. For two days, Tilly had heard nothing and was getting upset. Two days, and Ina was sure she'd phoned Mrs. Jacob and sent her over. Nicholas had had two years of nothing.

In the renewed quiet, Mrs. Jacob said, "Did you know Kathleen?" Her soft regard worried Ina, because she sensed nothing casual in the question. She said, "No, not really."

"She was a nice woman, a bit shy and quiet. I felt sorry for her when she was pregnant. You could see she was scared and nervous. She didn't like to be left alone, so I'd sit with her when Nicholas went to work."

Ina watched Mrs. Jacob's mouth open and close Her cheeks wobbled and her mouth stretched into a smile, before she said, "It drove Tilly mad to go in there. Your mother was always better out in the garden than indoors. I didn't mind though, especially when Kathleen got bigger and was so nervous. Not that she was the only one — Nicholas was nervous too. He treated her like she was made of glass."

Ina's head was spinning with the thought of Kathleen pregnant with Kate. Ina hadn't allowed herself to think of Kathleen growing with Nicholas's child and the intimacy of the two of them sharing this when she'd first heard about Kathleen's pregnancy. She had kept her mind blank because it hurt to consider how easy it was for others. Ina's pregnancies had never lasted beyond four months.

A hollow emptiness spread inside her and she

was afraid that she'd cry. She might have if Mrs. Jacob hadn't kept talking. "Kathleen was nervous with Kate when she was first born. Such a tiny thing and she was afraid of hurting her."

Ina felt dizzy. "What are you talking about?" she wanted to demand, but it was hard to speak. A ball of dread had formed in her chest.

"She was sick," Ina said.

"Yes, I know, schizophrenia. That's the one where people hear voices, isn't it? I saw a woman like that once outside the train station, walking in circles and having an argument with herself, but Kathleen was never like that. She was quiet and shy."

You can't trust anyone in here. All night, lines from Nicholas kept coming to Ina, and she thought of them now as she watched Mrs. Jacob shake her head and glance at the paper. The attic stairs were still pulled down and the light was on. Ina hadn't been able to go back after her visit with Nicholas. She didn't think she'd survive reading those letters again after seeing his fear when he held his child and understanding that he'd hardly changed.

Mrs. Jacob wiped the crumbs from the table with a stiff-backed authority that got to Ina. She wanted to be alone. "I saw her in your garden and I heard you shouting," Mrs. Jacob said.

Ina felt like stone in her seat. It was hard to read

Mrs. Jacob's face. There was some worry there, but also a determination that might have had a little distress, as if she didn't know how Ina would react.

She said, "She had no reason to come to my house, and I told her to leave."

Mrs. Jacob nodded, but her cobalt eyes were stern and made Ina feel tiny. She could imagine what Mrs. Jacob was thinking, that Kathleen was her neighbor and that was reason enough to visit. There was no reason for Ina to scream at her to leave.

In her natural state, Ina would have said that Kathleen had come to her house and stared through the window, and there was nothing normal about that. But Ina was drained and it was impossible to think straight, though it was the guilt that made her avert her gaze from Mrs. Jacob. Ina's hands shook as she gathered the mugs and the plate that still held two biscuits. A dog barked in a nearby house.

Ina said, "Thank you for coming, but I need to get some work done now."

Her voice came out low and she was afraid if she spoke much more the words would rip open the hole inside her. She walked into the kitchen. Through the window, she saw the bird feeder was empty, and that between white clouds were patches of blue sky. Ina found some comfort in rinsing the mugs, but she was too aware of the shuffling from the living room to relax fully. Ina felt sick at the thought of going to Nicholas's house last night, and how her late visit must have looked after everything. Her cheeks burned with the memory of the kiss. Mrs. Jacob was at the door. "You should call Tilly, she's worried."

The water ran over Ina's hands. She nodded and said, okay, and didn't feel any ease until she heard her visitor walk through the living room and close the door behind her.

"Is this how you feel all the time, hemmed in, like you can't move without someone watching? Mrs. Jacob was here and now, I want to close all my blinds."

Ina's voice moved inside Nicholas's skin and made him lean against the wall. It had been a particularly bad morning with Kate not wanting to put on her clothes and then screaming because she didn't want him to brush her hair, and he couldn't help thinking that Kate had been reacting to Ina's visit. He'd gone for a drive afterwards, unsure how to deal with having Ina so close. He hadn't been back long when the phone rang.

"Not all the time," he said. He thought he heard her smile.

Ina told him about not sleeping all night, and that Mrs. Jacob had showed her the article about Kathleen. She asked if he'd seen the article and he said no. He didn't want it in the house with Kate.

After a second, she said, "I used to go to your mother after she visited you in prison. I hated it. The house was always so dark, and she'd talk about how you were and I never got the courage to ask if you'd said anything about me. Every time, I thought I would, but I couldn't."

Kate's cereal bowl was still on the table. Milk was splattered beside it, and Nicholas felt Ina's breathing come down the line. She might have been waiting for him to say something but he had no idea what to say.

"You knew the week I graduated. In one letter, you congratulated me," Ina said.

"Mom told me. I didn't have to ask. After the first month, she wrote down things to tell me. It was easier for her to be prepared when she came." The silence was like a rope holding the two of them together. After a pause, Nicholas said his mother didn't know about the letters. "I didn't talk to anyone about them."

He thought Ina was crying but her voice came out steady when she said, "I need to see you."

"You can't come here."

"I know."

She gathered some of the letters, the ones that had hurt a lot to read, the ones where his loneliness, youth and regret screamed from the page.

Remember O'Keefe's dog? He used to dig holes all over their garden. They couldn't let him out without him ruining it. We used to laugh at him but I don't think it's funny anymore. I think he was scared or nervous and he couldn't sit still outside. He had to keep digging and digging just so he wouldn't have to look around him.

I used to think time dragged in school. I'd sit at the table and watch the clock and feel like it couldn't get any slower. I was wrong. Where are you? I imagine you on the porch steps of your house. I know you can't be there all the time, but I don't like to think of those steps empty.

On her knees in the attic, she reread some and put them back in their envelopes. She'd slept for a few hours, a deep sleep that held dreams she couldn't remember, though there was an immediate unsettling sensation when she woke, and she knew it would probably be like this for a while. She remembered after the death of her father when she would wake, and for a moment, forget her loss, only for it to come crashing in on her. She knew there was no forgetting what her mother had done.

With the letters in hand, she put on her jacket and left the house.

"Nicholas, I haven't heard you on the airwaves for a while," Ted said, pausing to cough. "Is everything okay?"

"Yeah. You miss me?" Nicholas said. Ted told him to fuck off. Kate had ketchup on her cheeks and was picking at her chicken pieces with her fingers.

"I had some family stuff. I'll be back to work in a couple of weeks."

"I don't give a fuck when you're back. I just wanted to make sure you weren't lying on some street somewhere."

"I hope you're not disappointed," Nicholas said. Ted laughed and Nicholas realized he'd missed his nights working and listening to Ted's banter. He said he'd be in touch soon. Ted grunted and hung up.

The phone rang seconds later, and Nicholas was smiling when he answered. "Did you forget something, Ted?" Nicholas heard crying on the other end and stiffened.

"Daddy, I don't want my milk. Daddy?" Kate said.

"Okay," he said, without looking at Kate. She must have pushed the glass away, because he heard it fall on its side, and the remnants of the milk splatter. "Daddy, look."

"Not now," he told Kate. He saw the effect of his impatient tone before she started to whimper, but it was impossible to worry about that now. He considered Kathleen might be on the other end of the phone and felt cold at the thought.

"I thought I was doing the best thing for her," a voice said, and he realized it was Tilly.

She took a breath. "Ina brought some letters. She wouldn't talk to me. She just dropped them on the bed and left."

Nicholas felt a blast of rage rush through him. "What do you want, Tilly?" Kate was still whimpering.

Tilly said, "I'm sorry Nicholas. You were just a kid."

Nicholas hung up. He was trembling when he wiped up the milk with paper towels. Kate's whimpers were burrowing inside his skin. He thought of Tilly on the bed, his letters around her, and felt exposed and volatile.

CHAPTER TEN

THE ROOM HAD BEIGE walls and a brown carpet. The bedspread and curtains were white. Ina phoned Nicholas the moment the door closed behind her. When he answered, she said, "Porter Square Hotel, room 201."

He hung up without saying anything. She'd hardly felt him on the phone, as if he'd kept the handset at a distance. He hadn't been happy when she'd phoned him the previous night. Kate was in bed and he said they'd had a bad day, but didn't go into detail.

"Tilly phoned," he'd said, and Ina had tensed. She'd refused to feel guilty.

"Yeah?" she'd said. She'd felt like the old Ina, before Stefano and San Francisco, and her failed pregnancies. She thought maybe Nicholas recognized this too, because he didn't say anything for a while. And then he'd said, "Yeah, she said you gave her some letters."

Ina said she didn't know any other way to make her mother understand. She didn't admit that she hadn't thought how Nicholas would feel about someone else reading his letters until then. There was nothing too personal in the ones she gave her mother, yet she knew every line had cost him.

"She needed to see them," she'd said. She received nothing but his breathing in return. Still, it eased her to know he wasn't hurt or angry enough to hang up. He'd waited to hear what else she had to say. "I'll call you in the morning," she'd said. "After you bring Kate to school, please be home."

He'd asked why and she'd said she wanted to see him. She'd said she had an idea. His responding chuckle could have opened all the regrets inside her, but she'd refused to think of how they used to be, and all the years they'd missed, because another night of crying and no sleep would have done her in.

"Now I'm curious," he'd told her.

In the hotel room, she was tempted to call him back. "Did you hear what I said?" she wanted to ask, or "Was that you earlier?"

She had an idea he was still waiting for the phone. When she tried phoning back there was no answer, and she imagined him standing in the kitchen, tense until the sound stopped. It was terrible to think that he might still be upset about the letters, and to know that Nicholas was inclined to stay distant and silent rather than say how he was feeling.

Ina tried sitting at the chair by the desk, but was restless and up within seconds. The bed was hard. Her hand tested it and she sat down. Street traffic was a distant hum outside. She opened the window and felt a blast of cool air as she watched the streets and the morning traffic, hoping to see Nicholas walking towards her with his hands in his pockets and back erect.

She closed the window. Fifty minutes had passed since she'd phoned Nicholas. She felt sick now, a weakening kind of nausea that made her knees shake. He wasn't coming. She lay on the bed and closed her eyes. When the knock came, she almost missed it.

Despite the cold, he wasn't wearing a jacket. His unsmiling face and intent gaze made her stomach toss and made speech impossible. She stepped back and he entered the room. There'd been moments throughout the last twelve years when they'd been in each other's company and the tension was such that Ina would never have walked into a room that held only Nicholas. The air would have been too thick, and she felt something of that now when the door closed behind him. Her mouth opened. She wanted to say that she was afraid he wouldn't come, but he was kissing her before she had a chance to speak. His hands were all over her, and when he pulled back, she was breathless and shaky. She wanted to reach out and grab him and tell him not to go. She wanted to cry from the fear of him walking away and the need in her that made her feel her body in a way she never had before. The rush between her legs burned.

"Take off your clothes," he said.

She undid the buttons of her blouse. "Slower," he said. The anticipation of finally having his hands on her skin made it hard to look at him. It was a kind of sweet torture to move slowly and let the blouse fall from her shoulders and then unfasten her bra. Topless, with the cool air on her skin, her hands went to her jeans. He told her to wait. He kissed her again. His lips were on her neck. Her hands gripped his waist. She wanted to pull him closer, to feel him pressed against her, but she also wanted his lips all over her. "I love this part of you," he said. He kissed her neck, before bringing his lips to her breasts and nipples.

A moan escaped her when his tongue traced the line of her belly to the rim of her jeans. He kissed her stomach and pulled opened her jeans. He helped her out of them one foot at a time. His breath fell on her thin panties and he kissed the soft cloth before pulling the panties down. His mouth was between her legs. Her hands were on his hair and she held him tight, trying to keep in control as his tongue explored, as if he'd always known the places to linger and touch. She was trembling by the time he finally stood and pressed his body against her. His hand was between her legs. His breath fell on her ear.

He whispered, "Lie down."

She watched him undress. Pale and lean, he was beautiful before her, and different too. This was the quiet, intent Nicholas she knew, yet also a Nicholas she had never seen before. There was a slowness to his movements that he'd never seemed capable of, and it was driving her mad. He was kissing her feet and she felt an urge to pull him up but couldn't move. And then he was over her, his body pressed against her. "I've always wanted to hear you come," he said, and she felt him press inside her.

She was supple on the bed and sweeter than he'd ever thought possible. He'd loved the scent on his finger as he undressed. He'd always thought that he'd take her quickly after waiting for so long. So many times, he'd imagined finding her in a room and taking her from behind or bringing her onto his lap and holding her down on him. He'd always wanted to be in charge of her in the bedroom, but to have her in front of him meant to know every part of her and take his time. She was enveloping him completely. His hips moved in a slow, circular motion and she was moving against him, drawing him in and then pushing him back, tightening and loosening around him until he couldn't take it any longer. He wanted her to writhe under him and cry out for more. She didn't cry out, but her fingers dug into him and her neck was taut. When he was so close and trying to hold back, he felt the ripples run through her and heard the sound of her pleasure move through her open mouth. He dissolved inside her and they lay panting and entwined.

"Jesus Christ," he said, and she laughed.

He knew they would have to do that again, and he knew she knew it by the way her hand moved down his neck and back.

Three hours they spent in that room, three hours in which they forgot completely the outside world and themselves. In the months to follow, they would meet in hotel rooms once a week and during that time together, they'd discard their lives and who they were. They would arrive in those rooms with their minds as naked as their bodies would soon be. For a while, they could pretend the world didn't exist, but outside there was always Kate and Kathleen.

CHAPTER ELEVEN

"HELLO, MR. GIOVANNI." HE didn't recognize the voice on the other end of the line. "This is Kate's teacher, Miss Jenson."

He sat up in bed. He'd only been asleep a few hours after working the night shift. Ina had watched Kate. He'd been relieved to get out and work, but it had been difficult too. Twice during the night, he'd pulled up outside the house on Summer Street and turned off the engine, but he felt different than he had when Kathleen lived there. He'd felt like an intruder on the scene, or someone extra who was not needed. Ina would have been asleep on the couch. She would have woken once he entered, and he would have felt foolish for checking up on them.

"Is everything okay?" he asked the teacher.

"Yes, Kate's fine, but I need you to come in this afternoon. Is that possible?" There were voices behind the teacher. He wondered if one was Kate's.

"What's this about?" he asked.

"Kate bit a student today," she said, and the background murmurs stopped. He felt light-headed.

"Why?" he asked.

There was a pause. "I'm not sure, but she hasn't wanted to play with the other students lately." She sounded more concerned than angry. "Can you come in?"

"Of course," he said.

Ina was on her way out. She paused on her porch to watch him approach. Two days ago, they'd met in the Veritas Hotel. As they'd lain entwined, he'd told her that he still hadn't been able to see Kathleen and she'd put her finger to his lips.

"Don't," she'd said, and that had gotten to him. He'd pulled away from her and sat on the bed. After a while, he'd said, "I don't know what to do about Kate."

It hurt to admit this. Kate had stopped asking about her mother and had grown quiet and troubled. Ina had tried to convince him that Kate would be okay. She'd said that Kate seemed fine whenever she came to her house after school, and Nicholas couldn't say that Ina didn't know what Kate was like before Kathleen left. She'd been a relaxed and happy child, but was not anymore. She'd been content in her own company, now she was restless and nervous. At night, she couldn't fall asleep without gripping Nicholas's hand. But there was more than that, a quiet surrounded her and made her seem distant and impossible to reach.

"What is it?" Ina asked now. She was wearing a light jacket. The air was fresh and becoming warmer.

"Kate's teacher called. She bit someone today. Has she said anything to you about school?"

"No, but she seems to like it," Ina said. Across the street, Mrs. Jacob's front door slammed. Nicholas heard her dog yapping.

"She bit someone," he repeated.

"Kids do that," she said.

"No Ina, kids don't do that," he told her. "Kate did." Ina waved to Mrs. Jacob and said hello.

Nicholas kept his gaze on Ina. "And we both know why."

Ina stiffened. He saw her shoulders go back and she seemed to be egging him on. Years ago, she would have hit him. Now the hit was all in her eyes.

"Has she ever talked to you about Kathleen?" Ina shook her head.

❋

The children were at recess. Kate sat in the corner of the classroom with a book. She glanced at her father, but remained seated. Miss Jenson brought him out to the hall. She told him Kate was happy to play alone, but if anyone annoyed her, she was quick to strike.

"Don't get me wrong," she said. "Kate's a good girl, that's why I haven't phoned you until now. I thought her hitting might stop. I'm sorry. I should have talked to you sooner."

Miss Jenson was young. With her dark hair falling over her face and her hands joined, she reminded Nicholas of his mother somehow, and it might have been the worry in her eyes.

"What hitting?" Nicholas asked.

"She's hit a couple of boys in the playground. She's attentive in class, and most of the time gets on well with her classmates, but her edginess worries me. I am sorry, but I need to ask. Is there anything going on at home? Is there anything I should know?"

Nicholas glanced into the classroom. There were posters on the wall showing numbers and the alphabet, and a twine ran from one corner of the room to the other, on which paintings were hung to dry. He wondered which painting was his daughter's.

The young teacher said, "Mr. Giovanni?"

"Her mother left a few months ago," he said, and saw her surprise.

"You should have told us. Has Kate talked about it?"

"Yes," he lied. A bell rang. He heard the click of high heels before a young woman hurried past.

Miss Jenson sighed. "Okay, maybe more one-on-one time with me will help. I'll see if it's okay for her to stay with me during recess. But if the behaviors persist, I'd recommend Kate see a psychologist. How do you feel about that?"

Nicholas thought of Stein's office and a shiver went up his spine. "I appreciate your help," he told her, "but I'm sure it won't come to that. I'll speak with Kate."

The teacher didn't look convinced, yet she said okay. He said goodbye to Kate from the classroom door. She didn't look up from her book.

"Well?" Ina looked worried, her brown eyes soft. She'd run out to the car before he'd turned off the engine.

"She's hitting a lot. Her teacher will spend time with her, but if she doesn't improve the teacher wants Kate to see a psychologist." A car passed. The window was down and a woman was singing. The voice filled the silence and then dragged it along with her.

Finally, Ina nodded, "Okay."

Nicholas couldn't believe it. "No, it's not okay. I don't want her to be picked apart and studied. She's just a kid."

Ina said, "A kid who has been through a traumatic experience. She needs to talk about it."

"She has us," Nicholas told her. He saw the effect of the word 'us' on her face, though it didn't last long. Her head tilted. He recognized this as her pensive look, and it unnerved him.

Eventually, Ina told him, "I don't know if that's enough."

There weren't many photos of Kate as a baby. One showed Kathleen holding Kate after she was born. The baby was swaddled in a blanket, her face pink and heart-shaped. Wisps of fair hair covered her head, and her eyes were closed. She looked content, while her mother stared at the camera with a look of surprise. Kathleen's cheeks were flushed. Her hair was disheveled and tossed. Whenever Nicholas looked at the photograph, he tried to remember what had happened in the moments after it was taken. He wondered if he'd sat on the bed beside Kathleen but couldn't imagine that he had. The woman in the photo seemed to take up too much room.

A picture was supposed to speak a thousand words, but any time Nicholas saw his daughter looking at the photos and frowning, he knew that wasn't true. He knew those images confused Kate. To her little mind, it was like reading books with pages missing. At Kate's second birthday, Kathleen was captured watching her daughter blow out the candles. She was sitting opposite Kate at the table, and Kate was standing up on the chair in order to reach the flickering flame. Kathleen's hands lay flat on the table, and her gaze was fixed on the cake. Another photo showed them side by side on the couch. Kathleen had her legs crossed and Kate was leaning towards her. That was the one Kate would look at the longest. In another photo, Kate was looking up at the camera. She held a doll by her chest while Kathleen was looking away. When Kate was a toddler, Nicholas would watch her climb onto the couch and hold her mother's arm. Nicholas took one photo of the two of them side by side, Kate's head leaning against Kathleen. Kate was falling asleep and Kathleen was looking at her, red hair falling onto the child's face, and her lips slightly parted.

After Kathleen left, Kate would take those photos out from the drawer. Nicholas noticed she always did this when he was not in the living room. Usually, he would be making breakfast, and he would hear the sliding wood and stand at the kitchen door to look at his five-year-old daughter, who seemed too small to take on those images. She would be so absorbed in the images that he could watch her without being noticed. Sometimes, if breakfast was already done, he would observe her for a good ten minutes. He would think about his daughter's total preoccupation and wonder what she was thinking of. Was she remembering the house when her mother was here? Was she trying to understand how she was feeling with seeing her mother's face in the photos? She never talked about Kathleen. Nicholas didn't know what was going through her head. If he came towards her while she was looking at the photos, she'd glance at him and he'd read nervousness in her gaze.

"It's okay," he'd tell her, wishing he could say something better. It was his refrain to her. "It's okay," though nothing was okay anymore.

Kate was afraid. The light had to remain on at night while she slept. More often than not she'd wake in the middle of the night and go to his bedroom.

"I had a nightmare," she'd tell him. Nicholas would remember when he was a boy and unable to sleep, feeling that some presence had slipped in through the window and was waiting under the bed. He'd felt weak with fright and stumbled to the living room. He'd tell his parents, 'I had a nightmare', because he couldn't explain his fear. And now he wondered what sent his daughter to him, if it was a dream as she said, or a memory pushing through.

He found the photo frames in the drawer. They were still in their boxes a year after he'd bought them. That day, his family had been sitting at the kitchen table finishing dinner when Kathleen said, "You know, there's nothing in this house that's mine."

He'd thought of her old apartment and its lack of possessions.

Kathleen had said, "You wouldn't even know I existed. You'd think it was a man and his child. Is that what you want?"

She'd led him to the living room and said, "Show me one thing that's mine."

He'd gone directly to the drawer and pulled out the photos. Her face had fallen, and he'd felt sorry for her then. He'd seen himself through her eyes, a man holding up limp photos and thinking this was enough to keep her happy, as though all she'd needed was a click of a camera every now and again. By the time he'd stood holding the photos in a weak peace offering, he hadn't touched Kathleen in months, and Kate was a quiet four-year-old. She had climbed from her seat at the kitchen table and stood beside her mother. Spaghetti sauce had been smeared around her mouth, which would have been comical if not for the worry in her eyes. Kate assimilated every detail, which scared Nicholas. She'd stand in the corner, taking in the harsh words, the screaming tones, and not move until Kathleen told her, 'Go to your room', or Nicholas took her hand and led her there.

Kathleen had glanced at her daughter, then back at Nicholas, before retreating to her room. He'd wanted to pick his daughter up and shield her from that glance, but it was already too late.

"Why is Mom mad?" Kate asked.

"Come on," he'd said. He'd liked to do things with her, camping out on her bed with books for hours, or wandering through shops. That day, he'd grabbed her hand and run out the door. She'd giggled with surprise. He'd ignored the spaghetti sauce on her face. He'd hoped they could ignore the anger that lay resolute in their house, and his inability to get down on Kate's level and talk to her about any of it.

He'd thought he could handle Kathleen leaving in the same way he had handled the aftermath of their arguments. Instead of answering Kate's question, "Why is Mom mad?", he'd driven to Target in Somerville Avenue. They'd chosen the frames together.

Kathleen was waiting for them in the living room. She'd pretended to watch television, but he knew different. He could hear her annoyance when she asked, "Where did you go?"

He'd brandished the bag and taken the photo frames out.

"You think that's what I want?" she'd said.

"I don't know what you want," he'd told her, surprised by the icy tone of his voice.

"Kate, go to your room," Kathleen had demanded.

"I'll take you." He'd taken hold of Kate's hand. Her warmth always surprised him.

"No, you will not," Kathleen had said, and Nicholas froze. He knew it was better to hold her off and keep her from storming into Kate's room, rabid with anger.

When Nicholas saw Kate's little body drifting towards the room, he'd thought she should have had a teddy bear or a blanket tucked to their chin, like one of the children at play school, but she was empty-handed and defenseless.

He'd gone to her later. She was curled up on the bed, and he held her until they fell asleep. They never talked about the shouting, or the sauce that had so hardened on her skin that the next morning, she whimpered as he scrubbed her clean.

In the car on the way home from school, Kate started telling Nicholas that she was going to paint with Ina today.

"You're not going to Ina's," Nicholas told her. The rear-view mirror caught her little face. Her mouth was open in surprise. For a moment, it looked as if she would cry. When he looked again, she was sitting back and looking out the window. Her lack of protest made him feel worse. She might have considered this punishment for her behavior at school.

At home, she stalled by the front door, staring at the photos in the frames. He had put them on the living room cabinet and in Kate's room. She glanced at him before continuing inside and looking behind the couch. He thought his heart would break. She must have believed those images meant her mother was back. He remembered once Kathleen had hidden behind the couch when she and Kate played hide and seek. Kate had pretended not to see her. Nicholas had watched her walk past Kathleen with her eyes trained ahead. Later, she'd told him she did it because she wanted the game to last.

The house would never be this quiet if Kathleen was present. She had a way of making noise wherever she was. If she was in the kitchen, she'd be grumbling or slamming doors. Still Kate stood rigid at the kitchen door, as if she expected to see Kathleen sitting there in her red dressing gown with her hair tied up. Her back would have been to the door, and she might have been tapping a tune on the table with her fingers. When she was like this, no one bothered her. Kathleen never liked to be surprised; she'd jump in the seat and tell them, "Didn't I tell you not to do that?"

The chairs were tucked under the table now. They'd never been this orderly when Kathleen was there. Nicholas was beside Kate. She seemed on the verge of crying, and was biting her lip. She slowly inspected the bathroom and bedrooms. Nicholas wanted to take his daughter's hand and tell her to stop looking. He thought of a story he'd heard once about a Doberman Pinscher who had followed a visitor around his owner's house in Vermont. No one was home. The woman went from room to room with the dog trailing after her. When she told her friends, they said it was a good thing she didn't pick up anything, even a pen, because the dog would have changed immediately, growling and rigid. It wouldn't have let the visitor leave. Nicholas felt something like that now, some kind of delicate balance between his daughter's calm searching and her reaction to the truth. He was sure that if he succumbed to the temptation to take his daughter's hand and tell her to stop looking, their relationship could turn.

The covers on his bed were pulled up neatly. He never slept on the couch anymore. He wondered if she missed his presence outside her door, and if this was why she rose most nights to seek him.

She looked under his bed and didn't glance at him as she left the room. He followed her to the living room. She seemed tired now. Her shoulders had slackened. Nicholas stood in front of her. She searched his face. She used to like observing him; when he read to her, she'd keep her gaze on him, waiting for changes in his face.

"Do you remember what happened?" he asked now. Her head shook. She was starting to cry.

She said, "I want to see Ina."

"Kate?" he said.

She said, "Please."

The sadness in her voice killed him.

"Okay, I'll get her. Wait here." He couldn't let her run away from the images, or what was going on inside her. She had to tell him what she remembered, let him know where to start so he could pick up the pieces. But when he came back with Ina in tow, Kate was sitting on the rocking chair outside, her legs dangling.

"What's wrong, love?" Ina sat in the chair beside her, but had to bring Kate's chin up with her hand to meet her eyes.

"Are you okay?" Ina asked.

Kate nodded and took her hand. Nicholas watched as she led the woman into the living room. He saw Ina's body freeze, and knew it all depended on her now. He had given Kate the responsibility and she was handing it back to the only person she could. Nicholas couldn't move. The two people before him seemed miles away rather than on the other side of a door. He felt Ina's emotion, the hurt and surprise was like ice on his skin. She could have walked to those photos and swept them away. She had as much right as Kate did. Instead, Ina's grip tightened around Kate's hand.

"That's your mom," she said.

She moved into the room and sat on the couch, lifting Kate onto her knee. "So how was school?" Ina said. She was good; only Nicholas heard the slight tremble in her voice.

"It was okay," Kate said. Ina looked over Kate's head to Nicholas. He had to move away from the pain and confusion in her eyes. He walked past them to the kitchen. After a few minutes, he heard the television turn on and felt Ina's presence. He was frying sausages in the pan.

"Look at me," she said.

He felt his stomach drop. It was unfair to seek her help with Kate, while not wanting her opinion on Kathleen's role in their lives, yet he had hoped Ina would let the photos pass. She had a restraint now that he had never experienced when they were younger. He had never known Ina to withhold a comment. Yet, when she'd suggested playdates for Kate, he'd told her Kate didn't want any, and Ina had surprised him by refraining from argument. Maybe she knew he wasn't ready for more little girls in his house. He could barely deal with one.

"Why?" Ina said.

He was holding the spatula over the sizzling pan. There were grease spots on the counter. An empty can of tomatoes was in the sink and its contents had left a stain on his t-shirt. Lately, Nicholas liked to make a mess when he cooked. He felt freer during those moments when he chopped with abandon and let onion peels fall to the ground.

"She needs to talk about it," he said. Ina wrapped her arms around her waist. In her sweater and jeans, she looked like the teenager he'd once known.

"You should have seen her all alone in the classroom while the other kids played. I had to do something," he said.

Ina said, "You're wrong."

CHAPTER TWELVE

THE DAYS WERE GETTING warmer and some light clung to the evening. Nicholas felt exhausted. He'd had a tough time putting Kate to bed. She'd wanted Ina to put on her pajamas, to brush her teeth with her, and read her bedtime stories. Their night-time ritual had been marred by Kate's whining and grumbling. He understood how Kathleen might have felt those nights when Kate had wanted only him. Although Kate had followed Kathleen around like a lost puppy, she never wanted her at bedtime. "Mom reads too fast," she'd say. "I don't understand the words."

"Tonight," Kate kept telling him, "I want Ina to read my story. I want to wait for her."

Eventually, when she refused to settle, Nicholas shouted at Kate to stop asking for Ina. He'd only raised his voice twice before; once when Kate was going near an electric outlet and another when she went too close to the road. Both times, Kate had burst out crying. But this time, her protests stopped. She burrowed down into the blankets and did not cry.

"Now let me read, okay?" Nicholas said to his daughter. He liked to pretend that she nodded.

He hated to think that he was falling into unknown territory. It was as if he were only starting fatherhood. With Kathleen gone, a space had opened between him and Kate. He read *Goodnight Moon* and kissed her cheek. Her eyes were closed. Nicholas rose from her bed with heavy limbs. He felt cruel for shouting, but mostly scared that he couldn't reach his daughter.

So, when Ina came to the house to watch Kate and told him, "She thinks you put those photos up to punish her," Nicholas was not ready to listen.

"She didn't tell you that," he said.

Ina said, "She didn't have to."

He stood for a moment. The house was silent. He rarely put on the television anymore, unless there was a game or Kate wanted to watch a cartoon. He wasn't sure how he felt about the quiet that seemed thick enough to crack. Ina had not moved. Her hand lightly touched the top of the couch. Nicholas told her there had been no incidents in school for over a week, and that Kate was now going outside without argument. Her teacher said she was doing well, and she had started to play with the girl from the apartment across the road.

"Yes, because you scared her," Ina answered.

"Kathleen is her mother!"

Ina winced, and in the light of the lamp, he thought he saw her cheeks flush and hoped it was because she knew she was overstepping. He waited for her to say something and was surprised when she didn't.

Finally, he asked, "When do you think I should take the photos down, while Kate's sleeping, or should I let her watch while I take her mother away again?" When Ina didn't respond, he asked, "You see what I mean?"

She didn't answer, and he left her standing in the living room. In the morning, she waited for his arrival and left seconds later, a habit they'd started so as to avoid Mrs. Jacob and Adrial's suspicions.

"Where are you?"

He told her the name of the hotel and she hung up. His window faced the back of the hotel and overlooked a small concrete area with tables and chairs that was probably nice during the summer. The room was small with barely enough space between the television and bed. He took his shoes off, but couldn't rest. He was struck with the thought that Ina would not come because of his anger the previous night, and the distance he'd set when they were at home.

The knock on the door brought him to his feet. Ina looked tired and drawn as she stepped into the room. There was a tension that kept Nicholas away from her. Although he wanted to pull her close to him, he waited.

"I nearly didn't come," she said. "I hate that you put those photos up. I hate that Kate has to see her face all time and we have no idea what's going on in her head."

Nicholas was standing behind her now, an inch between their bodies. He smelled the familiar scent of coconut in her hair that he loved. "I'm sorry," he said, and she turned to face him.

"Are you?"

"Yeah, I'm sorry that she hurt Kate and I don't know how to get her to talk, but mostly I'm sorry that I upset you." She hit his arm, but he felt her ease.

His hands went to her waist. He was pulling her to him. Once, not long ago, he'd gone into her house and found her in the kitchen and the look on his face must have told her exactly what he'd wanted.

"No, not here," she'd said, but she didn't stop him from kissing her and leaving her disheveled.

All day he'd wanted to go back to her and it was a torment he was getting used to, having Ina and not having her. The first touches in the hotel rooms were always urgent because of that. Sometimes they didn't make it to the bed. He pulled her jeans down and turned her around. The curtains were open. Anyone on the chairs outside would have seen her half-naked figure. Her hands were against the wall. The second time in this room would be slow and tame, a sense of drawing each other out by their touches, tracing every part of their bodies, so they could remember until the next time.

Nothing had changed with Kate when Nicholas and Ina met in La Quinta, on Cummins Street. Kate existed with the images of her mother without speaking about the photos.She was quiet at home, but lively in Ina's house. Oftentimes, when he collected her, Nicholas would hear his daughter's bright laughter and he would pause at Ina's door, afraid to put an end to it.

He didn't talk about Kate in the room. This was Ina and Nicholas's time for themselves. They soaked in the bath and lay like prunes on the bed. But Ina told him about visiting her mother. For nearly a month, she'd stayed away. Her mother phoned once a day and left messages apologizing. One day, she didn't phone, and Ina refused to feel anything. At first, she'd steeled herself against the notion that something might have happened to her mother. Her mother didn't deserve sympathy. The third day with no call, Ina grew worried. She remembered when her father was sick, how hard it had been to take care of him in the house, her desire to stay out after school for as long as she could, and her guilt when he died. She realized that no matter how much she wanted to stay away from Tilly, she couldn't do so indefinitely, because if something were to happen, Ina would never forgive herself. So the morning of the fourth day, Ina walked to the nursing home to see Tilly, though every step was an effort. When she arrived, Tilly was in the garden at the back of the nursing home. She liked to go there after breakfast. She was sitting on a bench, and when she saw Ina she started to cry.

"She wants to see you," Ina told him.

It was the end of April. They were in a double room on the third floor of the Liberty Hotel, the sun slicing through the window, and her hair wet after a shower. He picked a different hotel every time. The routine of meeting her in the same room would have been too difficult.

Ina lay naked beside him. He'd been quieter

than usual. The competency hearing was in eight days, on Wednesday morning at 10 a.m. Nicholas had hardly been able to sleep. Twice he'd driven to the hospital, and twice he'd been turned away.

And now, Ina was watching him. She was lying on her side and he felt tense with the thought of Tilly or having to see her.

"I want to bring her home for Sunday dinner. Will you come?"

"Please," she said seconds later.

Kate shouted, "She's here."

She'd been keeping watch from the bedroom window. The days were getting longer and warmer, but this didn't help Nicholas's mood. He'd been uneasy throughout the morning with the thought of seeing Tilly. Still, he smiled at his daughter and told her they would go over to Ina's in a minute. "Let Tilly get settled."

He knew Tilly would have to be helped from the nursing home van. A few months ago, he would have gone to help her. Now, he stayed at the kitchen table with his tea and the radio on in the background. Ina had gotten a portable ramp so her mother could be wheeled into the house. Earlier in the morning, Kate had spent some time running up and down the ramp. Kate had wanted to stay with

Ina, but she was busy cooking. Nicholas thought she seemed worried and distracted, too, and he wondered if Tilly had asked to see him, or if it were Ina's idea.

"Daddy, she's going up," Kate shouted from the bedroom.

She'd been excited to see the wheelchair on the ramp. Within minutes, she was back at the kitchen door in a dress that Ina had bought for her, her hair in braids. Kate could hardly stand still. "Can we go?"

"In a minute," he said. She frowned and disappeared. He knew she'd gone back to the window to watch, and that in a little while, her impatience would make her cry, but it was hard for Nicholas to move. Finally, the phone rang.

"Are you coming?" Ina said.

The house was filled with the aroma of roast meat. Tilly was sitting in the seat opposite her front window. She looked a lot older than she had the last time Nicholas saw her. Her face had extra lines around the mouth, and her gaze was unsure when she lighted on Nicholas. For a second, there was a pause where the room seemed to expand and contract. Kate slipped from her father's hands and ran to Ina, who'd appeared at the kitchen door with a tea towel in hand, and she bent down to hug the girl. She looked worried when she glanced at Nicholas over Kate's shoulder.

"I forgot to get dessert," she said. Tilly bowed her head, and Nicholas felt a burst of rage with their planning and scheming. He was tempted to say he'd get it, and turn around and walk out the door, but he stayed silent. His decision to remain had nothing to do with Tilly or Ina, but was due to Kate and the way she lit up when she was with Ina. If he called their bluff and walked out the door on the pretense of getting dessert, he would not come back, and he needed to see his daughter's lightness in this house. "Can I come?" Kate asked. Ina must have known that would happen too. She shot another glance at Nicholas and he said okay. They'd put a booster seat in Ina's car weeks ago.

Ina got her coat, and he wondered whose idea this was until he saw her nervous smile, and then knew Tilly had asked for a moment alone with him. It must have been when she was already in the house, and Ina would have felt pressured. She'd never been good at arguing with her mom, and Tilly wasn't the type to let something go.

"Everything's ready. We can eat when I get back," Ina said. Nicholas stepped out of her way and heard Kate's excited chatter before the door closed behind them.

He had only taken a single step into the house. Face to face with Tilly, he was surprised by his anger. For the last few months, if he'd thought about what

Tilly did, he'd felt a lethargic, weary sadness. But now his body felt stiff as Tilly asked how he was. He told her he was fine. There was expectation with his rage that made it impossible to move.

"I've been thinking about your mother a lot lately," Tilly said. Her voice was lower than he was used to, and it lacked her usual authority. She seemed nervous, and yet he couldn't fully believe in her anxiety. He heard Ina's car start outside.

"I never told her about the letters, but I nearly did once. Ina was seeing Stefano then, and she was starting to feel happy. I stood in your kitchen with one of your letters in my hand, but I couldn't show it to her."

The thought of his mother softened Nicholas, and he hated Tilly for that. It wasn't enough that Tilly had kept those letters, but she'd also used his mother as a way of explanation and apology. He would have liked to forget how much his time in prison had cost her. He'd taken years from his mother, and he knew Tilly wanted him to remember that, and think of how Ina would have been drained by every visit.

Behind him, the table was set.

In just under half an hour, they would all be sitting at the table, and Kate would kneel on her chair halfway through dinner and edge closer to Ina. After dessert, Ina would rise and tell Kate that, "The poor elephants can't do this," and proceed to jump around the table. Tilly would laugh, and Kate would clap her hands. But now, there was only Tilly's sad, brief smile, until she glanced away from him to take a breath, and in that moment, he felt his body as if it were a heavy sack stuck to the chair. Still, he couldn't conjure anything more than cold curiosity.

"What do you think she would have said?" Tilly asked.

He didn't know what to say. His mother had loved him deeply and had stayed by his side, but he could imagine her staring at the letter in Tilly's hand and feeling the same heavy sorrow she did whenever she visited, and he imagined that his mother would have understood when Tilly said that she was scared for Ina. Still, it was impossible to say this aloud. "It was hard enough for her," Nicholas said. "You showing the letter would have only made it worse. She might have understood, but she wouldn't have been able to keep it secret for long. She would have wanted Ina to know."

Tilly sighed, and said, "Yes, I think so too, and I think if she was here now and I told her, she wouldn't forgive me."

"There's no point thinking that," Nicholas said. He received a small smile. She might have wanted more — an assurance that his mother would have forgiven her, that everything was all right — but Nicholas couldn't give that to her.

Tilly frowned and shuffled in her seat, and he wondered if her hip was sore. A glass of water sat beside her, and a shawl was over her knees. She was studying him with a soft gaze.

"I did what I thought was best for my daughter. I'd tell Maureen that now, if she were here."

He couldn't help but laugh. "Is that an apology?"

She smiled, though her eyes seemed withdrawn. "It's the truth. I'd tell her that, and she'd ask, 'What about my son?' She'd remind me that you had no one in there."

He wished Tilly would stop talking about his mother. She was rising in the room, a tall, slim woman with hair that had turned grey too young and sad eyes that had never lost their worry.

"I know I shouldn't have done it," Tilly said, "but if I were to do it again, I don't think I'd do anything different. I don't think I had a choice, do you understand?"

He was staring at her. It was impossible for Nicholas to comprehend how he was feeling, struck by the thought that she would have hidden those letters again and again.

"Wouldn't you do anything to protect Kate?" she said.

He didn't know where she was going with this. The last time he'd spoken to Tilly, she'd accused him of hurting Kathleen on their final morning together.

She'd said she didn't believe in his innocence and now she was trying to tug on his love of his daughter. He walked to the front door, his hands dug deep into his pockets and he watched the breeze ruffle the grass. She waited and he felt her gaze on his back the whole time.

After a while, he said, "Yeah, I'd do anything to protect my daughter."

Tilly sighed and said, "Then maybe, we're more alike than I care to admit."

CHAPTER THIRTEEN

CRIMINAL CASE- 105645 PEOPLE v. Kathleen Lehanne, we are convened as the mental health court of the district court as requested for a competency evaluation.

Michael O'Neill, the assistant district attorney, presented himself to the judge. His suit had been pressed for today, and his hair combed. Once he was seated, Kathleen's attorney, the sharp-faced woman from the previous hearing, stood to present herself as Nadine Parson. Kathleen sat beside her in an orange jumpsuit. Her hair was pulled back from her face, and she sat straighter in her chair than she had two months ago. Stein was in a chair behind her, on the other side of the partition. He looked taller outside the hospital, and not less certain — Nicholas could never say that — but less cocky than usual, with a feigned humility that Nicholas didn't believe in, no more than he believed that Stein wasn't aware of his presence on the other side of the room.

It was a smaller room than the last time, with red walls and wooden partitions, and a sense of time stopping amid the thick air and carpeted floors. There were only a few people. Some of them must have been reporters, Nicholas thought, and he hated the thought of once again seeing Kathleen's name in the newspaper.

"I believe you have what has been previously marked as People's exhibit one, a forensic competency evaluation dated April 20th," O'Neill said.

The courtroom door opened behind Nicholas, and he sensed a change in the room before he turned to see his neighbors. Mrs. Jacob was dressed in a skirt and blouse, a change to her sweatpants and sweaters. Adrial was in jeans.

Parson was disagreeing with the report's conclusions, stating that they may have been accurate at the time they were written, but weren't now. Kathleen wasn't fit to proceed.

Adrial followed Mrs. Jacob to their seats on the same side of the room as Kathleen. When she'd taken her seat, Adrial glanced at Nicholas. It was not a hard look. She seemed nervous. Nicholas smiled and nodded, but was quick to look away.

His heart had swelled and seemed to fill his head, and there was a low drumming between his ears. Not once had he considered that his neighbors might take an interest in the case beyond the newspaper article. But he should have known Mrs. Jacob would. She'd been kind to Kathleen when she'd first arrived on Summer Street. She'd helped them get ready for Kate and visited throughout the years.

The doctor O'Neill called was in her early fifties. She had a round face and probing eyes, and was dressed in a sombre grey suit. Nicholas could not imagine Kathleen opening up to the woman. Still, he saw Kathleen straighten in her seat and look intently at the doctor as she stated that her name was Doctor Lisweitz, and that she worked as part of the outpatients' team at Bridgewater State Hospital.

"Doctor, you have before you what has been marked as People's exhibit one, forensic competency evaluation, dated April 20th. Is that the evaluation you completed?"

"Yes, it is."

"Is the subject of that evaluation the person to my left and your right?"

"Yes, it is."

"Before you prepared the evaluation, did you review any collateral sources?"

"Yes, I reviewed all the police reports and investigative reports that were written regarding the incident."

"Were there any other sources of collateral information?"

Nicholas wanted to leave the courtroom. His hands had begun to sweat.

"I also talked to Ms. Lehanne's partner, Nicholas Giovanni, who was living with her at the time."

It was impossible to look at them, but he was sure Adrial and Mrs. Jacob were watching him, and he knew Stein was too.

"Does Mr. Giovanni believe that Ms. Lehanne is capable of understanding her defense?"

"Yes."

"Does Mr. Giovanni believe she was aware of what she was doing?" If they asked him now in front everyone, he didn't think he would be able to give the same answer.

"Yes."

He could see Kathleen folding inward. It was like watching her wither. He'd seen her in all her guises, at her most beautiful and vulnerable and at her most needy and cruel. It was her cruelty — those moments she'd push Kate away, or he'd catch her watching Kate with an unforgiving gaze — that had let him say yes to the doctor.

Parson had risen and was arguing that Nicholas's opinion was irrelevant, and their only concern should be whether or not her client was competent to stand trial. The judge agreed, and the prosecution asked if Doctor Lisweitz had given the defendant a diagnosis.

"No, I didn't need to come up with a diagnosis. The records show that Ms. Lehanne suffers from schizophrenia and has been in St. John's for treatment three times. The records also show that when Ms. Lehanne is taking her medications, her symptoms cease."

Nicholas's head was ringing. The voices were like pinpricks. O'Neill asked if, after resuming her medication, Kathleen would be able to assist her defense. The doctor didn't bat an eyelid before she said yes. O'Neill asked if Kathleen was rational during the interview.

"Yes. I told her this report was being done in response to a court order, and that copies would be sent to the judge and district attorney, as well as the district court and defense attorney, and nothing she said would be confidential. She said she understood."

"Did she indicate she was willing to continue?"

"Yes."

"And how do you know she was able to continue?"

"She was able to take in what I said and repeat it in a logical fashion."

"Did she talk about her living situation?"

"She said that she lived with her partner and

daughter. I asked if she would be going back to them, and she remained silent. When I asked again, she said she didn't know." Either Adrial or Mrs. Jacob was looking at Nicholas.

He felt the burn on his skin that was already hot from the thought of Kathleen at the table in St. John's with her steely grey eyes.

"Did you ask why she would not be going back?"

"Yes."

"And what did she say?"

"She said I must know why, otherwise I would not be there to speak to her."

There was a murmur in the room, or it may have been a communal breath. The words sounded cold. O'Neill asked about Kathleen's work. Kathleen had told the doctor she used to work in a nursing home before she fell pregnant. *Fell. Would she have used that word?* Nicholas wondered. It didn't seem right and made him uncomfortable, as if there were layers to this he would never understand.

"Did she say anything about medication?"

"She said she has been taking her medication since she was brought to the hospital." Nicholas was afraid he would be sick.

I'm not a child, she had told him. And instead of arguing, he'd stopped going to the bathroom to get her pills. Stein already held Nicholas responsible, and he could imagine Kathleen pointing her finger at him. *He stopped giving them to me.* Since the day Kathleen had been arrested, he'd been expecting the blame to come flying towards him, and there was little he would have been able to do with it.

"Can you please tell us what led you to the opinion that she has the capacity to understand the charges against her?"

The doctor said that Kathleen was able to speak about the charges and the reasons why she was on trial. Nicholas felt weak in his seat. In the hospital, he'd grabbed her hand. "Do you know what you did?" he'd said. "You nearly killed her. You put a pillow over her face." He'd spat at her, and she'd shaken her head and shouted that he was wrong.

"So, it is your opinion that Ms. Lehanne is competent to stand trial?"

"Yes."

"Thank you. Your Honor. I have nothing further."

O'Neill sat down. The air in the courtroom was still and stuffy. Parson stood and asked when the doctor spoke to Kathleen, and was told they had spoken ten days ago. After looking through her paperwork, Parson asked about the information the doctor had received from the community. The doctor said she'd spoken to Nicholas and the community health nurse. Nicholas wondered if he was imagining the doctor's discomfort, a minor shuffle in her seat and a glance towards Kathleen, when she was asked what the nurse had said.

"The nurse said Ms. Lehanne was distant and quiet and showed a disinterest in her child whenever she visited."

"A hard thing to grasp, isn't it, a woman not able to look after her child?"

"No, it's not. Many women suffer from depression after childbirth."

"But this didn't end quickly, did it? It built up, is that not what the nurse said?"

The doctor sat straighter before saying that the nurse had admitted that she'd seen little change before visits to Kathleen stopped.

Parson flicked through her notes. "Did you ask my client about her daughter during the interview?"

"Yes."

"What did my client say?"

"She didn't want to talk about her daughter." Parson nodded and asked how Kathleen had reacted to the question. Nicholas had to close his eyes.

"She became upset."

"She started to tremble, didn't she?"

"Yes."

"And when you asked why she hurt her, what did my client say?"

"She said it wasn't her fault. She had no choice."

"My client felt she had no choice but to act, and

she still feels as if she'd had no choice — is that the mind of a competent person? Shouldn't a person on trial understand their responsibility?"

"Yes, anyone on trial should understand responsibility and, as I have already stated, I believe Ms. Lehanne is in full understanding of hers. She reacted to my questions in a way that suggested guilt rather than incomprehension."

"But my client has not been found guilty of anything."

Parson seemed happy. She wasn't smiling, and with her thin, sharp features, her delight had nowhere to go, but to push at the boundaries and make her stand a little straighter, as she called Stein to the stand. He walked slowly to the chair. He glanced over at Nicholas while Parson checked her notes, and his gaze was dismissive.

"Doctor Stein, how long have you known my client?"

"Nearly fifteen years."

The defense asked Stein to describe how he knew her. Stein spoke about his history of treating Kathleen, a history that Nicholas had learned in the doctor's office nearly six years ago. In September of 1975, at the age of eighteen, she was brought to St. John's after a psychotic episode, and stayed in the hospital for nearly a year. Stein didn't mention the foster homes before her stay, nor her parents, whom Kathleen had spoken to Nicholas about only once. He'd tried to forget the image she'd conjured of her bloodstained sheets and her mother closing the door on her husband's naked body without a word, but there were times when Nicholas had seen that girl inside Kathleen in the flashes of fear in her eyes and the needy clinging of her hands that could never be eased.

Stein told the court that he diagnosed Ms. Lehanne as a paranoid schizophrenic, and she started to take Clozaril. They had to monitor her closely for the first six months, but she was lucky and responded well to the drug. That was not the last time he saw Ms. Lehanne. In 1994, she had a second psychotic episode because she stopped taking her medication. She was kept in for six months. I saw her again in 1999. That time was different though — that time, Nicholas had rushed her to hospital after a suicide attempt, and she was involuntarily admitted.

"In 1999, had she stopped taking her medication again?"

"Yes."

"And did she give a reason for her suicide attempt?"

"She was pregnant."

"Your Honor, the defense is digressing," O'Neill said. "We are only interested in the evaluation made on April 20th."

"Your Honor, I want to make it clear to the court that my client's illness can be exacerbated at any time," Parson said. "Doctor Lisweitz may have been correct in her evaluation the day she made it, but not today."

"I will allow that," the judge said.

"Did the pregnancy scare my client?" Parson said.

"Very much so," Stein said.

Nicholas could see Adrial and Mrs. Jacob stiffen in their chairs. The clock on the wall showed that half an hour had passed, and every second of it hung on Nicholas.

Stein said he'd issued a Section 12 the moment he'd heard of her recent breakdown. Breakdown, he'd said, not attempted murder, not crime. Nicholas felt the tension riding on his shoulders. His hands were balled into fists.

"Doctor Stein, how long has my client been in the hospital this time?"

"Nearly three months."

"And how many interviews have you had with her?"

"I have spoken with Ms. Lehanne at least once a week."

"So that means at least twelve interviews?"

"No, when she was first brought in, Ms. Lehanne was not capable of giving an interview."

"Why?"

"She had discontinued her medication." Nicholas's heart had reached his ears. Stein was not looking at him, but he felt as if the doctor had been speaking directly to him. There was a low note of contempt Nicholas thought no one else would have noticed.

"Why would she stop?"

"She has impaired awareness of her illness. It's biological in origin, similar to that seen in Alzheimer's disease. She really doesn't think she needs to take her medication."

"So, at any time, my client could refuse her medications with the belief that she doesn't need them."

"Yes."

"And what would happen then?"

"The main characteristic is a loss of reality. Ms. Lehanne has auditory, and sometimes visual, hallucinations, but medication can stop them."

"She hears voices."

"Yes."

"When you first interviewed her, did she appear to understand what was going on?"

"No, she maintained some delusion. I believe it is very difficult for her to admit what happened. She kept asking where her daughter was, and if Mr. Giovanni was coming in to get her."

Nicholas's fists tightened. Stein had said nothing about this to him and it was hard to imagine Kathleen asking for Kate. A buzzing had started between Nicholas's ears. Stein was speaking again. "…put her hands over her ears and told me to stop speaking. She became very agitated when asked why she was in the hospital."

"Did she know why?"

"No, I don't think so. She insisted that she had no choice."

"Yet, Doctor Lisweitz has testified that she was able to answer questions."

"She may have been able to that day. Ms. Lehanne can have moments of lucidity and quiet calm, but her rationality can break at any time, and the stress from a trial could easily bring a psychosis. I don't believe we can take the risk."

"Do you believe she is competent to stand trial?"

"No, I do not. Ms. Lehanne is having an extremely difficult time coming to terms with what happened."

Parson was not looking at Stein. "Do you believe, Doctor Stein, that she might be competent within the time frame of one year?"

"I could not claim that Ms. Lehanne would be competent today, or in a year. Schizophrenia is not a mental illness that you can predict."

"Has my client spoken to you at all about what happened on the morning of March 2nd?"

"No, she has not."

"Doctor Stein, are you the only one who believes Ms. Lehanne is not competent to stand trial?"

"No, I am not."

"Your colleagues are in agreement."

"Yes."

"Your Honor, you can see the evaluations written by Doctor O'Keefe and Doctor McKenzie."

"Yes, I have read the reports," the judge said.

"For the record," Parson said, "I would like to stipulate that they found my client unresponsive to questions."

Kathleen grasped her attorney's jacket sleeve. The movement was a jarring surprise, and Nicholas felt as if she'd hit him in the chest. During Stein's testimony, she had been so still and folded inward as though sleeping, and now she was whispering to her attorney. Nicholas was sure she knew of his presence. He was sure she'd glanced at him before she started to speak.

The judge looked on, impassive, or maybe impatient. It was impossible for Nicholas to guess. He couldn't take his eyes off Kathleen and her thin, agitated lawyer, who eventually saw no choice but to concede. She nodded briskly.

"Your Honor, my client has just consulted with me, and I want to say before she speaks..." Parson paused to check her paperwork. Nicholas felt the blood drain from his face. "...that she has given me authorization today to tell the court my opinion on whether she is able to proceed, and to elucidate to the court my belief that she is not. I have no reason to doubt that on the day Doctor Lisweitz saw my client, she was responsive, but I think we will all see, if we ask my client a few questions, a different story."

"You have no further questions for the doctor?" the judge asked.

"I do not. Thank you for your time," Parson said. Stein nodded and returned to his seat, but Nicholas was hardly aware. His attention was fixed on Kathleen, and he felt sick and hollow.

"Ms. Lehanne, I will ask you to talk to the judge about your case, if that is okay."

Kathleen glanced at her attorney and nodded. Her arms were on the table and she was pulling at the sleeves of her jumpsuit. It reminded Nicholas of the first time he'd visited her in hospital, and the shock her appearance had given him.

"Ms. Lehanne, do you have something to say?" the judge asked. Kathleen nodded and was looking straight at the judge when she said, "She screamed." The words made everyone sit straighter.

"Who screamed?" the judge asked. Parson made a motion to get Kathleen's attention but was ignored.

"She was always screaming at me and telling me what I did wrong." Parson looked worried. She shuffled in her seat and extended her hand, but stopped inches from Kathleen, who was refusing to look at her.

"But you didn't know it was Kate, did you?"

Parson's said. Kathleen's head was lowered, and she let out a deep, audible sigh. "Did you know it was Kate?"

Kathleen's fists were clenching and unclenching. Her attorney leaned forward. "Ms. Lehanne, who did you think she was?" Parson asked. "Do you hear me? Do you know where you are right now?" Kathleen nodded. Her head was down, but Nicholas was sure she was saying something and it felt as if everyone else in the room had stopped breathing

"Who were you just talking to?" Parson asked.

"You."

"No. Just there, your lips were moving. Who were you talking to?"

"That doesn't matter. It's not important. I know where I am. I'm at a hearing. You are my defense attorney."

"Who else is with you?" Kathleen didn't seem to hear her. She nodded to the judge and might have been smiling.

"He is the judge and he wants to know if I realize what I did," Kathleen said. The judge was watching her with a frown.

"Does God ever talk to you?" Parson's said.

"I don't want to talk about God. I know where I am, and I know what happened. She disappeared under the pillow. I wanted her to be quiet. She loved him more than me, she always did, and I hated her for it."

Chapter Fourteen

NICHOLAS CRIED IN THE car. It came upon him fast, a rupturing from the inside, and then he was sobbing with the thought of his daughter disappearing under the pillow and Kathleen's words. *I hated her*. She'd said the same thing about her mother, and she'd sounded confused in the courtroom, but he knew from the crowd's chatter and commotion and the way the judge had sat back that he was the only one to realize it. Nicholas had sat in his seat waiting for her to look at him. What would he have seen on her face? The thought scared him. His chest hurt and his mouth was so dry it tasted like dirt. On his way home, he was distracted and had to pull over to calm down. He felt drunk and disorientated and by the time he parked in front of his house, he was trembling.

Kate was still at school. She could have been drawing or writing or looking out the window when the judge ruled that her mother engaged in an overt act causing serious bodily harm to another, and that this held a sentence of fifteen years. The judge also found that, due to the evidence and the evaluations, Kathleen qualified as mentally ill and dangerous, and he ordered her to be committed indeterminately to St. John's psychiatric hospital. Throughout her treatment, Kathleen would be periodically evaluated, and the court would hold additional competency hearings. If Kathleen were not restored to competency within the timeframe that she would be prosecuted, the court must dismiss without any charges.

Kathleen remained silent throughout the speech. After she'd spoken, she seemed drained. It was as if she'd been possessed by something outside herself and then was suddenly empty. Nicholas wondered if she knew what was being said, and if she understood that Stein would never deem her competent to stand trial. Every year for fifteen years, she'd be evaluated and sent back to the hospital, and he felt sick with the thought of the questions she would be continually asked.

Ina saw him arrive home. She stood at the window

and watched his loose form sit still in the driver's seat. It was impossible to go to him and ask what had happened after the way he'd behaved yesterday evening. She'd known he would be uncomfortable letting her inside. The neighbors would talk, and then there was Kate and the difficulties she was going through, which he didn't speak to Ina about, but didn't have to. Kate spent enough time at her house, and more than once she'd seen Kate complain to her father that she didn't want to go home, and she'd seen the pained uncertainty in Nicholas's face. Still, Ina had gone to the house to talk about accompanying him to court. He and Kate had finished dinner, and Kate was in the bath. Nicholas and Ina stood in the dimly lit living room so that they could hear Kate splash. Ina noticed he left the front door open.

"I want to go to court with you tomorrow."

His answer was immediate. "No."

She'd felt a flush of heat on her cheeks, not least because she still hadn't grown used to the photos he'd put up. "I think I'm entitled to know what's going on," she'd said. And maybe she shouldn't have used the word entitled, maybe she should have concentrated on the time she spent with Kate, and the fact that she'd like to know what was happening because she had started to love the little girl. But she'd been agitated from the get go, and Nicholas balked.

"So, you want a front seat to this fucking mess? Do you think it's going to help my situation or Kate's if Kathleen sees you with me? Jesus Christ Ina, this isn't about you."

Ina would not cry in front of Nicholas, though she'd felt her heart shatter. And it wasn't the first time he'd done this to her. Only days previously, in the Holiday Inn, she'd watched him slide from the bed and put on his jeans, and she'd felt some anxiousness with his reluctance to look at her. Then she'd seen him place the envelope with her name scrawled in his handwriting onto the bed "You forgot this," he'd said.

"No, I didn't forget it," she'd told him. She'd wanted him to have that letter, to have a reminder of how much they'd lost, and feel even a fraction of what she felt at home with all the other letters. It was a part of him, as much as it was a part of her, and he seemed reluctant to hold it. "I can't keep it," he'd said, and Ina knew he must have been thinking of Kate, and the guilt that had never really left him and made him hardly glance at her on their street.

She didn't answer. Instead she went into the bathroom and locked the door, where she remained, even when he'd knocked and begged her to come out. She'd heard him get dressed and leave, and she'd prayed that the letter would not be on the bed when she emerged because it would feel like a heart exposed. It was there, discarded, and she'd lain on the bed with an empty, lost feeling.

Then to have him keep her outside and to hear him say, *this is not about you.*

She thought of all this, as she watched him finally get out of his car, and she thought of her mother in the nursing home garden, asking if something was going on between them. Ina had felt no delight, no compulsion to share anything of who they were together. "Be careful," Tilly had told her, and the words had made Ina want to cry.

The slow ticking of the living room clock mixed with her breathing, while she waited for Nicholas to phone and tell her what had happened. She needed Nicholas to invite her into his life, instead of keeping her on the periphery, amid hotel rooms where all evidence of their presence was cleaned away within hours. She wouldn't continue like that. It was scary to realize that Nicholas wasn't able to open up fully; his unease and sharpness had shown her that. He'd attacked because he'd felt cornered, just like he'd done as a boy. He had not changed. The aggression might have been taken from him in prison, but his fear remained. She wondered what he feared most, feeling too much, or not feeling enough, and if he was even aware of how scared he was

After Kate finished school, she ran down to Ina's house. Nicholas hadn't known what time he'd get back from court, and had asked Ina to collect Kate if he was delayed. She'd agreed and had offered, before the visit to the house and his coldness, to take Kate for a few hours that afternoon regardless of when he was home, in case he needed some time. Kate's arrival brought a great sense of loneliness over Ina. The little girl's ability to simultaneously bring Ina's emptiness to the surface and then ease it never ceased to amaze her.

The two tended to the garden and then Kate colored while Ina did some work. When Nicholas came to collect Kate for dinner, he looked awful. Still, Ina couldn't forgive the dismissive shake of his head when she asked how the hearing went.

"Civil commitment," he said, as if she knew what that meant. He wasn't working that night. He'd decided that weeks ago because he'd had a feeling the hearing would be draining. He thanked Ina when Kate was ready to go, and she had a strong urge to slap his face. She would have if Kate had not been there.

Ina didn't cry when Nicholas walked away, nor during the night when she harbored some hope that he'd phone. Every minute of silence wore on her. Eventually, she climbed into the attic and reread his letters and this time she felt distant from the boy who'd written them. She was dry-eyed, returning the pages to the envelopes, and throughout the night, she refused to look at his house as often. When he phoned the next morning, she didn't let the softness in his voice reach her. He asked if she would meet him.

She said, "You know what I figured out?"

She waited a moment, but he didn't ask what. All she heard was his breathing before she said, "You wouldn't have kept writing to me if I'd answered."

In the silence, she became aware of the hard, rhythmic beating of her heart. He didn't attempt to deny it, and she hated him at that moment. In the letter he'd given back to her, he'd written, *You need to know that I love you. I always have. I'm sorry for everything.*

She thought of that and said, "It's the most honest you've ever been, and you were talking to a ghost."

After Ina hung up, Nicholas stood for a long time against the kitchen wall. His legs were shaky, and he felt nauseous from his lack of sleep and thinking about Kathleen and Kate.

She loved him more than me. She always did, and I hated her for that.

It was his fault, he knew that, and he knew that he couldn't ever hope to bring Kate to her mother after she'd declared her hatred. His whole being was filled up with his daughter: worry, love, regret, guilt; there was too much to assess and hold and not enough for anyone else. Maybe Ina was right. Maybe he wouldn't have written to her so frequently if she'd responded, and maybe he wouldn't have been as honest in the letters, but he remembered the pain he'd felt each day he saw there was no answer from her, and he remembered how impossible it was to give up. Each time he wrote, he gave a little more to her, didn't he? Each letter had opened the wound further, yet he'd seen no other choice. He couldn't believe that he hadn't wanted to hear from her, that it was some exercise in honesty that he enjoyed on his own. But what did he know about honesty? He wasn't honest when he came home to Ina and Stefano together and kept everything in and refused to tell her how he felt, or when he brought Kathleen home to take care of her because of the child she bore, and his inability to walk away from that baby. He'd wished he'd been a man like his father then, but he was nothing like his father.

He loved his daughter with all his heart, and he'd wanted to live in a house where he could lie down beside her at night and tell her a story, or watch her smiling up at him from the kitchen table, or hear her screeches of laughter as they played, without worry of argument and tension, but the tension was still

the surface. He saw her sag a little. Her shoulders loosened, though her gaze stayed firm.

He said, "Kate is not an excuse."

"I love her, you know?" Ina said. The hollowness in her tone shocked him. There was a finality to it that made him stand still, unsure of how to react, though he felt a sinking in his stomach. "I want to be there for her." She paused and seemed to gather herself. Her voice was not shaky when she said, "I'll be over tomorrow night to watch her."

It was impossible to know exactly how to feel in this house that he'd known since he was a child, with the table, chairs and plants, and what he'd always thought of as theatrical domesticity, a lie as much as any house, though he'd never really known why until this moment. Ina was just like Tilly, with her need to protect and shield and keep safe from everything. He knew Ina wouldn't change her mind no matter what he said, and what could he say anyway? He wouldn't make promises to her. That was impossible given the precariousness of his position, and Kate being his first concern. But he clung to the softness in Ina's defiance. The uncertainty in her gaze let him bridge the distance between them.

He pulled her to him and sought her mouth, but she was limp in his hold. She did not kiss him back, and he pulled away to put his forehead on hers. He wanted nothing more than to lead her into the bedroom. His lips found her cheek and neck, and still she did not respond. There was no anger when he stepped back, only a deep sorrow that was mirrored in her eyes. She would let him undress her and kiss her, but she would not surrender to him. He wouldn't have wanted her like that, and he understood that this was what she wanted too — not part of him, but all.

"You need to go," Ina said.

"You don't have to do this," he said the following night, when Ina appeared at his door. He regretted the words straight away, not only for the hurt that flashed in her eyes, but the distance in them, too. *You don't have to do this*, as if everything before now hadn't been real, but he couldn't help it, given his frustration.

Ina said, "I brought some books for Kate."

She would not acknowledge his statement, and it was hard then not to close the door on her. He let her into the dim living room. The light from the corner barely illuminated the room's edges, yet even in the dark, he couldn't forget the photos of Kathleen. The air was thick, and his urge to reach out to Ina, as well as the thought of his earlier calls, calls which had never been answered, added to the tension. Yet, the relief when Kate came running from her bedroom saddened him because he knew how easy it would be to hide behind his daughter. He would learn to be happy with what little he had with Ina. He'd spent his life doing that.

"We saw a mouse at school," Kate said.

"A real mouse?" Ina asked. She'd bent down to the girl, and the softness that came to her face showed just how reserved she'd become with Nicholas. He had to walk away from the scene that seemed far removed from him. Getting ready for work, he could hear Kate's excited chatter and their movement to the bedroom, where Ina would lie beside Kate and tell stories.

In the morning, Ina would come out of that room with sleep softening her features, making her look like the child he'd once known, and she would tell him Tilly was coming home for dinner on Sunday, and she hoped to see him and Kate. His visits to the nursing home were infrequent, though no one mentioned that.

"How are you?" he'd ask.

She'd nod. The sun would be peeking through the gap in the curtain, and he'd be struck with the uneasy air before she'd tell him, "Kate asked where her mother was last night."

He wouldn't be able to hide his worry.

Her laugh would hold no mirth. "Isn't this what you wanted?"

Chapter Fifteen

Eventually, Kate would not remember the house without the photos. She would recall coming in and looking for her mother, thinking she was playing hide and seek while her father stood guard by the door, and she would also remember the images of her mother's dresses hanging in the wardrobe and the lonely feeling she'd gotten from them, but she would not be able to say what each dress looked like. Nor would she think of those days she had sought the fabric out, looking for hints of Kathleen. Concrete memories dissolved as she got older. Yet, there would always be the sensation that something important was just beyond her grasp.

Kate would dream of Kathleen with vibrant red hair and startling grey eyes. In a lot of the dreams,

Kathleen would be standing outside the house. She would be unable to enter, no matter how hard Kate tried to pull her in. Sometimes Kate would wake crying, and she would lie in the dark remembering her mother's face. She never told Nicholas about those dreams.

A few months after her mother left, Kate stopped going into her father's room at night. It was not because she had moved past her fears. Rather, they became more alive when she rose from her bed, under her mother's photographed gaze. It never helped that her father would hold her and ask what was wrong. She would stiffen with his curiosity and her inability to put her feelings into words.

For a while, Nicholas had been persistent with his questions about what Kate remembered. She hated his questions, just as she had hated Miss Jenson's interest in her and the way she'd look at her with pity. When she went to Mrs. Teller's class the next year, she was determined to keep the teacher from noticing her. Mrs. Teller was a stout woman with intense green eyes. Kate learned to keep those eyes off her; all she had to do was work. She discovered she enjoyed the distraction of reading and maths. Books were a way to survive in her house, where each day she'd come home to the strange quiet made from her mother's absence.

The teacher after Mrs. Teller was Miss Hersh. Miss Hersh tended towards favoritism. Whenever her interest veered towards Kate, the girl dove into her books or activities, reluctant to meet the teacher's gaze or start a discussion.

Each year, the reports were the same. *She's a good worker, but quiet.*

The notion of her timidness irritated Kate, almost as much as her father's easy acceptance of it. She wasn't shy. She liked going out alone. She never minded walking up to the neighborhood kids, yet she didn't like when kids trailed behind her. And she was uncomfortable with the way adults lingered, as if waiting for her to say something. After school, she tended to go directly to her room and take out her homework. Nicholas would bring a snack to her. He'd sit on the bed and ask about her day. Her cuddly toys lay against the pillow as they'd done for years. She had a bookcase filled with the children's books Nicholas used to read to her, *The Hungry Caterpillar, Racing in the Rain, The Last Fish*, and other books that she had started to read herself, *The Secret Garden, The Living Tree*. She'd sit sideways in her seat and wait until he'd finished with his questions. He was always reluctant to leave her, and she would bite her tongue, afraid to say, "Please Dad, leave me alone."

There were moments throughout the day when she would feel her mother's presence like a ghost.

Afternoons, when Nicholas rose and reluctantly walked out of her room, she'd watch her father's back and imagine her mother in the room, her bright eyes lingering, not on the departing figure, but on Kate and she'd feel a weight of sadness too big for a little girl.

She felt like that in school, too. When the teachers or kids badgered her to play, she wanted to scream at them to go away. But she'd hold it in, not wanting to sit in the principal's office under a barrage of personal questions and fake concern. Occasionally, when she could forget about her mother, she was able to enjoy the games her classmates played, but this was rare. The open playground that faced the street distracted her with thoughts of her mother's disappearance because every time Kate looked up, she hoped to see her.

She wondered constantly where her mother was, if she had fallen and hurt herself, if she had forgotten where she lived, if she was wandering around the streets close-by. It would have been easier if there were a goodbye note, if her father had something concrete to give her instead of, "She's gone." There was a void from her mother's unexplained absence that grew each day.

She remembered small details from the day her mother left; the cold on her legs, the smell of cookies in Ina's house, her father leaving to look for Kathleen.

He didn't find her, yet he continued living as if nothing was amiss. The photos reminded her every day of their "missing person," but her father didn't like to speak about Kathleen. He pretended he wanted to. He'd stand at her bedroom door or sit at the kitchen table and say, "We should talk about your mom." But the moment she asked where she was, he'd clam up and shake his head. So, she started to avoid him like she did her classmates at school.

Apart from Ina, the only person she liked was Christine, who lived in the apartment across the road. Christine was nearly as tall as Kate. She had blonde curly hair, blue eyes, and a quiet assured air about her. She went to the same school, but they weren't in the same class, so Kate saw her mostly in the local playground. Christine floated around Kate, garnering her attention and curiosity. Most of the time, Christine was with her little brother, helping him on the swings or seesaw. Sometimes though, she'd be alone, and she'd sit on the swing beside Kate and talk in a low voice about her cat and his habit of bringing dead birds to the door, which she thought was pretty gross, or how she had to wait until her brother was napping to run outside, because she didn't always want him trailing behind her. She never seemed bothered if Kate didn't respond. Christine would eventually slow the swing and drift to some other play area with an indifference that made Kate start to follow her. After a while, Kate would run straight to Christine. Nicholas accompanied Kate to the park, and he and Christine's dad would lean against the park fence chatting, but this ended when Kate wanted to walk to the park alone.

"I'm old enough," she told him. She was nine.

"Yeah," Nicholas said. "But I like to walk with you." He had put his jacket on and was facing the door, but was barred from leaving by his daughter. She was so quiet most of the time that her determination shocked him. There was no uncertainty in her stare or in the hand that held the door.

"I want to go by myself." He heard no apology or doubt. "Toby goes alone and he's only seven." Toby lived a few doors down and cursed like an old man.

"I don't care about Toby," Nicholas told her, and his heart skipped with relief when her hand fell.

"Okay, I won't go." She was brushing past him with her head down. Her red hair fell over her shoulders.

"Come on, Kate," he said.

She went into her bedroom and closed the door. Nicholas would have liked to ask Ina what she thought. "She's only nine," he wanted to say. "Is she really old enough to go alone?" But he knew Ina would tell him, "She'll be fine, she's a smart girl."

And besides, Ina was busy. Jeff's car was parked next door. Nicholas had met him a few Sundays ago, a smiling, big-shouldered man in his suit and tie. Ina was nervous beside him, as she used to be with Stefano, which got to Nicholas more than the presence of Jeff himself. Ina had shown that same nervousness around Pete, too, a friend of a client who was around for a few months and then not. When Nicholas said he hadn't seen Pete for a while, Ina had laughed and made some comment about his powers of observation. In the last couple of years, an easier acceptance and a more relaxed way of being had developed between them, but he had not forgotten their meetings in the hotel rooms. When he slept with Marcy, the sister of one of his co-workers, or June, a woman he'd met in the supermarket (each one never more than a handful of times), he'd thought of Ina's body. Ina might not have forgotten him either. She'd been hard-edged and angry for a long time, but now there was softness to her resignation; an easier lingering in the mornings after she watched Kate and she was more relaxed during their Sunday dinners with Tilly. When had the change occurred? Nicholas couldn't be sure if it coincided with Pete's appearance, or if one Sunday he arrived in her house and found her easier to be with, more prone to laugh and meet his gaze.

All he knew was that it had gotten better with Ina, but with Kate he was still floundering. He wanted to have her by his side a little longer and not have to worry about strangers and the wrong places to go. They'd talked about the dangers out there before, but it was like talking about violence happening in a different country. He never thought he'd be going there so soon.

He couldn't say yes. His threw his jacket on the couch and sat beside it, for once turning on the television to let Kate know his decision had been made. She didn't come out of her room until dinnertime.

The next day, she asked him again. Nicholas had had hours to get used to the idea and knew he had to let her do this. Yet the moment she passed Ina's front door, he was out of house. He was sure Kate heard him. She was good at listening. There was a pause in her movement, and he imagined she would have a childish need to turn around and seek approval. He liked to think that his presence relieved her, though she kept walking without a glance.

Her pace quickened on Central Street. He wondered what he would do if she started to run. Would he yell her name? He felt trapped and out of his depth. At Somerville Avenue, she stopped before crossing the road. For weeks she had practiced the art of waiting for the walk signal. Patience was one of her strong points, which was one of the reasons her father acquiesced to this venture.

Somerville Avenue was wide at this point. Another girl might have been nervous, but Nicholas was sure Kate was too busy watching everything around her. She would have noticed not only the cars on the road, but an older lady coming towards her dressed in a coat, though the weather was warm enough for a t-shirt, and a young boy and girl standing outside the playground fence, giggling at a book they were looking at. There were a few kids in the playground, a young mother following her toddler around, and Manuel with one of his friends. Manuel was watching Kate, and Nicholas wondered if that was why she hesitated before crossing the road.

She was still considered shy. Her new teacher, Mr. Cohen, was middle aged and smart. He'd started walking with her during recess. It was to him that Kate had said, "You know, people just disappear." The teacher told Nicholas he was awed by the even tone of her statement as much as the immensity of it. "Who disappears?" he had asked, but she refused to say anything else.

Nicholas imagined his daughter walking around the playground, watching for her mother, looking out for that red hair. He imagined her throwing furtive glances toward the classroom door, nervous and fidgety with the notion of her mother coming back for her.

Kate started to walk across the street. His little girl was alone on the concrete road with the vast sky over her head, and not once did she glance back to show her delight in her new found independence, not once did she seek his approval. Even when her hand fell on the gate of the playground, when she might have stolen a glimpse at Nicholas, she did not.

Kate had a watch with an alarm set for when she had to go home. Nicholas told her he'd be waiting, and she would not be allowed to go alone again if she were late. He thought he might stay for a few minutes and then leave, but he couldn't drag himself away.

Manuel was watching Kate. Nicholas was sure she was aware of him, but she kept her head down and went to the swings the long way around to avoid him. He didn't know how he felt about Manuel. He rarely saw Adrial anymore, now that she worked full time. When they passed each other, there was never anything more than a polite nod, sometimes a smile. He saw her husband infrequently, but saw the boy a lot, playing outside or cycling his bike. He was only a few months older than Kate, but seemed more mature when he nodded at Nicholas with a direct stare. Nicholas was relieved to see Kate was cautious around him. He watched his daughter lean back on the swings and bring her legs forward, saw the liquid movement of her body and her red hair flying backwards and wished he could go to her now, just stand by the fence so they might smile at each other. He wished he could bridge the distance that had widened today. Only now, when it was too late, he realized he had let his daughter take a step further away.

For the next couple of weeks, Nicholas stood many times on that corner between Central Street and Somerville Avenue. He would never pass it again without thinking of his daughter. He knew her routine, her wait for the walk signal, her stroll into the park, her dart for the swings. Sometimes, Christine would manage to lure her with a game, and she would play for the time that remained. He'd spied on her until the day she stood in the living room and said, "Don't follow me, okay? I'm not stupid."

He had to let her go, but the moment she walked out of sight, he grew nervous. It was terrible not to know if Kate was okay. He thought Ina could check on her. Approaching her house, he saw the front door was open. Ina was standing in the living room. He was sure she saw him, until he got to the steps and heard voices, distant and high pitched. He noticed then that she was looking towards the floor and seemed deep in thought. She looked up just as he opened the screen door. A man was speaking. "Accountants as magicians, a whole company disappearing in one day, who would have thought it was possible?" Nicholas stepped inside her house. A woman was speaking now. "It's not a joking matter, 30,000 people have lost their jobs and retirement funds."

"I'm not laughing, I'm shocked," the reporter said.

Ina shook her head. In the years since the incompetency hearing, Nicholas had gone to her house alone only once. For the first sixteen months, he'd phoned the hospital every few weeks to see how Kathleen was. The calls were always made after Kate had gone to school. He'd dial the number he knew by heart and would ask to speak to Kathleen. The music playing down the line would add to his nerves, brought from the expectation of hearing her voice that never came. She refused to speak to him, and without her consent, he couldn't get information from anyone else. Eventually, he stopped calling, though he couldn't remember making a conscious decision to do so. There was only an awareness of time since his last attempt, and a sense of relief with the silence.

"For anyone who has just joined us, we are talking about the company Nerrel, who have declared bankruptcy. $63.4 billion in assets makes it the largest corporate bankruptcy in U.S. history. Billions of dollars of debt were hidden from shareholders and customers. The question is how many people were involved."

Ina tilted her head. Her eyes had narrowed. Nicholas wondered if she was really listening to the news and if it was large enough to silence her, or if she were waiting for him to do something. He decided he didn't really care. He was glad to have the radio between them.

"How could they have done that? Livelihoods are gone, retirement funds evaporated," a reporter said.

"This cover up was on all levels."

A man was speaking. His voice was deep. Nicholas couldn't tell when he had started. Ina was going towards the radio. He'd always thought her a person frugal with her movements. She walked with a minute grace.

"Too many people are accountable," the reporter said.

"Finger pointing isn't going to change anything — what we need now is new legislation and regulation to expand the accuracy."

The woman's voice was cut off. Nicholas felt as if he had just surfaced from water. His chest was heavy.

"It's bad enough being an accountant without this shit," Ina said.

Nicholas smiled. After a moment, he said,

"Kate's gone. I don't like her in the playground alone. Can you walk down?"

Ina found her flip flops and asked, "Are you coming?"

"She doesn't want me to."

Ina's lack of argument hurt. He moved out of her way and watched her disappear down the road. When Ina came back, she told him Kate was playing with Christine.

"Everything's fine," she said. He would have loved to believe her.

CHAPTER SIXTEEN

CHRISTINE'S MOTHER, HELEN, WAS an office manager at Somerville Hospital. She was small and slim and full of nervous energy. Her hair was dark brown and her face was narrow. It was easy to mistake her for a younger woman. She was a vegan. When Christine turned eleven, she stopped eating meat too.

"Do you know how many lectures I've gotten from Christine about cooking meat?" Nicholas told Helen weeks after the conversion.

"Oh no," Helen laughed. They were standing in Helen's apartment. The hallway was littered with shoes, and Nicholas had to slip his off before following Helen. The apartment had light green carpets, and the living room, kitchen, and dining room was one large room to the left. Double windows led out to the concrete space in back where Helen had put pots of flowers that made Nicholas wish he knew more about gardening. He imagined Helen and Ina could speak for hours on the subject. Some of the flowers Helen had chosen sat in Ina's garden too, but Ina had never been one for neighborhood chats. Above their heads was the sound of running feet. The first time Nicholas heard this, Helen told him, "The twins. At least they stop around 9 p.m."

The girls were in Christine's bedroom. Alex was watching a movie. "Say hello," Helen told her son.

"Hello," he said, without looking at Nicholas. He was more like his mother, with darker hair and a slender body, while Christine took after her father. A pot was boiling on the cooker. There was the smell of lemon and garlic.

Usually, Helen would be calling for Kate to get ready to go home by now and Nicholas would wait in the bright room with the white walls covered by tapestries, amid dark leather couches and a disgruntled Alex, who had tried and failed to play with the girls. But that day, Helen said, "I know it's hard for you, working and taking care of Kate."

He had bristled at this. He found in sympathy an inclination to criticize. "If ever you need Kate to stay the night, we'd be happy to have her," Helen continued quickly. Nicholas managed to smile and say thanks.

He would resist the sleepovers for as long as he could. He liked to come home to Kate and check on her in bed, and he loved their mornings together when she'd come out of the room, sleepy and unguarded. She'd sit at the table while he cooked breakfast and it seemed the only part of the day that they had kept intact. But as the girls got older, Kate would spend more and more time away. It was hardly surprising, since Helen finished work at 2:30 p.m. and every evening she was home with the kids, busy cooking or writing letters for the prevention of cruelty against animals. Her presence was reassuring and eventually, he'd go to collect Kate for dinner, only for the two girls to come out, hands joined together as though in prayer.

"Please let her stay," Christine would plead.

"I can go to school with Christine in the morning. Please, come on Dad. You have to work, and Ina might want the night off."

Kate would always look tired the following day. Mike, Christine's father, a wide-set man with a fashionably shaved head, who spoke in a slow Texan drawl, said the girls spent hours giggling together.

When Kate started high school, she walked to school with Christine, and they hung out in the evenings. She seemed to be doing well at the new school. There were no reports of missing classes or bad behavior. Her grades were good, but she rarely talked about her day to day activities. If she wasn't with Christine, she was on her computer in her room.

The day Nicholas bought her the computer, Ina said, "You're trying to make up for everything by letting her have whatever she wants." He hated to think what she meant by "everything," and that maybe she was right. Nicholas had wanted to set the computer up in the living room.

"I need to study on it. I need quiet," Kate said.

Nicholas said, "But I need to know what you're looking at."

"Just like you used to follow me to the playground. You have to trust me," Kate said.

In the preceding years, she'd often used Nicholas's over-protectiveness against him. She told him he needed to trust her, and then started to slip out of the house without telling him where she was going.

The day of Kate's fight, Ina was in the living room when Nicholas arrived looking for his daughter. The news was on. Ina reached for the remote and turned the television off. Her smile disappeared as she studied at his face. "Not again," Ina said. She usually stood up for Kate, reminding Nicholas that they'd been her age too, and asking him to cut Kate some slack. But he could tell Ina was getting tired of her theatrics. Nicholas had started to dislike those long evenings when his daughter would amble around the neighborhood and could be anywhere. He'd grounded her the week before. But the nights he had to work, Ina would arrive with movies and popcorn, which hardly felt like punishment. Besides, there were times when Ina couldn't stay with Kate, and she would have to spend the night with Christine. He'd have no choice but to back down, so it had gotten to a stage where Kate hardly blinked when he reprimanded her. Twice, he tried taking her computer, but that only meant she spent more time at Christine's. Once, he'd seen her mother's name typed on the computer. *Kathleen Giovanni*. His heart had stopped at the thought of Kathleen in hospital, and Kate looking for her. Kate never mentioned Kathleen to him anymore, but she didn't have to. She kept the photo of her mother beside her computer in pride of place.

Ina was looking over his shoulder. He saw her alarm spread, and turned to see his daughter and Christine. Kate's nose was bleeding. Her knees were scraped. The laces of her sneakers were undone. She was squinting into the sun and crying. Christine had a firm grasp on her hand and was bringing her towards the house. Nicholas ran to Kate. She resisted his hand under her cheek. He said, "Kate, my God." She shook her head.

Ina was beside him, and she looked small and timid as she searched Kate's face. "What happened?" Nicholas asked.

"Manuel started it," Christine said.

"Shut up," Kate said, and her vehemence shocked everyone. Nicholas was aware of birdsong and a lawn mower in the distance. Down the road, a ball was being bounced.

"Kate?" Christine said. Her tone was surprised and hurt. Kate glanced at her. The blood had stopped flowing from her nose, but her shirt was ruined. She seemed to take in and disregard Christine in a glance, before ambling towards the house with Ina at her heels.

Nicholas said, "Are you okay?"

Christine shrugged. "You better go to her."

In the dark living room, Kate and Ina looked like ghosts. The distance between them made Nicholas wonder what he had missed. He imagined Ina had tried to comfort her and had been pushed back.

Kate said, "Manuel said Mom was crazy." Her voice was low and resolute. "He said she screamed all the time. She used to lock me in my room and his mom used to save me."

Kate reminded Nicholas of Kathleen, with her straight arms pushed towards the ground and the tense line of her neck, but her disgusted gaze was all her own.

"That's ridiculous," he told her. "Adrial took you for walks sometimes, that's all."

Kate let his comment sit for a while before shaking her head and telling him, "An ambulance took her away. She didn't just run off."

"That's enough." Ina was beside her. "Manuel's just a bully."

Nicholas had adjusted to the light and could see Ina's impatience. Kate read it too. She was taller than Ina now. He wondered how much longer she would let Ina take hold of her hand and dictate things to her. Dried blood had darkened around Kate's nose. Nicholas saw that her lip was cut.

Ina said, "Come with me, I need to clean you up. Then we can talk." There was a moment in which Nicholas thought Ina had lost Kate too, a moment where Kate seemed to consider her possibilities. Nicholas imagined her darting for the door. But eventually she nodded. Alone, Nicholas wandered to the armchair and sat. He heard the water running, Kate's yelp of pain, and Ina's apology. He thought of Adrial in court and remembered the days after, when she came to see if Kate wanted to go to the playground with Manuel. Nicholas had seen pity in her eyes and he'd told her no, Kate didn't need to go. He hadn't cared about her surprise or how cold he'd sounded, and he hadn't thought about what Adrial might have said to her son, but he should have.

Finally, Kate stood before Nicholas with a clean face. When he looked at her, he couldn't believe she was only fourteen. Her blue eyes seemed older. They had an ice-like quality. Before she had a chance to ask him anything, he said, "I don't know where she is."

He wanted to believe he wasn't lying, that Kathleen could have gone anywhere at this stage. She could have been moved from the hospital. Kate's eyes flashed with hurt. Her head shook. She said, "She can't have just disappeared."

Ina said, "People disappear all the time." There was a shout from outside, a hoot of laughter. People were arriving home from work.

"I knew my mom, okay? She was here and now she's not."

Kate's tears were starting. "An ambulance came. What was wrong with her?"

"Sit down," Nicholas said.

He gestured to the couch, and felt a pause before Kate obeyed. They sat facing each other. Nicholas was leaning forward while Kate sat back, giving him the impression that she wanted to hide.

"Your mother was sick," Nicholas said.

Kate asked, "What was wrong?"

He avoided the temptation to look at Ina, though he could feel her anxiety from the other side of the room. His daughter looked frightened now, and he knew he couldn't tell her the whole truth. It would be too much to deal with all at once, so he told her that Kathleen suffered from depression.

Ina's phone rang in her pocket, but she ignored it. Nicholas imagined Tilly in the nursing home, oblivious to the trouble.

Kate asked, "Was she happy before me?"

"Her depression had nothing to do with you," Nicholas said.

"Did she have a family?" Kate asked.

"I never met her mother and father," Nicholas told her.

"Where are they?"

Nicholas could tell by her wide eyes that she had never thought of her maternal grandmother and grandfather. She was clinging to the idea now, and he was the villain again, taking it from her. "They're dead," he said, because that was what Kathleen had said. They were dead to her — only that wasn't true either. Parts of them had stayed with her, digging deep inside her skin.

"How?"

"I don't know," Nicholas said.

"How could you not know?" Kate said. "They were my grandparents." Kate looked tiny and fragile, but there was a maturity in the way she gazed at Nicholas. For once, Ina was speechless. Nicholas couldn't tell if she was worried or surprised. Later, she would ask, "When did Kate grow up?"

"I just don't," Nicholas said.

"Fine," Kate said and stood. Alone, he would think on the finality of that word, *Fine*.

But then he asked, "Why is Manuel talking about her after so long?"

Kate paused in her retreat. Her gaze seemed detached, as if they were discussing something that had happened years ago.

She said, "How am I supposed to know?" He was sure she was lying.

Kate closed her bedroom door. They heard a child's screech from outside. There was a small yard behind the apartment building where the twins played ball every now and again. Their laughter intensified the silence in the house. A car door slammed and brought Ina to the window.

"Adrial's home," she said.

Nicholas didn't answer. After a few moments, Ina drifted from him, too.

Ina stalled outside Nicholas's house. The sound of children playing was sometimes difficult to hear, though she couldn't pinpoint exactly why. She didn't think it was because she mourned her childlessness. Rather, their laughter left her feeling that there was something wrong in her life. Kate was starting to worry her. Ina had always argued with Nicholas to give her the benefit of the doubt, but whatever freedom Kate received only made her want more. She was like a horse biting at the bit. A few evenings ago, a school night when Ina was supposed to stay with her, Kate had come into the house at 9 p.m. Ina had been reading *The Boston Globe* with her legs curled up on the couch. It had taken her a long time to get used to Nicholas's house, and to stop jumping with every sound, expecting Kathleen to appear behind her, but she had never said anything because she wanted to be able to come and go, like she'd done as a child. Things were different now. There was a distance with Nicholas that she needed to keep in order to maintain some control. Pete had given her the space she'd needed, and Jeff for a time, though she'd wanted little else from them. Sometimes, she felt her control slipping. At night, she'd lie awake and think of going to Nicholas, and she knew if she didn't go to the house to watch Kate, she would not have been able to stay away from him. The little she had was enough for her.

That night, Ina's body had unfolded with Kate's quick entry into the house. Kate hardly looked at her. "I'm staying with a friend tonight," she said as she passed through the living room.

"What friend?" Ina asked. She threw the newspaper on the couch and followed Kate.

"Someone from school," Kate said.

"No, you are not!" Ina told her.

Kate was packing some things in a bag. She didn't look up while she said, "Dad won't mind."

"Don't be ridiculous," Ina said. Kate stopped with her pajama bottoms hanging out of her bag and shrugged, as if she didn't care either way. She said, "What's the difference between one girlfriend and another?"

Ina said, "The difference is I have no idea where you'll be, and I don't even know it's a girl."

"So?"

"So, if you go, don't bother coming to me with your problems. And I certainly won't be waiting for you next week," Ina told her.

Kate stalled with her bag on her back. It was still hard for Ina to get used to Kate being taller than her, though with Ina's threat, Kate seemed to deflate and looked as young as she ought to. Still, there was a depth in Kate's eyes that threw Ina every now and again, as if Kate had the ability to see right through her. Ina could imagine how disconcerting this might be for Nicholas. She held steadfast that night. Her heart knew what was at stake. It beat wildly as Kate cocked her head and said, "Please Ina."

"No," Ina said. "You're staying here tonight."

Kate dropped her bag on the bed. The rest of the night was strained. Kate was noncommittal, and her disinterest in the movie and takeout hurt Ina more than a screaming match might have. She wondered how much longer before Kate would not want her around. How long before she would lose the girl?

A blast of music erupted from Manuel's house and was lowered immediately. Ina realized that Nicholas hadn't said anything about talking to Manuel. Knowing Nicholas, he'd want to have a quiet word. He'd wait for Manuel after school on some corner, or visit before Adrial came home to tell him not to go near his daughter. He wouldn't think of getting Manuel to apologize, or of Kate's discomfort whenever she left her house.

The Barba's house was narrow and long. The family had put an extension on the back years ago, soon after Ina's return. She knocked on the door. When Manuel answered, Ina said, "I need to talk to your mom."

Manuel hesitated for a moment. Ina saw worry in his dark eyes. He had a budding bruise on his cheek. His lips were parted as though he wanted to say something but couldn't remember what it was. She could smell spices from the kitchen, and Ina recognized the scent of cumin. Music drifted from a bedroom to the side. A man was singing about his girl leaving him.

Manuel stepped back to reveal a dark corridor in which a mirror hung on one wall, taking in his reflection. There was a coat rack further down. The floor was dark wood, and the space made Ina think of a tunnel.

"Who is it?" Adrial asked, before appearing at the kitchen door wearing a white apron. She was still in her tights, but had taken off her shoes. Her eyes narrowed when she saw Ina, and Ina realized how irate she must look. "Is everything okay?" Adrial was walking towards the front door and rubbing her hands on her apron.

"No," Ina said.

Adrial took a breath. Manuel had his head down. Ina could feel his desire to flee. She was glad they hadn't asked her in. She didn't want to step inside their cocoon of smells and darkness, and hated the idea of sitting with tea and making small talk. For years, she'd avoided getting to know any of her new neighbors. It was easier coming home when she didn't have to nod hello or remember names.

She'd seen Adrial's husband many times, and thought he looked aloof and strict, with his chin held high and his shoulders straight. She wondered if it was his influence that made the boy stay at the door with his head down in anticipation of a scolding. She couldn't imagine Adrial eliciting such behavior. There was softness to the woman, even as she gazed at her son and her lips tightened with impatience.

"Do you want to tell me what's going on?" Adrial asked her son.

Ina watched the two of them. The chubby woman and tall lean boy were so alike in the way they held themselves. They made her feel like an outsider. A world was held in their exchange of glances and the hand that came up to touch Manuel's cheek.

"Has it got anything to do with this?" Adrial asked. Manuel looked at Ina, who was not surprised to see resentment in his eyes. He looked older now.

"She attacked me," he said.

Adrial flinched. There was shock in her voice when she asked, "Who attacked you?" It was obvious she knew. She would have seen Kate and Ina together many times. She would have known why Ina was here the moment she saw her. Kate was their common denominator.

Manuel turned to his mother. "I didn't touch her."

"Her nose was bleeding," Ina said.

Adrial's hand went to her mouth. Ina didn't know what to think of her easy acceptance. She wished there were some denial to lighten the strain that had filled the hall.

Manuel said, "She ran at me and we fell to the ground. It wasn't my fault."

"Manuel?" Adrial said. She seemed on the verge of tears. He was looking at her with shoulders barred, and it reminded Ina of the way his dad walked. "It wasn't my fault," he said.

Ina sighed. "So, she attacked you for no reason."

"Yeah, she's crazy like her mother," Manuel said.

"Manuel?" Adrial managed before her voice trailed off. Her shoulders had sagged. She was falling apart before Ina. Ina imagined Adrial was praying for her to leave and the door to close behind her so that she could go back to her cooking and pretend this had never happened. She imagined Manuel hiding in his room, listening to music, and the subdued quiet in the house, until his father came home and Adrial whispered, "I have something to tell you." But Ina had no intention of walking away, or letting them believe that his bullying had not occurred.

"Kate is not crazy and neither was her mother," Ina said. She couldn't believe she was the one to say this. "And you need to apologize."

Manuel merely shrugged at Ina's order.

Adrial said, "I'll go with you," and disappeared into the kitchen to take off her apron. Maybe she turned her dinner off too. Ina didn't care. She slipped away before they went to Nicholas's door. She did not feel the need to witness Manuel and Kate together. She didn't know how Kate would accept Manuel's apology, but she hoped it might help her move on from the notion that her mother was insane.

Manuel was standing beside Adrial when Nicholas opened the door.

"Manuel wants to apologize," Adrial told him. Nicholas was silent for long enough to be impolite. Manuel shifted on his feet and kept his head down. Nicholas wanted Manuel to look him in the eye. He wanted to see what Kate saw before the boy had turned her world upside down. Adrial's eyes were a soft black. He imagined Manuel to be harder, to have no remorse. When he finally looked up, Nicholas saw his eyes were more green than brown, and there was worry in them, but also pride. The boy seemed not to care that a girl had given him the bruise on his right cheek and a cut on his lip. Nicholas didn't think the boy wanted to apologize, but he couldn't tell if he was completely averse to the idea. His mouth threw Nicholas off. Manuel had inherited his mother's full lips, and though he wasn't quite smiling, he wasn't tight lipped either. The resemblance to Adrial softened Nicholas and let him step back and allow Manuel to enter his home. He'd regret this long before he discovered Kate missing one morning, the bed neat and tidy, and her cuddly toys on the pillow looking like some cruel joke.

He told the mother and son to wait in the living room and knocked on Kate's door. She didn't answer. "Kate, someone's here to see you," Nicholas told her.

He heard her shuffling before the door opened. Her gaze was too neutral, and gave Nicholas the impression that she hardly saw him. When they entered the living room, her shoulders straightened. Manuel was putting out his hand. Nicholas noticed he had long fingers.

"I'm sorry," he said. "I shouldn't have said that."

Kate glanced at his hand before looking back at Manuel's face. "Is it true?" Kate asked.

Manuel shrugged. Adrial seemed to have grown pale.

Nicholas said, "That's enough." He had to fight the urge to kick them out and lock the door. He stepped beside Kate and told her, "It isn't true."

Adrial's gaze was on him and he felt her surprise and refused to look at her. His voice had come out hard and a ball of nerves sat in his belly.

Manuel glanced at his mother, who said they should go. And Nicholas knew that in front of her son she must have said, "That woman was crazy." He was sure she was the person Manuel had taken the idea from. She was going for the door. But Manuel hadn't moved. He was standing across from Kate. He apologized again.

"Okay," Kate finally said. "Apology accepted." She put her hand out towards Manuel.

Nicholas wondered later if he imagined her smile. It was there and gone within seconds, and then her hand was in his. The boy and girl nodded to each other.

CHAPTER SEVENTEEN

AFTER THE FIGHT, NICHOLAS didn't see Christine for weeks. He thought Kate's violence and the gruffness in her "Shut up" must have kept her away, since Christine always seemed more grown up than his daughter, and not likely to accept that behavior. Whenever she stayed over, she'd get up early and sit with Nicholas, on the couch or in the kitchen, telling him about the videos she'd watched on animal rescue. She wanted a dog but wasn't allowed one, and a slight Texan twang would be audible in her accent whenever she grew irate, talking about the dogs that were maltreated. The accent came from her father. Nicholas thought her confidence came from him too. Where Helen was all nervous gestures and jumps, Mike was calm and easy going.

Nicholas had often witnessed his saunter to the swings after Alex had fallen. He would pick his son up and whisper something to him before putting him back on the swing. Nicholas believed Helen would have screamed in fright, and this was why he never saw Helen at the playground. She was better at coolly scrutinizing disaster from her kitchen table.

Christine had gotten her parents' best traits. She believed in everything her mother was doing, but had a poise that Helen did not. When Helen talked about eating meat, or an animal that had been left abandoned in a drainpipe, her voice would go high and her hands would flutter around her face. Christine, on the other hand, would take the beef out of Nicholas's fridge and say evenly, "You know that buying this is helping to destroy the rain forest," with an authoritative calm by the time she was twelve.

Kate never said anything to these comments, though after a while she stopped eating meat in front of her friend, and would lift the plate of bacon off the table to hide it. Nicholas always thought Kate was the quieter of the two. He imagined her trailing behind Christine, listening to her talk about this and that, while being as reticent as she was at home. He never thought that Kate might be a completely different person outside her house, until she told Christine to shut up in the tone of a bully, and Manuel started to appear in Christine's absence. It scared him to think how much he didn't know and how much Kate kept from him. In many ways, Kate reminded him of Kathleen: her inward gaze, her love of roaming, the red hair that she grew long. More than once, Nicholas was struck with the sight of Kate at the kitchen table with her back to the door. She always sat in the seat her mother had used, and she resembled Kathleen, with the rounded shoulders and stillness. Nicholas felt lonely for Kate then. It was impossible to go to her when Kathleen had risen in his head, and he wondered how often Kathleen came to life for Kate. How many times did she study the photos and envision her mother beside her? Kate would never have told him. She kept her feelings to herself. She and Nicholas only skimmed the surface with each other. When he asked about Manuel, she merely shrugged and said, "It's nothing serious, Dad."

Manuel never came into the house. It might have been better if he had. Then there would be an acknowledgment of Nicholas as the father, a nod of respect, and a "How are you?" Instead, he waited outside with his hands in his pockets, shuffling his feet with his head down. Nicholas believed that if Manuel had a car, he would have blown the horn and Kate would have run out, until one hot afternoon, when he realized he had it all wrong. Kate was in her room, which was the coolest in the house due to the window fan. The living room had a large fan that tossed the air around rather than cooled it, and made a whirring noise that used to drive Kathleen mad. Nicholas was standing at Kate's bedroom door, asking what she wanted for dinner when her mobile alert went off. She glanced at the text message, before shrugging and telling him, "Whatever. Just not pasta, okay?"

In the living room, Nicholas saw Manuel was waiting outside. He was sixteen and nearly as tall as Nicholas. He was leaning against the fence, staring up at the house, as if willing Kate to appear. He looked impatient and ruffled, and Nicholas realized he must have texted Kate minutes ago. Yet she kept him waiting, sometimes for ten minutes. When Kate eventually came out of her room, Nicholas couldn't resist asking, "Does Christine not like Manuel?"

She paused at the front door. There was a second when Kate seemed to consider what he was saying. Then she nodded, and said, "Yeah, she doesn't like Manuel," with a matter of fact ease that was strange.

Not long after this exchange, Helen approached Nicholas when he was leaving for work. Kate was alone in the house. Ina would check on her every few hours, but Kate had started to dislike the idea of being babysat. They had refused to listen to her at first, but the last few occasions, Kate had stayed in her bedroom for the evening and not spoken to Ina. "If she wanted to go, she only has to climb out the window," Ina told Nicholas. "I'll check up on her."

Helen looked worried and tired. Her hair was pulled back from her face with a clip. She said her daughter had been very quiet since the beginning of summer. "I'd hoped she would talk to me," Helen said, "but she clams up whenever I ask about Kate. Do you have any idea what's wrong?"

The interior of the taxi felt uncomfortably hot. Helen was leaning on the door. "She doesn't like Manuel," he told her.

Helen nodded, and said, "Maybe," but it was obvious she thought it was more than that.

Nicholas sat outside and fought his desire to sleep. His red eyes were hidden behind sunglasses. He'd been working all night. A ball was being kicked down the street, and he could hear boys shouting names at each other. Someone was vacuuming with their windows open. He remembered when Kate and Christine were young, and he'd hose them down at the side of the house, and laugh at their screeches whenever they heard the music of the ice cream van. He felt Kate's note in his hand.

The paper had gotten soggy from sweat. She had written that she was out and would be back in the evening. He had no idea when she'd left, but couldn't imagine she'd gotten out of bed before 8 a. m. Finally, Christine and Alex came out of the apartment. He was surprised at Christine's reluctance when he called her over. Her hair was shorter. Her smile was thin, and she didn't seem to want to look Nicholas in the eye. He was sitting on the rocking chair. A book sat on his lap, hardly touched.

"What's going on?" Nicholas asked. She shrugged and looked down the empty street. Her body was tense with discomfort.

"Is it Manuel?" he asked.

Alex was watching his sister with curiosity. He must have asked her the same question many times and gotten nothing. She finally looked at Nicholas, and he was struck by the dullness in her eyes. "I guess," she said. "I have to go."

Nicholas was cooking dinner when Kate got home later that evening. "Hey," she said, as she entered the house. He had slept a little, but he'd kept waking up, hoping to see his daughter home. It was summer, and he'd told himself not to worry too much, but Christine's behavior had put him on edge. His daughter was fourteen and he had no idea where she'd been. Still, he knew shouting would only make her storm off. "Hey," he said. "How was your day?"

Her red-cheeked smile made his stomach lurch because he didn't trust that it would remain. "Great," she said. "I went to the beach." She came into the kitchen and picked a piece of penne from the dish. It was smothered with butter, just as she liked it.

"Kate, I need to know where you are."

She looked at him and he knew she was thinking of Kathleen. *You don't know where Mom is*, she might have said, but her indifference was worse when she shrugged and said, "Okay. I need to shower."

A few nights later, Kate didn't come home. After an hour of waiting, Nicholas went to Manuel's house. Adrial's husband opened the door to him. Nicholas was struck by the man's dissimilarity to his son and wife. His blonde hair was receding and he had angry, olive eyes.

"What do you want?" he asked.

Nicholas wanted to be angry, but a sinking feeling had started in his belly. Manuel hadn't been in front of the house for at least a week. Kate said she was meeting him at the playground.

"Is Kate here?" he asked, keeping his eyes on the man's arrogant face. Nicholas wouldn't show his worry. He wished he knew the man's name.

"No," Manuel's father said. He was still wearing his suit, but the tie was loose. Adrial appeared behind him. "Manuel hasn't talked to your daughter in over a week."

Adrial was telling him to stop, but a glint had entered her husband's eyes. He was enjoying himself. Nicholas would have walked away if he could have, but he felt like everything was caving in on him. It was possible that if he took one step he'd collapse. "She's seeing someone else," Adrial's husband said. "Manuel doesn't know who he is, but he's a lot older."

Ina was on her way to visit her mother when Nicholas appeared shaky and pale faced.

"I don't know where she is," he said. "She's with a man. Did she tell you anything?" Ina was standing at the door with her bag in her hand. She was speechless. "Ina?"

Kate had mentioned someone. She'd said something about him working with the homeless. Or maybe she said he was homeless. *Jesus*, Ina thought. Kate had burst in the door and started talking about a guy. Ina had been in the middle of an account, her head tied to columns and numbers, and had put up her hand and said, "Wait a sec." But Kate didn't wait. She said something about meeting him. Ina didn't catch what she'd said. By the time Ina looked up, Kate had finished talking. She was flushed, and her eyes were bright. Ina was annoyed at her then; Kate irritated her a lot lately because she never showed this side to Nicholas. If he walked into the room, the light inside her would switch off, and Ina thought it cruel and dishonest. It was getting harder to be with the two of them. Even when Kate wasn't there, Nicholas couldn't move past his failings with his daughter, but mostly, Ina was damned tired of Kate's selfish theatrics. Maybe this was why she said, "What about Manuel?"

Ina wished she hadn't asked because Kate's excitement had waned along with her openness. So now, Ina had nothing concrete. "I don't know," she said.

"She talked about a guy a while ago, but I don't know anything, not even his name."

Nicholas's eyes flared. He rubbed his face. She had the impression that he wanted to rip his hair out.

He said, "It's getting late."

She said, "Let's take separate cars. You go ahead, I need to phone Mom first."

She phoned her mother and told her she couldn't make it. Tilly said it was okay. She wanted to get a good sleep anyway. She was feeling very tired. An early night would do her good.

Nicholas ran to Christine's apartment. She said she had no idea where Kate was. Nicholas was too restless to go into the apartment, while Christine listed places Kate liked to go to. They searched the streets for four hours. It was dark, and Summer Street was quiet when Ina pulled up to her house after midnight. She sat listening to the ticking of her engine for a long time. She felt tired and listless. When Nicholas arrived, she wanted to tell him they were overreacting, that kids did this these days. Kate would come home soon. But she couldn't say any of it. They sat in his house, pretending to watch TV. The volume was low. They hardly spoke, as if any sound might make them miss some clue to Kate's whereabouts. Nicholas sent Ina home an hour later. "One of us needs to sleep," he told her.

CHAPTER EIGHTEEN

INA'S PHONE RANG AT 6 a. m. Kate was the first thing on her mind, but it wasn't her. The woman's voice was familiar and her tone was soft and sad. "Hello, Miss Alderman," Ina's mind struggled. Who was this?

"Ina," the voice said, and then the nurse rose like a genie from the telephone line, dark haired, with glasses and full cheeks.

"I'm afraid we have some sad news," the nurse said. She waited a moment before telling Ina that Tilly had died during the night. Ina hung up with the image of mother dead on the bed, her eyelids translucent amid a pale face. She thought of the nurse touching her cooling skin and wished she was the one to find her. If she had visited her last night, maybe she would have known. She might have been there when Tilly's life started to slip away.

How could she have missed it? How could she have slept here oblivious, and then think of Kate when the phone rang? She felt ashamed and small. For a long time, Ina lay curled up in her bed. She knew Tilly wouldn't hold it against her. But this knowledge didn't help, because Ina couldn't forgive herself.

Nicholas opened the door to a sobbing, shaking Ina. Later, he wouldn't be able to remember if she told him the news, or if he knew the moment he saw her. She collapsed into his arms, her body trembling. He was holding her when Kate appeared in her pajamas, her hair messy. "What is it?" she asked.

Nicholas had tears in his eyes. "Tilly," he told her, and watched her face fall. He managed to bring Ina in and close the door. His daughter looked like a little girl as she sobbed and put her arms around them. It was after 2 a.m. by the time Kate had come home the previous night. Nicholas was waiting on the couch.

"Where were you?" he'd said the moment she clicked the door closed.

"Out," she'd said.

He'd risen to his full height. "That's not good enough. You're only fourteen for God's sake. I have to know where you are."

"I was at a friend's house." In the lamplight, she'd looked ageless, like a ghost.

"What friend?" he'd asked.

"I'm tired, I'm going to bed," she'd said.

He'd grabbed her arm and heard her yelp. "If you want to live here, you've got to follow the rules."

"Or what? Are you going to kick me out like you did to Mom?" she'd said, and his grip had loosened.

"Go ahead Dad, see if I care." She'd pulled away, leaving a lingering smell of cigarettes. Her bedroom door had slammed, and light appeared in the gap on the floor. Nicholas hadn't been able to move until it was turned off again.

Now Kate was standing beside them, holding them and crying. Ina's sobbing stalled when she moved back and looked at Kate. She seemed to straighten, and though her eyes were red and her mouth loose, Nicholas detected anger. He heard Kate's snivels. He waited for Ina to say something, to bring Kate back to the child she was, to have her realize what she was doing to them. Tears were running down Kate's cheeks. He wasn't sure if she noticed Ina's scrutiny, if she felt anything other than her grief. He thought that this was what she was like every day now, so fixated on her mother that she had stopped caring about the two people in the room.

The silence dragged and Kate rubbed her face. "I'm so sorry," she said to Ina.

Ina nodded. Maybe it was the thought of Tilly that kept her from haranguing Kate. Perhaps, she didn't have the energy. But Nicholas wished she said something instead of treating her so coldly. When Nicholas offered to take Ina to the mortuary, Kate started for her room. "I'll get dressed."

"No." The word seemed too large for the room. Kate's blue eyes showed confusion. Her mouth twitched again.

"You can stay here," Ina said. Her voice was shaky, yet this didn't take from the finality of her words. "I know you don't mind being alone."

Kate's face collapsed. There were minute traces of makeup on her cheeks, black dots of mascara that Nicholas might have missed were he not looking so intently. Her hair still smelled of smoke, and even with all this she looked inconceivably young as she shook her head.

"Please," she said.

Ina said, "It's better this way." Her hand went to her mouth and her head lowered. She missed Kate's beseeching glances towards Nicholas. He had nothing to say. Watching his daughter, he was left with a sensation of dryness, as if all his words had turned to dust.

Ina turned to him and said, "We need to go."

Kate put her hand out towards Ina and then took it back. She was crying so hard she had started to hiccup. Nicholas wanted to run to his daughter and tell her it was going to be all right. He wanted to hold her like he did when she was five, but he knew she would not let him.

"I'm sorry," Kate wept.

Ina nodded without looking at anyone. "So am I," she said.

"I'll be back as soon as I can," Nicholas told Kate. "Don't go anywhere."

He wondered if she heard him at all. All her attention was on the diminutive woman leaving, whose hair was wild on her head. Ina was wearing an old pair of sweatpants and a t-shirt. Her feet were bare. Outside, she flinched at the sun's brightness and paused at the top step. Nicholas put his arm around her and felt her body slacken and lean on him.

"You sure you don't want her to come," Nicholas said. He wanted to say that it wasn't Kate's fault Tilly died, and he felt bad leaving her alone at home, but Ina had tensed in his hold before pulling away. She started down the steps and said, "I'm sure."

Nicholas followed Ina to her house. He sat on the couch in the living room and waited for her to change and he thought of all those Sundays he'd brought Tilly home. Their weekly tradition of Sunday dinners had started because of Tilly and had been an important part of Kate's childhood. Years ago, Tilly had kept Ina and Nicholas apart, only to become the glue that would hold them together. He was sure Tilly had known this. Sundays, when Kate was young and had difficulty sitting at the table, when she would ask constantly for dessert and Ina started to keep her fascinating facts as a treat for when Kate finished dinner, Tilly often sat back with a gloating gleam in her eye, and said simply, "Isn't this nice."

Ina came out wearing a pair of jeans and a blouse. She wore flip flops and her hair was tied back. She didn't bother with makeup. She looked drained, as if she hadn't slept in weeks, and asked, "Are you ready?" with a cursive glance.

Nicholas wondered if she was missing Kate too and if she felt that her absence was another thing to mourn. He knew Ina was doing what she thought was right. "She has to know there are boundaries," she'd often said, but this was something bigger. This was shutting Kate out from Ina's grief. This was putting a wall between them.

He called her name as she was going for the passenger door. She stopped. Her brown eyes were sunken. "I can't," she said. She was a small bundle of sorrow. He watched her go to his car with those words ringing in his ears. The soft whisper of "I can't" scared him.

Ina leaned against the locked car. Kate was at the

front door when he reached the driver's side. She'd stopped crying, but was red faced and trembling. She had put on a pair of jeans and a black t-shirt. Her hair was in a ponytail. He wondered if Ina had heard the door open and kept her head away on purpose or if she was unaware of everything except the woman laid out in a mortuary waiting for her.

Nicholas couldn't stop thinking of Kate, even as he drove. Ina gazed out the window and was silent for the journey. Every now and again, she'd wipe tears from her face. The funeral home was an impressive two-story building, that looked like a residential home.

Inside, they were brought to Tilly, who was laid out in a white blouse and skirt. Her hands were resting on her belly. Ina reached for Tilly's hand. Her fingers traced her mother's rings. When Ina glanced at Nicholas, he realized she wanted to be alone. He withdrew to the front office, and decided to phone Stefano. They only talked a couple of times a year. When Kate was young, she used to run for the phone and spend some time nodding into the mouth piece. Nicholas's conversations with Stefano's son Cooper were just as reticent, with Nicholas asking questions and getting little response. Stefano had phoned a few months ago. Kate had answered the phone, and said, "Hello. Yes. Okay, do you want Dad?" She held the phone outward, afraid to get stuck in conversation.

It was early morning in San Francisco, but Stefano sounded all business when he answered the phone. His voice was deep and full of authority. A woman's voice came from somewhere in the background. Nicholas had talked to Audrey once or twice. She never stayed on the phone long, and he couldn't tell if she was shy or aloof.

"Is everything okay?" Stefano had asked a similar question nine years ago. Then Nicholas had said, "I nearly lost Kate."

Now, he said, "It's Tilly. She died last night in her sleep; I'm at the mortuary with Ina. I'll phone the priest in a bit and organize the funeral."

He told Stefano about the nursing home already sending a bouquet to the mortuary. He talked about the phone calls Ina had received on the car ride there from men and women he'd met in the nursing home and used to hear about every Sunday. Nicholas didn't know why he was talking so much, but he couldn't stop. His voice brought him away from the idea of his daughter curled up on the couch, waiting for them to come home.

"We'll be there for the funeral," Stefano said.

Nicholas had never thought that Stefano would come home.

"You don't have to," Nicholas said, and was surprised by the irritation in Stefano's voice.

"Of course, we have to. It's Tilly we're talking

about. Let me know when you have a date; I might as well start looking for flights now." After a pause he said, "I'm lucky there's not much going on at work." Nicholas almost smiled at Stefano's typical remark, but all he could think of was his photos of Kathleen.

"Nicholas?" Stefano urged.

Nicholas said, "I'll call with the times, okay."

"Okay, see you soon." Stefano hung up.

The door of the office was open. The funeral director, Mr. Sheehan, a thin man with watery eyes and blood vessels visible under the pale skin of his cheeks, was on the phone at his desk. He was dressed in a pinstriped suit. His voice made Nicholas think of the Ivy League and holiday homes in the country. In his agitated state, the talking sat on Nicholas's nerves. What would Stefano say when he saw the photos of Kathleen? He knew the story of what she had done. He'd heard it all in the days after Kathleen's arrest. Nicholas wasn't sure why he'd opened up so much to Stefano. It was hard to remember the searing loneliness he'd felt in the days after Kathleen was gone, and how the weight of nearly losing Kate had sat like a sledgehammer on his heart. For a while, the act of rising in the morning had been mountainous.

Stefano had offered to come home for a few days, but Nicholas had managed to put him off. Nicholas never thought of Stefano stepping back into his house. At that stage, it had been ten years since Stefano had visited home. It didn't take long for their relationship to revert to the yearly postcards and brief "How are you doing?" chats that never went deeper than, "My ten year old son just beat me in chess again," or, "Audrey's thinking of going back to work, but she's been saying that for fifteen years." Nicholas never mentioned Ina's input in their life. He refused to bring her up and sensed the growing curiosity on the end of the line. It would be Stefano's style, to throw Ina back at his brother.

Nicholas didn't realize Mr. Sheehan had finished his conversation until he was beside Nicholas asking, "Are you all right?" Nicholas looked at the man and saw concern. *How many people went through here?* Nicholas wondered. Still, Mr. Sheehan had reached out for Ina's hand, when they'd arrived and had expressed his sympathies in a way that made Nicholas wonder if he'd known Tilly. Was it a role he put on the moment he entered the mortuary, a soft exterior put over his indifference, a uniform of grieving? At Nicholas's pause, Mr. Sheehan's concern heightened. He leaned towards Nicholas, as though he were about to touch his hand, and Nicholas stepped back from the prospect of the man's sympathy.

"I have to phone the priest." Ina's voice surprised him.

The funeral would be in four days, Friday, at

midday. Stefano said he'd get a flight for Thursday. When Nicholas told Ina, he was sure she would make some smart remark. A frown appeared and she shook her head, but said nothing. Later, in the car on the way home, she complained of a headache and put her head back on the seat. Her face was pale and drawn, and her hair was tied back tightly. She closed her eyes, and murmured, "I suppose it's only right," which was as close as she came to saying that she didn't like the thought of Stefano coming. Nicholas glanced at her. She seemed smaller since the news of her mother's death. All her stubborn energy had dissolved in her grief so that she was like a child, huddled on the passenger seat of his car.

All day, Nicholas had imagined his daughter crying and upset. The image was reminiscent of those afternoons he'd return home after Kathleen had a particularly bad rage towards Kate. Kate's little body would be curled up on the bed. He used to pick her up and hold her until she unwrapped in his arms. Then, they'd start to talk in conspiratorial whispers. He'd ask what she'd like to do. He'd never thought they were spoiling her. He and Kathleen had pulled and pushed. They'd upset and coddled her. They gave and took in the same breath, so that she must have started to associate rage with treats. When the rages stopped, she didn't know how to handle the hugs.

Before he had turned off the engine, Kate was out of the house. Her face was dry of tears and her steps towards them were forceful, as if they were late for some important event, and not returning from a funeral home. The image of his remorseful daughter, who had spent hours feeling guilty turned to dust. Nicholas was reluctant to get out of the car and see what she would be replaced with.

Kate kept her gaze fixed on Ina. "It's not my fault she died," Kate said.

Without missing a beat, Ina told her, "I didn't see her yesterday." She didn't have to say *because of you*; the knowledge was thick between them.

"I never asked you," Kate started, but was cut off by Ina slamming the passenger door.

"That's not true," Ina said. "You wanted me to care."

Kate's mouth dropped open. Her justification had been whipped away. Nicholas saw her stance soften. He expected her to ask for forgiveness, but instead she turned and marched back to the house.

Chapter Nineteen

Nicholas walked into his empty living room. Music blared behind Kate's closed door. Usually Nicholas would knock, but he couldn't afford her this grace, not with the memory of her advance on Ina. He had sat with Ina in her house for a while. Every now and again, Ina would shake her head, but neither could put words to what had just happened. Eventually, Ina told him she needed to sleep. He was reluctant to leave her, but also lost for words. Kate had robbed him of expression.

Kate was in front of the computer, her shoulders slumped forward. The screen lit up her face in the otherwise dark room. She was wearing headphones. "I know. It's the pits," she was saying. She didn't hear Nicholas open the door. Whenever Nicholas was outside the room, he could feel the bass or hear the strain of a guitar, but he had never been able to make out the words. Now, a man was singing about leaving, and Nicholas realized the music was playing for his benefit, so he wouldn't hear her voice. The curtains were closed. The air was stale and her bed was unmade. Clothes lay on the floor. He kicked a pair of jeans on his way to his daughter. Her eyes widened when she noticed him.

"What are you doing?" Kate said.

He'd expected her to jump up and shout at him to get out, but instead she folded towards the computer, as if she could hide the man with blonde hair who was leaning towards her. His mouth was moving and a muffled voice was coming from the headphones. Nicholas could make out an open wardrobe, clothes hanging over the door. There was a bed behind him.

"I have to go," Kate said. The screen turned blank. Kate jumped up. Her headphones clattered to the side.

"Who is he?" Nicholas asked.

Kate said, "A friend."

In the background, the man sung. *You tell me you're tipsy; I tell you you're pretty. We could spend the night if you're still sure.* It was hard for Nicholas to restrain himself from grabbing Kate's arms. He could still see the frown on the man's face

and the stubble that lined his chin. He was no teenager. Nicholas's head was starting to buzz.

He said, "What does he want with you?"

"What's that supposed to mean? You don't
think he'd be interested in me?" she said.

"Jesus, Kate, you're fourteen."

"He's only twenty-six," Kate told him with a
hint of satisfaction that made his skin crawl. The
evenness of his daughter's gaze and her complete
disregard shocked him. Kate didn't back down. It
seemed she was egging him on. Her gaze said, "Go
on then."

He was getting lightheaded. Darkness was
moving behind his eyes, distorting her features.
The music was running around his head. The
singer was talking about tears on the phone, feeling so alone, and Kate was moving backward, her
body an outline. He couldn't let her walk away.
Right in the morning. C'mon c'mon c'mon. He
grabbed her computer. Kate screamed. Her fingers were on his arm. "Stop it," she said, sounding
scared and far away, as if her voice were traveling
through a tunnel to reach him. He pulled away
from her grasp and smashed the computer on the
ground. He didn't think he pushed her, but could
see her falling backwards. He was conscious of
his breathing. The air came in and out his nose.
His chest moved up and down rapidly and he was

aware of Kate's presence on the bed and how quiet she was. The black dots that had floated behind his eyes were fading. His stomach was heavy with the memory of that blonde man, who had frowned at him, as if Nicholas had barged into his home, and not the other way around.

"You see him again Kate," he said, "and I'll have him arrested."

Her body was a mass of black, a shape folding inward. She was crying softly. He hated that she didn't want to look at him. What had she expected when she was spending time with a twenty-six-year-old and staying out at all hours of the night? Had she really thought Nicholas would continue to sit back and let her ruin herself? The song had changed. *He's a teenager, a teenager in love. What a tragic attraction.* Nicholas wasn't sorry. The floor was littered, and the table was leaning back on its hind legs. The wall had stopped it from falling. He righted it. *With a curse and a crush, what a magical distraction....*

She stayed on the bed and watched, as he picked up the pieces of her computer. He'd opened the curtains. Sun spilled into her room. Her schoolbag lay on the floor at the end of the bed. Two days ago, he'd gotten her school supplies. Next week, she would start ninth grade. She would be going nowhere until he found out who that man was. The stupid thing was all traces of him had gone with her computer.

Everything you want in this world, first things first, get what you deserve. The music was starting to grind him down, but he couldn't imagine turning it off and have nothing between them. He couldn't remember the last time he'd been in this room for so long. Years ago, he'd spend Saturday mornings cleaning. Kathleen had never been one for household chores. She'd advocated for a cleaner, but Nicholas hated the idea of a stranger going into their bedroom or cleaning the bathroom after them. Kate used to love to vacuum. She'd squeeze between the handle and Nicholas. He'd take twice as long because he'd have to guide her through the rooms without tripping over her. At some point, she stopped running to help him, and then a year or two ago, she blocked him from entering her room. "I can do it," she'd said.

He felt like an intruder now, sweeping the vacuum over the small specks of glass with Kate watching stony faced from the bed. He would have liked to sit beside her and apologize, say how sorry he was, but she had long ago stopped respecting his need for approval.

By the time he'd finished vacuuming, the music had stopped. He left her door open as he put everything away. She didn't jump off the bed to close it, as he expected. Maybe with the computer gone, she had no secrets to hide from him, or maybe she was still in shock. He was out of the room for at least ten minutes when he remembered her cell and felt hot with stupidity.

"I want your phone," he said at the door.

He expected her to argue. The cell lay beside her. She picked it up and handed it to him, and he knew by her lack of panic that she'd foreseen this and had taken precaution ,while he'd been out of the room. Her blank expression told him he wouldn't find anything. With a quick glance, he saw no suspicious names. Her text messages were empty.

"Stefano and his family are coming for the funeral," Nicholas said. She didn't look at him.

He continued, "They'll be here Thursday."

"Well, I won't be," she said.

A day ago, he might have felt less irritation and more panic; a day ago he might have tried to reason with her. But now he said, "If you're not here for Tilly's funeral, don't bother coming back."

Christine visited later that day. She seemed awkward, and it reminded Nicholas of when she was nine and had stood shyly at the door, asking if Kate wanted to go to the park. She was the first one to bridge the distance of the street and offer a friendship that surpassed the playground. When she was a little girl, Nicholas thought the gloom of his house might scare her. He had left her at the door to get Kate. Now, he stepped back and Christine came in. Her gaze flitted over the room, as if unsure this was where she meant to be, before resting uneasily on Nicholas. Clouds had massed in the sky. The day was hot and muggy, and Nicholas had spent a long time staring out the living room window, hoping for a storm.

Christine told him, "I'm sorry about Tilly." Music came from Kate's room. A woman was singing now, but Nicholas couldn't concentrate on her words.

He nodded and said, "Who is he?"

Christine didn't seem surprised. Her unease could have been in expectation of the questions. Nicholas realized Kate must have texted her after the computer was destroyed, reaching out to complain, but more likely to warn her. He imagined her typing, *Dad knows, don't say anything.* Christine looked towards the bedroom. "His name is Colin, but I don't know where he lives. She wouldn't tell me."

Nicholas was aware of two boys passing the house on a bike. One was laughing. They'll get soaked if it rains, he thought. He said, "How long has she been seeing him?"

He could sense Christine's discomfort. She had never been timid or unsure, and it worried him. The music stopped, and the brief pause added tension to the room. Eventually, she mumbled that she wasn't sure.

Nicholas was glad when the woman started singing again. The quiet was unbearable. She was singing about trouble. The rain started and darkened the room. He told Christine that he had believed Manuel's presence had kept her from seeing Kate. She said, "Well, I didn't like him. He was always teasing her."

She paused, and glanced towards Kate's room. Finally, after many minutes, she told him that after the first week, Kate had only pretended to date Manuel. Nicholas remembered his daughter's pause when he'd asked if Christine didn't like Manuel. He had handed her an excuse for their estrangement. He should have been more aware. He should never have let her spend all that time in the room on that computer. Still, he couldn't believe Christine had known about Colin, and had let Kate go to him in that room with the double bed. The thought sickened him. Christine dropped her gaze. For a moment, he believed she might cry. He felt no sympathy and heard only the rain spattering against the window and felt an ache opening in his chest.

It occurred to Nicholas that he should have been grateful to Christine for telling him the man's name. The effort was obvious, but he had no space for thanks. She stood still, probably expecting some reprimand. He had to walk away before he said something he would regret. This wasn't Christine's fault.

In the kitchen, Kate's plate was still on the table. The bread's packaging had not been tied and slices spilled out. He heard Christine's steps towards Kate's room. Her pause before knocking was upsetting. He would have liked to think Christine was a positive influence, but he was beginning to understand that Kate had stopped listening to anyone a long time ago. When Kate opened the door, it took a moment before Christine stepped inside.

CHAPTER TWENTY

NICHOLAS ONLY SAW KATE when she came out to take her meals or darted for the bathroom. Christine came every day, though there was a slowness in her movement and a slump in her shoulders that made Nicholas wonder about their time spent together. On the second day, Kate started to wear headphones after Nicholas shouted at her to turn her damn music down. His head was about to burst from the noise. Whenever Christine arrived, he heard the music played low. There were times when he considered barging in on her, asking, "Where does he live?" He'd refuse to leave until she gave him something. But he could imagine her eyes hardening, her flinching and lack of remorse. He couldn't demand she talk; it never worked with Kate, and only served to bring her further away.

He hated to leave the house unless Christine was there. A quick run to the store would make him nauseous with worry. He knew it was stupid; this house arrest could be easily broken. Whether he was there or not, all Kate had to do was walk out of her room. Yet he clung to the semblance of control, just as he had done the first months of her life, when he pretended he could curtail her mother's moods, and later when he cooked dinner for them and set the table, trying to act as if they were a normal family.

Nights were worse, as he could no longer pretend to watch television. With the lights off and the streets quiet, except for an occasional car that would make him stiffen, he would wonder if Kate was awake, listening for sounds of an approach, if somehow without her computer and phone she was still in communication with Colin, or if she was curled up and innocent in her sleep.

In the two days he was entrenched at home — sitting on the couch or wandering around the house, knocking on her door, telling her lunch was ready, peeking in to see her still asleep at noon, so that he'd wonder how late she stayed awake — he was reminded of Kate's first days, when he couldn't move past his front door. Only now, she didn't cry out for him. Now, she had moved so far back, she was more like Kathleen lying lost in her bed than the baby who had smiled at him.

Ina had been coming and going from her house over the last few days, and she looked exhausted. There were dark circles around her eyes. He wished he could help her with the funeral arrangements. He told her this outside her house, after she'd arrived home with a bag full of shopping. It was late morning. He'd already watched all the children go to school. Car doors had slammed and shouts resounded, until it seemed they had been deserted. Ina thanked him and reminded him that the wake was the next day. In the pause, he was sure she would ask how Kate was doing. He would have said she was fine, not wanting to give Ina more to think about, but she brushed away the unspoken inquiry with a "See you soon."

Neither mentioned Stefano's imminent arrival. He was due the night of the wake but would arrive too late to attend. He was staying at the Boston Harbor Hotel, but said he'd come straight to Nicholas from the airport. Cooper would be with him, but Audrey wasn't coming. There was some excuse given, but Nicholas had hardly been listening. He knew Audrey had worked in the same company as Stefano, and they'd been having an affair for many years before Ina left California, so

Nicholas could understand her reluctance to meet Ina at her mother's funeral.

Christine went to the wake with Kate and Nicholas. Nicholas and the girls were quiet in the car. Christine stared out the window and there was none of her easy chatter. Ina was standing in the lobby of the funeral home when they arrived. Her hair was pulled back, and she wore a black knee length dress with short sleeves. She was shaking hands with an elderly couple. Murmurs were coming from the room ahead. Against the wall was a table filled with refreshments. Soft music played from the intercoms.

Apart from "Are you hungry?", Nicholas and Kate hadn't talked in three days.

Kate was wearing black pants and a cream blouse, and her hair flowed down her back. She fell in behind the couple, and Nicholas watched, scared Ina was going to treat her coolly. Ina's hand had dropped. The couple was gone, and she seemed frozen by Kate's presence, as if she were the last person Ina expected. Kate moved forward. She might have said something, but all Nicholas saw was Ina's stark expression dissolving. She melted into Kate's hug.

A bus had been sent from the nursing home, and some of Tilly's friends sat on chairs in front of the casket. Linda was one of them. Her grey hair had been cut short. She was a thin woman, wearing dark pants and a rain jacket. Her rheumy green eyes were red from crying. She rose and told Kate, "She was so proud of you."

Kate hugged her. Beside her, Christine looked uneasy, her gaze turned inward. Her glances towards Kate were full of query, as if waiting for Kate to give her direction. For a moment, she paused by Kate and then followed Nicholas to the casket. With her chin lifted and white blouse on, Tilly looked too stern. Kate appeared between them and started to cry. She said, "That's not Tilly."

Nicholas's arm went around her shoulders. "I know." In her grief, Kate forgot herself. She became untethered, floating towards him. He held onto her for the first time in years. His arm ached for the feel of her shoulder, the simplicity of that body that he had taken care of since it had come into the world. For the rest of their time in the funeral home, they stayed close by each other.

But the moment they stepped out into the night, he could sense Kate's distance. She sat in the back seat. He concentrated on driving, focusing on his hands holding the steering wheel, his foot on the pedal, the traffic lights coming towards him and moving away, so that he would not think of his daughter gazing out of the window. She was already withdrawing from the two people in the car, focusing on something out there.

✳

Nicholas did not think about Stefano's visit until his phone rang and his brother told him they had landed. Christine had gone straight home when he parked the car and Kate had retreated to her bedroom. Nicholas waited for Stefano and Cooper by the living room window. He had stopped worrying about Stefano seeing the photos when he realized Stefano might think they had been put up while Kathleen lived with them. He hoped his brother would have enough sense not to mention Kathleen. The last time they spoke of her, Nicholas told Stefano she refused to see him. "So that's that then," Stefano had said, and Nicholas agreed.

Yet, a sinking sensation came upon Nicholas the moment he saw the car stop outside his house and Stefano and his son get out. Cooper was a taller, more angular version of Stefano. With his dark eyes and fine features, he could have been described as beautiful. This was enhanced by his shy, timid air. He remained by the door, as his father gave Nicholas a hug, which was different from the handshake at their mother's funeral fifteen years ago. Stefano smelled of expensive cologne and mint. His hair was brushed back. There were streaks of grey and his forehead was lined. He had put on weight, but it suited him. It made him look less shifty.

"This is Cooper," he said, and the boy came over. He was holding a book in one hand and reached out with the free one.

"Hi." His voice was soft, and Nicholas thought he must be more like his mother, who whispered on the phone and was prudent with her words.

"Nice to finally meet you," Nicholas said.

Cooper said, "You too."

Stefano asked, "Where's Kate?" Nicholas became aware of Stefano's curious gaze. His eyebrows had lifted in anticipation of finally meeting the girl who had gone through so much. Nicholas's chest tightened. They were probably expecting someone timid like Cooper, who was overly aware of the people around him. Cooper's gaze contained a nervous empathy that scared Nicholas. He could imagine how Kate would react to his pity. He wanted to usher them out, to tell them, "Shh, quiet. Kate's asleep, you'll meet her tomorrow."

He wanted to protect her from the arrogance and compassion, from the "We heard what happened," or, "You must have been so scared." But he couldn't do anything. He was frozen in a room that seemed unfamiliar all of a sudden, as if he were not the person who had lived with a woman he didn't love in order to gain custody of their baby, and who had foolishly, stupidly, in a fit of helplessness and guilt, placed that woman's face in frames and put her on the cabinets. He wanted to ask that man "Why?', grab him by the cuff of the neck and spit at him, call him a coward and a fucking idiot, because as Kate started to stir in her room, Cooper was gazing at the photos. His mouth had dropped open. Stefano noticed the photos a second later, and Nicholas understood that, no matter, when the photos had been put up they should have been taken down, instead of being a constant reminder to Kate.

"So that's that then," Stefano had said years ago, but it wasn't, was it? Nothing had ended. Cooper and Stefano had walked into a house where something terrible had happened, and though the disaster had occurred years ago, father and daughter had never come out of their shock to speak about it.

Kate stepped out of her room to see the two visitors looking at the photos. They were drawn by the madness they associated with Kathleen. The woman might as well have been in the room. Stefano managed to smile at his niece. Nicholas had often seen him collect himself like this. When he'd come home and heard about their father leaving, or later walked in to the sound of their mother sobbing, Stefano's eyes had glazed over in the same way. But Nicholas thought Cooper was nothing like his father.

Nicholas wished Audrey had come. She might have noticed Kate's face, the fire and defiance in her eyes, when Stefano introduced himself and said, "It's good to finally meet you." Her gaze went from father to son. She read their unease too clearly. Audrey might have glared at her son, told him to get a grip. She might have gone to Kate, and said she was sorry to hear about Tilly, and reminded Stefano of their loss and their reason for being here, which had nothing to do with Kathleen.

Later, Nicholas would think that he should have done something. He should have offered a drink and stepped between the visitors and Kate. He should have asked about their flight and hotel. But it was like standing at the edge of a hole and realizing just how far you had to drop. He was dizzy at the sight of Stefano smiling at Kate, who was probably convinced that saying, "You look more like your father," would make her fall under his charm. Instead, she seemed to move back without taking a step. Her eyes showed hurt. Nicholas could imagine the thoughts going around in her head, and the notion that this was yet another person who disliked her mother. Stefano was talking about her lovely red hair and how it had been in his family on his mother's side, because, as Kate must know, her grandmother was Irish.

Nicholas said, "This is your cousin, Cooper." He wanted to take her attention from Stefano, who was getting flustered with Kate's brooding silence.

"Hi," Cooper said. His voice came out a whisper.

Kate glanced at Nicholas. His chest loosened at the glint in her eyes. He saw in her face an urge to laugh, and stepped back from the abyss. For a brief, lovely moment, he believed it would be okay, that maybe they could laugh at Stefano's banter and Cooper's nervousness.

In the days that followed, when Nicholas went to the police, when he searched the streets for her and lay in bed, wondering where she was and what she was doing, he would try to remember how he felt during that speck of time, when Kate might have shaken her head and rolled her eyes. But no matter how hard he tried, he could never return to that moment, because her voice was inside him. Her cold tone made Stefano flinch when she said, "I look like my mom."

Cooper was taken aback. "Don't you care...?" he started, but stopped when he saw Kate's face fall.

She asked, "Care about what?" Nicholas wanted to say "Nothing, never mind," but the air had turned thick.

Stefano asked, "Doesn't she know?"

"Know what?" Kate asked. She looked terrified. Her gaze took in the three people in the room as if she had no idea who they were. Finally, she settled on Nicholas. He saw her terror harden into a hatred so fine he could feel it on his skin.

"What did you tell them?" she asked. The clock ticked once, before she screeched, "Tell me!"

He thought of Kathleen looming over her small body, but it wasn't just her shadow, it was his, too, and his silence had only let it grow, until he was left with a daughter who hated him for leaving her in the dark. He had no choice but to tell her, "She hurt you. That's why she left."

Kate's head was shaking. Stefano was saying that it was okay, that it happened long ago. Kate looked at him blankly. "Sometimes, she seems someplace else," Mr. Cohen had said. Her retreat scared Nicholas now.

Stefano's voice was low and held none of his usual self-assurance as he veered from topic and asked about the funeral arrangements. Somehow, Nicholas managed to pull the details up, Mass at 11 a.m., burial directly after. Kate was stepping back, and Nicholas didn't know how he was still standing. He was barely listening to Stefano and merely nodded at his inquiry about Ina.

Seconds after Kate's bedroom door slammed, they stopped the pretense of conversation. Nicholas glared at Stefano. "What the fuck is wrong with you?"

"Jesus, Nicholas, I'm sorry, but we didn't expect..." Stefano glanced towards the photos. "They're a bit weird."

"Maybe they are," Nicholas told him, "but that

doesn't make it okay to come in here and start talking about her." Nicholas was livid. He was afraid to move, lest he start on a rampage. Cooper sitting repentant on the couch infuriated him. "What a bloody stupid thing to say to her. Do you realize how heartless that was?" he said to the boy.

"Hey," Stefano said. "He's sorry, okay? You should have told us that she didn't know. Doesn't she remember?"

Nicholas glared at his brother. He understood now that Tilly's funeral was an excuse to come back. Stefano needed a reason to show Cooper off, to bring him across the country in order to compare his happy, together life with Nicholas's chaos.

"I think you better go," Nicholas said.

"But why do you have them up?" Stefano asked, and if Cooper hadn't risen and told his dad to come on, Nicholas would have thumped him.

Once Stefano and Cooper had gone, he knocked on Kate's door. She told him to go away but he couldn't. He stepped inside her room. The curtains were open and he could make out her figure lying curled in the bed. Some part of this scene reminded him of Kathleen, and the way she used to lie in bed so quietly. Nicholas wanted so much to go to his daughter and hold her that tears started in his eyes. He had never loved anyone as much as he loved Kate, and no one had ever made him feel so small and useless.

"I'm sorry Kate," he said.

She said, "If she hurt me, why would you put her photos up?"

"I did it for you, so you could talk." He felt dizzy from her antagonism, which made her seem so very far away.

"So you could tell me Mom hurt me? Why should I want to know that?" she asked. Before he could answer, she said, "You're a liar."

Chapter Twenty-One

Nicholas watched his reflection disappear from the window. The black night had faded into a day he felt incapable of. He hadn't slept. There was no way he could close his eyes after he'd pleaded with Kate, and she'd told him, with her body in a tight bundle, to leave her alone.

He had no idea what time it was, or how long he'd been sitting in the kitchen, when he heard Kate get out of bed. He knew his daughter would not come anywhere near him. After her shower, he was not surprised by her soft tread through the living room, and the click of the front door opening. Christine's parents were going to the funeral. Although they didn't know Ina well, they had expressed their condolences, and Christine had mentioned their desire to go for him and Kate. Nicholas heard the screen door and was sure Kate was going to them. Pulling his body up from the chair was a huge effort. The living room curtains were open. He didn't remember pulling them apart, and thought he had gone straight from her bedroom to the kitchen. Kate was at the top of the steps leading to the apartment building, her backpack over her shoulder. He wondered what she needed for the funeral, if she intended to stay with Christine, and decided he would have to speak to Helen. Christine's front door opened seconds after Kate knocked, and she faded into the dark corridor.

Ina was taken aback when Nicholas appeared at her door. It was an overcast day and the humidity was eased by a slight breeze. "Where's Kate?" Ina asked. She was standing, but hadn't moved from her table. Her fingertips lay on the surface and made him think of a defendant in court. She was scared. He could see the vulnerability in her eyes, but it was the silence between them, her lack of urging, that told him the extent of her fear.

"She's with Christine," he told her.

Ina took a moment with her relief, before she said "You look awful,"

"Thanks," he said.

Ina was wearing black. Her hair fell to her shoulders, and he saw streaks of grey. She asked if he wanted a coffee. He didn't, but he said yes just to do something. His hands were stuck in his pants pockets and there was an awkwardness to his stance. With the funeral on today, he didn't want to talk about Kate, but it was difficult to think of anything else, and he was sure Ina felt his strain. He followed her into the kitchen where she turned to him and said, "Stefano did something, didn't he?"

His heart dropped. "Why are you asking?"

Her hand went to the coffee pot, but stopped there. Coffee must have been an excuse for her too, something to do to help her avert her gaze. She said, "I know you talked to him about what happened."

Nicholas wanted to grab her shoulders and force her to look at him, but he couldn't move. He'd always thought Stefano's lack of probing was a sign of respect, and it was terrible to hear that he'd satisfied his curiosity on the line with Ina. He had never asked Nicholas about Ina because he didn't need to.

"And?" he said. His voice was cold and stronger than he thought it would be.

It was hard to read her face. The soft worry in her brown eyes was gone and in its stead was a focused study of him, as though he were the one with something to say. It cooled his anger and made him want to sit down.

"And," she said, "he phoned me after you told him about Kathleen's arrest to see if he should come to Boston. He was very busy, but said that if he had to, he would come." Her flat tone told Nicholas that she didn't believe Stefano's reason for calling. "He was also very interested in Kathleen, but I didn't tell him anything. Around a year ago, he told Cooper what happened, and he phoned to let me know. I have no idea why. Maybe he thought I'd have something to say."

Nicholas was nauseous. He imagined Cooper and Stefano talking about their crazy relatives. They would have leaned towards each other on the airplane, eating peanuts and wondering what they would find. It wouldn't have been a surprise if they'd called their journey an "adventure." Then, to see the photos up, to have their morbid curiosity met — what luck! — no wonder they didn't walk away from the images, no wonder they stared and prodded.

"Did you tell him Kate doesn't remember?" Nicholas asked. She shook her head, and his relief was immense. For all of Stefano's vanity and insensitivity, he had never thought of his brother as cruel.

Ina said, "I didn't stay on the phone long, but I was worried when you said he was coming."

"Why didn't you tell me?" Nicholas asked.

She said, "Because I didn't know what to say. I

was hoping it would be okay, that he'd have forgotten everything after so long."

He said, "You should have told me."

She asked him what happened. In the silence, he noticed the radio wasn't playing, and Ina was starting to get impatient. He said, "They went straight for the photos. They were shocked to see them. Cooper alluded to Kathleen hurting Kate."

Ina's head was shaking. He saw the fury in her eyes and thought it was directed at Stefano until she said, "Isn't that why you put them up, to get at the truth, to force it on her? Does it really matter how it happened?"

"I didn't want to force anything on her," he said.

She said, "What do think you would have done if you knew about Stefano's phone calls to me? Do you think you would have taken them down after all this time? You must have thought about it, you had to have. For God's sake, he knew the story, and you wanted Kate to know, too. You wanted her to know her mother hurt her, so she would stop blaming you."

Her gaze softened. "I'm sorry, but I won't let you blame Stefano. You wanted her to know."

His denial got caught in his throat, and it was a relief when Ina slipped past him to the living room. He needed to be alone. As he listened to her getting ready, he thought there was a good chance of rain. The idea seemed to come from some place outside of him.

Stefano came up to them the moment they arrived at the church. Ina allowed him to hug her and give his condolences before going to look for Kate. Nicholas knew Stefano had been waiting for him. He also knew that his cell phone would have a record of Stefano's attempts to call, and maybe a text message of apology. Nicholas had left it sitting on the kitchen table for that reason. Cooper was wearing a grey suit and his hair was pulled back from his face. He threw a shy smile at Nicholas, though he was more confident today. Maybe it was because he was not standing in Nicholas's house, or perhaps, it was from the quality of his suit, which hugged his body and was obviously tailored to fit. Nicholas was inclined to believe it was because his curiosity had been assuaged.

"We saw Kate," Stefano said. "She wasn't very talkative, though I can't say I blame her. We feel terrible." He paused to study Nicholas. "Are you okay? You don't look too good."

Nicholas said, "The service is about to start."

Stefano nodded. He apologized again and seemed hurt by Nicholas's aloofness. "We'll talk later."

The funeral wore on Nicholas. He listened to friends speak of Tilly and he realized how much he would miss her. The last few days had been so crazy with Kate that he had hardly any time to consider their loss, but sitting at the front of the church with Ina between him and Kate, he understood how much emptier their lives had become.

Helen and Mike came up to Nicholas and Ina outside the church. "I'm sorry," Helen said. He saw her concern and imagined how he must look, red eyed and withdrawn. His desire to crawl under a rock was probably visible to everyone. The Jacobs were there, but neither Adrial nor Manuel was, which was some relief. They walked the few yards to the grave site. It had started to drizzle. Kate shared an umbrella with Christine. Their arms were around one another. Cooper and Stefano had been waiting for Nicholas outside the church and to see them brought a deep exhaustion to his bones. Stefano walked beside him now, while Cooper stayed on the other side of his father. They were leaving in a couple of days, and Stefano wanted to take Nicholas and Kate to dinner. "After you've gotten some sleep," he said.

Once Nicholas had woken, sprawled on the bed, still dressed in his suit, his shoes tossed on the floor, he saw Stefano had phoned five times throughout the day and had left two voice messages. Nicholas didn't bother listening to them before he turned off his phone. It would have been easier if he were angry at Stefano. The previous night, his body had tingled with fury. He had imagined all the things he wanted to tell his brother, but Ina had robbed him of that and left him with nothing to say.

Stefano was not the type to come to a place where he was not wanted. He wouldn't face Kate's stubborn quietness again when he knew he had no chance of softening her. Hence, Nicholas was safe in his living room, sitting on the couch in front of the blank television. He tried to watch a movie, but the voices grated his nerves and he couldn't concentrate. Kate was still with Christine. He and Kate hadn't talked at the funeral. He fell asleep waiting for her to come home and woke stiff-necked. His mouth was dry and his stomach empty. Hours ago, Ina had suggested dinner, but he couldn't have imagined sitting in a restaurant, having to smile at a waitress. He'd declined. She had nodded and apologized before retreating to her house.

The words had stung him because they made him realize he and Kate couldn't just walk away from Stefano's visit. He drank two glasses of cold water and made a quick cheese sandwich. Kate's door was closed. He stood before it for a while before going to his room. He woke a few times during the night, unsettled and anxious, wondering if Kate had come back, but he didn't knock on her door until the morning.

There was no answer to his knock. "Kate?" he said, trying not to get worried. So what if she had not come home? She had stayed so many nights at Christine's house that it was second nature to her. He opened the door and saw her bed was empty, the sheets tossed to the side. A dresser drawer was open and clothes spilled out of it. He went to the wardrobe and looked inside, not sure what he was searching for until he saw the empty hangers. He switched on his mobile. A total of seven missed calls from Stefano and a text message that told him this was their final full day and Stefano hoped to meet before leaving. There was nothing from Helen. Kate could have told her she had gotten in touch with Nicholas and it was okay to stay the night. The girls were old enough now not to need such parental interference. It was 7:30 a.m., a Saturday. He decided to wait before calling in case they were asleep, but only made it to 8 a.m. He remembered he had Kate's phone when it went direct to voicemail. He hung up without saying anything. He tried Helen's mobile, a number he'd been given years ago when Kate started to stay over, though he'd only dialed it a handful of times.

She answered on the third ring and sounded spritely, yet he said, "I hope I didn't wake you."

"No, no," she said. His hand went to the kitchen

counter. He could feel her curiosity at his call. If Kate was there, she'd volunteer information. She'd tell him, "They're still asleep."

Instead, she said, "Nicholas, Kate isn't here. She went home before eight last night."

Christine was up by the time he arrived at their door. She was wearing pale blue pajamas. Her blonde hair was tossed, but it took nothing away from the fright in her eyes. She was sitting on the couch, her legs pulled up against her chest. Helen had opened the door for Nicholas. She was wearing jeans and a t-shirt and had never looked as helpless as she did then. Her hair was pulled back in a loose ponytail and tears were in her eyes.

"I didn't think," she said. "I should have phoned you, but she said she was going straight home."

"It's not your fault," Nicholas said, but he knew she didn't hear him. She was tense and restless, a ball of nerves. He followed her to the living room. He was glad that Alex was asleep and Mike was working. Christine glanced at him and quickly looked away.

"Where is she?" Nicholas asked.

Christine was starting to cry. Helen was crouching in front of her. "Christine," she asked, "What's going on?"

Christine took a breath and said, "You should ask him."

It took a moment before Nicholas realized she was talking about him. He forced himself to stay calm enough to ask where Colin lived. It was taking all of his effort not to explode. If he let that happen, he would be grabbing Christine by the arms and screaming at her. She was shaking her head and crying harder. Helen wrapped her arms around her.

"Where is she?" Nicholas asked.

"I don't know," Christine finally managed. She told them that all she knew was that he lived alone. Before Kate left, she said that he was going to help her find her mother. Kate had deactivated her Facebook account the night before. She said she'd e-mail eventually, but Christine wasn't so sure. Kate had become cagey and distant. In the days Christine had spent in Kate's bedroom, she'd hardly talked. Kate hadn't said anything about Stefano's visit, which didn't mean she wasn't thinking of it. Nicholas was sure that the worse the experience the less she would be willing to talk about it.

"I have her phone," he said, "and her computer broke."

Christine's eyebrows raised. She studied him for a minute, but he refused to feel bad about what he had done. He'd do it again if he had to. After a moment, Christine said, "She'd emailed his details to herself. She got them yesterday morning from my computer."

"You let her phone him from here?" Nicholas asked. Helen made a sound. She was sitting beside Christine with a hand on her shoulder. Christine looked at her, and Nicholas envied the silent communication between the two.

"Sorry," she murmured to her mother, who shook her head. Nicholas knew this house wouldn't be the same until Kate returned. He wondered if Kate considered her friend's worry and guilt when she asked if she could keep in touch with Colin from here.

"She didn't phone him," Christine said. "She emailed him, but she got rid of everything then."

It was hard to know how long he sat opposite Christine, watching her body unfold as she talked. He could imagine how tough it must have been for her to sit with her taciturn friend and hear about Colin, who Christine said scared her. At some stage, Alex got out of bed. While he ate cereal in the kitchen, Helen distracted him to let Nicholas and Christine talk in low voices. Nicholas sat on the white leather armchair opposite Christine. He was leaning forward, somehow feeling in control. It might have been the interview, or it might have been that the task of finding Kate was easier than talking to her, though he knew this thought was merely a defense mechanism, a technique to keep his fear away. He lingered in the apartment, where at least he was doing something, asking questions, getting Christine to repeat what she knew about Colin.

"Kate met him on one of the social sites. They were the only places she talked about her mom; it upset me because she never spoke to me about her. Even when we were kids, she'd close up whenever I asked questions. She said she didn't want pity."

"You don't know what site?" Nicholas asked.

Christine's head rested against the back of the couch. She looked tired, and he realized that she must have been expecting this since Kate left. "No," she said. "Kate's been on social sites for ages and tried a lot of them. Mom wouldn't allow me to have any accounts, and I don't like them anyway, so we didn't talk about them much. I should have asked, but when she told me about him, I didn't know what to do."

She started crying again. He wanted to reach out and touch her hand, tell her it was okay, but he couldn't. "She met him alone before, mostly at his place," Christine said, wiping the tears from her cheeks. Nicholas tensed. "I wanted to say something, but Kate would never have forgiven me, so I stopped talking to her. I hoped she'd see sense."

She was right, Kate would never have forgiven

her. No one would have been able to stop her from seeing Colin.

She said, "Colin gave her the idea that her mother might be homeless and that you abandoned her. She said she remembered dresses hanging in the closet, that it was really weird."

Nicholas nodded. He couldn't leave the apartment and go home to Kate's absence. He didn't think he had the strength. Christine seemed to know this. There was no impatience, no rush in her speech. She waited until he looked at her and said, "She'll come back, she has to." He wasn't too sure, but he couldn't argue with her. She seemed so young in her pajamas.

He said, "Is there anyone else she's friendly with at school, someone she might have gotten in touch with?" He was not surprised to see Christine shake her head.

Helen walked him to the door. For a moment, he was afraid she'd hug him, but she seemed to sense his reluctance and drew back a little. "It'll be okay," she told him.

Alone, without the distraction of questions, he understood the doubt that had flashed in Helen's eyes, and it scared him. His daughter could be anywhere, and she was with a man no one knew. He could still remember Colin's apartment: the tossed bed, the kitchen counter behind him, a window to the side. He imagined Kate there, waiting for Colin. She had little money of her own. Nicholas gave her some pocket money, but mostly she asked if she needed anything. Did she have to wait for Colin to feed her?

In the rain, Nicholas ran jacketless to his car with his head down. Ina was standing at her door and called to him. He got into his car without glancing in her direction, because to see his fear mirrored on Ina's face would have been too much to bear right now. As it was, he didn't know what kept him upright. He thought Ina shouted something before he slammed his car door. A pain started in his chest, a tight winding heat as if someone were drilling a hole in him. He parked at the police station and thought he might collapse. He had to force his breath out, and he clutched the steering wheel until the panic attack eased.

The station was a large building with double glass doors and a tiled hall. Inside, it was strangely quiet. There was an officer at the desk who looked to be in his thirties and had sad eyes and a bad complexion. Nicholas reported Kate as missing.

The officer reached for a form "You need to fill this out," he said, and asked for a photo.

In his wallet, Nicholas had a school portrait of Kate. He told the officer about Colin, as he filled in the form. "I'll put her on the National Crime

Missing Persons File, but there's not much we can do if she doesn't want to come back," the officer said. "Does she have a phone? We could try and track her calls."

"No," Nicholas said. "I have it."

The officer said that the amount of cases like this was rising every year. The internet made it harder to keep track of who kids were speaking to. Parents might as well unlock their doors.

Nicholas had no defense. He combed the streets for Kate. Twice, he thought he saw her. The first time, he swerved to a halt halfway up Winter Hill, causing a chorus of horns. He jumped out of the car. A man was screaming at him. The rain was getting in his eyes, obscuring the girl but bringing out her hair, making it seem too bright in the overcast day. She squealed when he grabbed her arm. The next time, he slowed down as he passed a girl he thought might be Kate.

Ina checked his house for Kate before going to Christine's apartment to see what was wrong with Nicholas. The moment she saw Helen, she knew something terrible had happened. Ina followed Helen inside to hear the news. Helen sat beside her but didn't touch her. There was a distance in Ina that could not be bridged. After a while, Ina started to cry softly. Every now and again, she'd shake her head.

"It will kill her," she said. Christine had risen to stretch her legs. She glanced at her mother when Ina said, "But we have no choice. We have to bring her to Kathleen."

No one said anything for a long time. The knowledge made Ina feel brittle, as if years had fled from her. She rose and, without another word, started for the front door. Her shoes were still on; she hadn't thought anything about the pairs tossed in the hallway. Helen broke her habit of walking guests out. She considered it bad luck to let them go alone, but she couldn't stand, nor could she look at her daughter. She focused on her hands, joined together and resting on her knees. The front door closed and they stayed rigid for a long time.

Ina didn't phone Nicholas. Her voice had dried up. Even if she had something to say, she wouldn't have the language to say it. All she could do was await his return. Christine said he'd gone to the police. What was he thinking? Was he afraid to tell her about Kate? The image of Tilly's coffin being laid into the ground, and the frightful urge to fall over it and scream for her to come back, added to Ina's sense of loneliness. After changing into dry sweatpants, she sat at the living room table. There were papers in a bundle in the corner. She tried unsuccessfully to work, hoping it would distract her, but the numbers before her meant nothing. The rain eventually stopped. There was a drowned out muted quality to the streets. There were few cars until the evening, and they passed slower than usual, sending a swish of puddles. No shouts from children were heard. The neighborhood kids were all getting older. The twins' parents had moved away two years ago.

It was getting late by the time Nicholas's car swerved in front of his house. His headlights went off immediately. There was none of his usual pause and deliberation. She thought he had become more cautious than nervous. Now, however, he was out of the car with a speed that surprised her. Kate's disappearance had spurred him on, while it had emptied Ina out. Her movements were slow and every task was monumental. She hadn't eaten all day, unable to find the will to rise, and she realized she was sitting in the dark.

Still, he would have seen her car and known she was there. His avoidance hurt enough to propel her into motion. She was not going to promise her help in searching the streets. She would not intrude where she was not wanted, but she needed Nicholas to know he could not fight Kate's need for her mother anymore. If he wanted his daughter back, he would have to give in to her wishes. He would have to bring her to Kathleen.

The street was quiet. She could hear her breathing as she strolled towards his house. The front door was open. Through the screen door, she saw Nicholas at the far end of the living room. He was holding one of the photos of Kathleen. Often, Ina had imagined those images being ripped up. She'd imagined an act of blind rage, with the frames smashing to the ground and the photos torn to pieces, but he was still. The living room lights seemed too bright. Ina wished for a dimness that would allow them to hardly see each other. Her attention was stuck on his face, which was kept downwards and away from her, so that she couldn't imagine what was going through his head. He might have been annoyed with her intrusion. She thought his jaw had tensed, and pictured his eyes narrowing. Ina was sure he stood staring at the photo because he didn't want to look at her, yet she stepped inside. A few moments ago, broken by Kate's leaving and Nicholas's failure to come to her with the news, she thought she would not come into this house, unless invited. If Nicholas turned away from her, she would not insist he listen. She had been determined that she would walk away. She'd learn to live without them, though already there was a space inside her where the silence entered and reverberated.

Her steps were shaky. She stopped by the couch.

Finally, he looked at her. The moment he met her eyes, she saw that fear had dulled his gaze in a way she had never seen before, and she wanted to withdraw. She expected him to say something about Kate and she wanted to leave him before he could say anything, but the hollowness of her body made her incapable of moving. A single step would send her folding onto the floor. As it was, her hand was on the couch for support. Only now, she realized how precarious it was to have loved Nicholas and Kate and keep nothing in reserve in order to survive their loss.

"Kate ran away," Nicholas said.

She nodded. She could have told him that she knew. She might have said, "I talked to Christine," but, somehow, she knew Kate's leaving was not the reason he was so nervous. He showed no surprise at her lack of response.

There was a pause and the house ticked. Ina felt a heavy weight in her chest, and she didn't know how she was standing straight. "We need to bring her to Kathleen," Ina said.

Nicholas nodded, and said yes before putting the photo back in its place on the shelf. Ina knew he'd run into this house full of anger, but something had caused the rage to leave him, so that he stood helpless, unable to break the frames, and she thought of him at eighteen at the docks in court with his limp shoulders. Guilty, he'd pleaded then, and he was doing it again.

"Whatever you did, I don't care," Ina said. Her voice was so low she would have wondered if Nicholas heard her had he not turned to her with a look on his face that hurt to see. His eyes had softened with surprise or relief, but there was argument there too, a pulling back that brought her forward as she said, "And I don't want to know."

Chapter Twenty-Two

Kate knew Colin was different from the first time she met him. She liked his confidence and the way he sat back in delight when he saw her. His appreciation of her was obvious in his smile and pause, which was so unlike the fumbling boys her age. With the sun shining on his blonde hair giving him an ethereal glow, he said, "Tell me about yourself."

His voice made Kate sit straighter. For a moment, she didn't know if she could speak. In every other encounter she'd been in control. She'd drifted from virtual room to room, seeing men lean towards her with that look of wanting something. More than once, she'd gone into a room where a man was holding his penis. The first time, she'd been shocked, and left the session in a hurry. She was angry with herself afterwards, for the glint of satisfaction in his eyes, and for showing weakness. It could have been weeks or months before she came across another man with that hard look in his eyes. He was completely naked and holding himself. Kate didn't flinch. Slowly, she rose up and, in a measured voice, told him he was disgusting. Her heart was pounding when she left the session, but she had been in no rush, sauntering in and out unperturbed. She was sure he had been surprised by her response, while she'd felt proud.

By the time she met Colin, she was more confident. She told Colin that she was eighteen and lived with her father, but couldn't wait to get her own place. He smiled. She noticed that he had a day's worth of stubble. He said, "I have a place you can come to anytime you like. But first, you need to tell me a secret."

"What do you want to know?" Kate asked. She heard her father in the living room, and then his pause by her door. When she first started on the sites, she was nervous of him entering, but he always knocked and gave her enough time to get rid of her company. Her father moved on, and she picked up her earphones.

"Tell me something important," Colin said. She liked his excitement. He didn't need to be perverse. Sitting fully clothed in jeans and a Manic Street

Preachers t-shirt, he seemed as turned on as the men who had masturbated in front of her.

"You first," she said.

"Okay," he said. "I was homeless when I was sixteen."

"Why?" she asked. She noticed the quietness of his room. Usually, people played music to drown out the noise of family members, and she thought it was cool that he didn't need the cover.

He said, "I didn't like my stepdad, so I ran away."

"I've thought about running away," Kate said, and was surprised by the admission and the truth in it. She remembered as a child saying to her father, "If Mom can disappear, why can't I?" and the fright it had given Nicholas, but she had never been sure if she wanted to leave until now.

"Why?" Colin asked.

She said, "To get back at my dad."

His head tilted. He was studying her, waiting for more, but she didn't know what to say, where to start. The quiet didn't get to her, and he seemed untroubled by it. There weren't many people like that. Christine had a tendency to fill the silences, talking about her mother's lost causes or her dreams to be a vet, while her father was always strained by the quiet. Ina was more like Colin. She could sit and wait for Kate to speak with no discomfort. The comparison would have made her smile, only she didn't want Colin to see how much she liked him.

She said, "My mom disappeared and Dad won't tell me anything."

"What do you think happened?" Colin asked. No one had asked her this. Christine might have if she'd had the space, but Kate was afraid to talk to her about it. Any speculation from Kate would lead to Christine giving her ideas about her mother, and she would have talked as if Kathleen were nothing more than some unsolved mystery.

"It's okay if you don't want to talk about it," Colin said.

She shrugged. She had never talked about her mom. She told Christine she used social sites as an outlet to do just that so that she'd stop harping on about their dangers. "There are crazy people out there," Christine said often, but Colin wasn't crazy. He was sweet and he saw her fully. He was taking in every detail of her and building her up into a girl worthy of time, a girl worth listening to. His interest let her tell him that it was okay, she didn't mind talking. She told him that her mother left one day, and that she had lived her life believing everyone was keeping a secret from her.

"Dad's hiding something," she told Colin. In the fading daylight, his room was growing duller and gave an ominous feel to her words. Did she mention the ambulance coming for her mother the first day she talked to him? Had she given everything so quickly, all her fears rolled out, so that there was no chance of hiding behind her façade of confidence?

It didn't take long before she told him about her attempts to look for her mother. She'd searched her father's room on the nights he worked and found nothing with her mother's name, which only heightened her suspicion and unease. There were also days when she'd typed Kathleen Giovanni and hoped to find some news on her computer, while also frightened by the thought. Her memories of her mother's last day with them were faint, but she knew her father had run out of the house holding her in his arms, and she knew something had happened. Once, she'd gone to the library with the idea of looking up newspaper articles from *The Somerville Times*, but, when she got the desk, she'd felt foolish at the thought of asking for them, and angry, because she had no idea of the date. It had been cold, and she was five. That was all she knew. She didn't tell Colin that she was also scared of finding her mother's name, and how lonely she'd felt when she'd left the library empty-handed, but she thought from his soft smile and promise to help that he knew these things without her voicing them. With him, she'd felt lighter than she ever remembered being, as if he'd torn a layer from her.

Their conversations rolled into one another and she became someone else with Colin; a person who, for the first time since she had run to Ina as a little girl, needed someone. She told him about Manuel asking her out. Manuel had stopped her and Christine on the way home from school and asked Christine if he could talk to Kate alone. She couldn't believe it when he asked her out. One minute, he was teasing her and saying horrible things about her mother, the next he was saying he really liked her. When Colin heard this, he was silent for a moment. She thought she'd overstepped, and wanted to take mention of Manuel back, and have no one else in the room except the two of them.

Finally, he said, "Well, maybe that's a good thing." When she looked surprised, he added, "It might be better if your Dad thinks you're meeting him instead of me."

At Davis Square, they met outside Blue Shirt Café. She had strolled there alongside Manuel, who had displayed a shyness that surprised her. The days he'd waited outside her house so they could walk to Davis or the playground, his silence had infuriated her. "What do you want?" she might have asked if she'd cared enough. During their second week dating, with traffic winding on the narrow road, music coming from the Joshua Tree, and pedestrians weaving in and out of each other's way, she was on the lookout

for Colin. She found him sitting on the chairs outside the Blue Shirt Café, wearing his usual jeans and
t-shirt. His blonde hair was tied back and his gaze
fixed steadily on her while she sent Manuel inside
the café to get drinks. By the time Manuel came out,
she was gone. She sent him a text message. *Sorry, felt
sick. Had to go.* She didn't think he'd seen anything,
until Christine confronted her. By that stage, she'd
been in Colin's apartment. The first night she'd visited him, she'd gotten up before her father arrived
home from work and walked to Davis Square. She
took the red line to Downtown Crossing. From
there, she changed to the Orange Line and stayed
on until the end of the tracks. Forest Hills Station
was orange and steel grey, and steps away from the
Forest Hills Cemetery. The station was known for
the amount of homeless who gathered there, colorful
characters, Colin called them, all streaming out of
Shattuck Homeless Shelter in the morning and gath-
ering to go back in the evening. "Just don't talk to
anyone," he'd said. "You need to wait there for the
bus to Cleary Square. I'll meet you there."

At Forest Hills, she felt as if she had stepped out
at the end of the world. It was the furthest she'd ever
gotten from Somerville, and she was exhilarated by
the impossibility of her father passing in his cab. His
world had revolved around Somerville for so long
that he was incapable of stepping further afield. The

stark greyness of the area and the cemetery did nothing to deter her delight. For the first time, she was free from the confines of her world. Here no one knew her, except Colin, who took her to his rundown apartment, where the tossed bed took up most of the room. Beside it, was the table he used for his computer. The kitchen was a small cubby hole beside the main door. The bathroom, a narrow aisle with only a shower and toilet, she could hear flushing from any part of the apartment, was on the other side of the kitchen. The place smelled of fried food. The blankets were messy on his bed. There was nowhere else to sit. She leaned against the counter separating the kitchen and bedroom. From the window, she could see a small garden and a fence. The place was very quiet.

Kate could hear Colin's breathing behind her. He smelled of soap. His lips touched the space between her neck and shoulders. A shock moved through her when his hands went to her waist, and then down to her thighs. The world became as small as the space between her legs. She thought she could crawl in there and die when his hand slipped inside her jeans. She might have pushed him away if she had not been so shocked. He touched her for a long time. When he finally stepped away, she was both diminished from what she had given him and proud that she could manage to say, "Yeah, sure," to his offer of a drink of water.

By the time Christine barged into her room demanding answers for her treatment of Manuel, Kate wanted to laugh at the silliness of teenagers complaining to each other. There were parts of her, of everyone, that could only be reached by the right person, and, at fourteen, she'd met that person. While Christine remained in her silly world, where there was only black and white, good and bad, where people like Manuel deserved to be treated with respect no matter what they did or how they used their power, Kate knew the world was really made up of the grey, hidden places, where people disappeared, or a girl could walk into an apartment and walk out someone else.

While the journey to the small apartment in Hyde Park had emboldened her, taking the bus home had been a different story. "I don't want to go," she told Colin at Cleary Square. The noise of the traffic helped her speak, where in the apartment the silence had dried her up. He wasn't as talkative in person. They had spent a long time on the bed. His handprints were all over her body.

"I don't want you to go either," he said and kissed her cheek. "But I have to work." She got on the #50 bus. Her feeling of despondency got worse the further she got from Colin. By the time she was on the Red Line, she was on the verge of crying. She thought she had left a part of herself inside the apartment, where the thread of heavy steps from upstairs broke the quiet every now and again, and her half-eaten sandwich still lay under the bed.

"You really think I could date Manuel?" Kate said to Christine days later.

She saw Christine's eyes glaze with confusion, and heard the worry in her voice when she said, "Well you are, aren't you?" A door slammed in her kitchen. The news was playing on the radio.

"Close the door," Kate said. Christine obeyed and sat on Kate's bed. Kate told her about Colin and how they'd met in Davis, and that she'd gone to his apartment. Christine was shocked.

Maybe if she had stayed beside Kate on the bed, if she had asked questions about the visit, Kate might not have been as quick to run to Colin after witnessing Nicholas's temper. Kate no longer doubted the reason for the ambulance taking her mother away after Nicholas had dug his hand into her skin and she'd seen his raging, red face. She'd thought he was going to hit her, and, in that second, she became sure that he'd hit her mother. The fact seemed to have been there all along, like a seed that needed only the faintest clue to sprout.

But Christine didn't ask Kate why she was with Colin, or if she had enjoyed the visit to his apartment.

She didn't let Kate talk about how strange it was to have his hands over her body, or explain how, all those times in the chatroom, he had built her up by looking straight at her and waiting for her to speak, yet had hardly uttered a word while she was in his room. Christine told her she was crazy. She talked about statutory rape and the possibility of Colin being arrested, as if she had taken for granted that Kate had given him everything, which hurt more than Kate thought possible. Kate became Colin's advocate, telling her how good he was to her, how he listened, how many conversations they had, how hard he worked in his job at the bar, his dream of going to night school to study business, so that by the time Christine finally quit trying to change her mind or extracting Colin's address, Kate was strengthened by the Colin who had been given form by her words.

When Kate went to see Colin the second time, she was prepared for what to expect. He gave her a couple of beers and she liked the way they made her feel. She was less tense and lost all track of time. He'd been surprised when she said she had to go home. The last bus had left, and she'd nearly cried with the thought of her father and Ina looking for her. There was no way she could sleep thinking of them. She would have walked home if she had to, but Colin phoned a friend and they went to the Dempsey's Bar where he worked, so he could borrow a car. She arrived home at 2 a.m. the night Tilly died.

After the funeral, she was back at his apartment. She'd sent him an email, but he hadn't replied. It was after 10 p.m. by the time she arrived at his place. No one was home. Dempsey's was a few blocks away. There were a few cars on the street and the street-lights lit her way. She passed two men smoking on the street, music ushering from the house behind them. One mumbled something and laughed. Kate's cheeks reddened and her steps quickened. She thought of having to pass those men on the way back and decided she'd get a cab, if Colin had to work. She hated the thought of going into his apart-ment alone and sitting on the bed, waiting for him to return, while footsteps resounded upstairs from the obese man Colin said would one day fall right through the floorboards.

Dempsey's was darker than she anticipated and had a long bar against the left wall. Colin stood at the corner on the far end. He was leaning over the counter and talking to customers. Kate made out long hair and an arm over a shoulder and realized they belonged to a couple draped over each other. A roar of laughter came from a table to her left, where a group of people, mostly men, older than Colin, were sitting. A scatter of customers sat around the bar. Low tables were dotted around the floor and were mostly empty. The place smelled of burgers and beer.

Kate waited at the counter to get Colin's attention. She had emailed him right after the funeral, and again at 3 p.m. *I need to get out of here.* She was aware of the urgency in the note, and hoped Colin would question her safety with her father. She'd already told Christine she was going. There was no way she could go back on it, though at the door with her bag on her back and her friend begging Kate to tell her where he lived, Kate had stalled, wishing Christine would plead with her not to go.

Colin was laughing. The boy at the counter pulled his arm from his girlfriend. His body was obscured by the girl, whose hair was long and fair. She said something, and Colin shook his head before finally turning in Kate's direction. A man from the large table came up to the bar. Colin nodded at him and put up his finger to ask the man to hang on. He walked over to Kate. His face eased into a smile. "Hey, what are you doing here?"

"Didn't you get my email?" she asked. He said he hadn't, and she wanted to believe him, even with his pause.

"I can't go back home," she said. The customer was getting impatient.

"You've run away?" he asked, incredulous.

"Yeah," she said.

"Kate, come on. You can't do that."

"You did," she said.

"Hey," the customer shouted.

Colin stepped closer to her. "I lasted a night."

"Please." She tried to remain calm but it was hard not to cry.

"Okay." His hand was in his pocket. "Here."

"Can a man not get a drink around here?" the customer asked.

"Hang on a sec'," Colin said. The key was before her. "Go on. I'll be there as soon as I can," Colin told her.

Night fell around Nicholas, but there would be no driving around the streets this time, no fruitless searches for Kate. Nicholas had to cling to Ina to keep himself steady; without her, he would probably be flying out the front door. He laughed when she asked when he last slept, and said he had no idea. Ina led him into the front room, where they lay side by side on the bed and spoke in whispers. The blinds were open to let in the light from the street, and it illuminated their bodies. He smelled rain off Ina. Her face was half hidden in shadow.

"All you have to do is phone St. John's. Finding

Kathleen is the easy part; the hard part is getting Kate to come home."

Nicholas could imagine Kathleen sitting in front of the large windows of the hospital visiting room, the sun causing a halo over her red hair. Her face would be devoid of expression, as it had been the last time he'd seen her. It hit him then. He jumped up. A horn blasted from outside. "I know how to bring Kate back."

Ina was sitting up. "What are you talking about?"

He said, "Kate doesn't know who she's looking for."

"What? Wait," Ina said. "Where are you going?"

Nicholas said, "I need Christine to email Kate."

The email was comprised of two sentences. There was no "How are you?" or "When will you be home?" Christine didn't think Kate would be interested. She wrote, *Did you notice your Mom's hands? Email me when you see what I mean.* She signed it *Christine.* The wording was her idea. "Kate won't come home if you tell her she has to," she'd told Nicholas.

She had been sleeping when Nicholas and Ina arrived at the apartment. Helen had let them in. She was quieter than earlier and not inclined to meet their eyes. Nicholas thought she was feeling for Christine now, for everything Kate had done, and he couldn't blame her. He read the email and was about to ask how Kate could notice her mother's hands when he thought of the photos in her room. Minutes later, he and Ina stood before the empty frames. They knew Kate had left the frames on purpose, to tell them she was choosing her mother over their silence.

Ina stayed with him that night. Neither could sleep. Once it started getting bright she went home to shower. At one point, Nicholas found himself standing in the middle of the living room, not knowing how long it had been since he'd risen from the armchair, where he had sat most of the night, barely illuminated by the lamp by the door. When Christine appeared, he knew by her face that there was still no news.

"I'm sorry," she said.

It was Ina's idea to print missing posters and send Kate's photo into local news channels. Above a photo of Kate were the words, "Missing Since 08/30/2013". Underneath her image was a description of her, and what she had been wearing when she left Christine. They wrote Nicholas's number and the number of the Somerville Police Department and spent hours driving around Somerville and Cambridge, putting the posters on telephone poles and inside train stations.

Looking at the posters made Nicholas feel small and useless. Nothing compared to the helplessness that made him alternate from wanting to tear his house apart or sit frozen, staring at the door, waiting for his daughter to walk in. He forced himself to stay calm, but he was jumpy. Any noise would make him whirl around, hoping to see his daughter. And each time his phone rang, his heart seized, and he found it difficult to breathe. After they'd returned from putting up the posters, while he made tea and Ina stood at the front door, he received his first call of the day. Ina was at the kitchen door in seconds. Her face fell when she heard him say, "No, I'm not coming in today...."

One woman phoned to say she thought she'd seen Kate on the Orange Line the previous day, and there were other callers whose information was just as opaque, and merely added to his helplessness. He gave the police the details.

On Wednesday, he called the school and talked to the principal. He knew he probably should have gone in person, but he couldn't have handled walking into that school and having to face their sympathy and suspicion. The principal was soft-spoken. She told him she was sorry and asked him to let her know as soon as he heard anything.

After her first morning visit, Christine started to phone rather than visit. It was easier, Nicholas imagined, than appearing at the door and feeling the strain. Plus, she might have realized that her presence made his hurt rawer. To see Christine with a schoolbag over her back brought home how young Kate was. She should have been walking to school with her, giggling about teenage things, instead of being in a foreign place, where Nicholas imagined that, despite her independence, she was feeling very alone. He knew there was no point in searching the streets. He needed to be home for her, yet he refused to watch the news. Ina kept it on in the background with the volume low. The local channels showed her photo, and Nicholas had to go outside to sit on the porch the first time he saw her peering out at him. They'd sent in school photographs of her staring out with a detached smile. Her blue eyes were distant, as if gazing at something beyond the camera, and Nicholas had the idea that they had given the public permission to take hold of his daughter. Strangers on the street could stop her now. He could picture Kate seeing herself on the screen and her anger with them for betraying her, because no matter how fearful he was, he couldn't think she was in any harm. His restlessness, his inability to eat and sleep, his need to have Ina, to be able to squeeze her hand, to have her touch his back in a soft gesture of reassurance had to be due only to Kate's absence.

She's okay. She'll be home soon. These were his silent mantras and the prayers he repeated over and over in his head to stop any other dark thoughts from defeating him. The thought of Kate being hurt would have destroyed him.

He saw the fear in Ina's eyes. The dark brown had turned soft with concern, and she seemed to have aged in the last few days, with the folding in of shoulders and tired lines around her mouth. He could not reassure her and say, "She's going to be okay." Because by voicing this, he would voice the possibility that she might not be. Sometimes, he would feel Ina looking at him and see the pleading in her eyes to talk about Kate, to say something, and he would go to her and hold her, to avoid that gaze that must have mirrored his own. He hadn't looked at his reflection since the first morning.

He didn't care about shaving, but on the fourth day, Ina took his hand and brought him to the kitchen. She told him to sit on the hard chair. She put a towel around his shoulders before he realized what she was planning to do. With a basin of hot water, she shaved his face, softly lathering the skin with the shaving foam and then skimming steadily with the razor. Her hands were soft and sure. The ease in Ina's face told him that in those few moments of concentration she managed to forget Kate. But, once she had dried his face, she left the room quickly. He followed to see her go outside, where she stood on the porch with her arms wrapped around herself and her head down, and Nicholas went back to the kitchen to empty the basin and hide all evidence of their domesticity. They didn't deserve such small moments of forgetting. Christine phoned every morning. "Maybe she has no internet access," she said to Nicholas, but they knew that Colin had a computer. This was the way he'd managed to infiltrate their lives.

"Why isn't she getting in touch?" Ina asked. There was no answer. It had been four days since the email. Ina had stopped going home after the first day. She said she couldn't bear to be alone and, if Kate needed her, she'd call her cell. As usual, Christine phoned before bed. Nicholas knew what she would say the moment he answered; her pause said enough. Still she said, "Maybe tomorrow," and he said, Yes, maybe, though tomorrow seemed so far away.

They had the night to go through first. He and Ina would sleep some, holding onto each other, and then one of them would wake with a start and wake the other, and that would be the beginning of their nighttime vigil. They would lie in the dark for a while, but eventually their restlessness would pull them up. Then they would drink tea in the kitchen, until their tired bodies needed the softer seats of the living room, where they would doze as the sun came up and another day started. Ina had talked about going back to work, and she'd told Nicholas he should too, but there was no confidence in her voice and he had not answered.

"You sleep," Nicholas told Ina on the fifth night. "We can take turns."

"Promise you'll wake me in three hours," Ina said, and Nicholas realized how tired she was. Nicholas promised and kissed her cheek. There had been no touching, bar the gentle assurances during the day and their arms wrapping around each other at night, yet he felt she'd managed to reach inside him. He turned on the light in the kitchen, where the window showed his faceless reflection, and made tea. He would not wake Ina, he thought.

At 3 a.m., when Nicholas was dozing on his chair, his phone rang. A faraway siren was reaching through the quiet streets. The phone read *Unknown caller*. Nicholas answered. "Hello?"

A man said, "I didn't know what age she was."

Nicholas jumped up. "Who is this?" he asked. He didn't know how he'd managed to talk through the dread. *Was*, the man had said. "I didn't know what age she *was*." The breathing on the other side was frantic.

"She told me she was eighteen."

Was again, and this time Nicholas pleaded, "Who is this? Where is my daughter?"

"If I tell you, you've got to promise not to press charges. I swear to God I didn't know."

Nicholas was crying when he asked if his daughter was okay. The man's mania scared him. He sounded drunk

"She's fine. She won't leave. I wanted her to go to you," the man said.

"Tell me where she is," Nicholas said.

"Not until you promise there'll be no police."

Nicholas didn't notice Ina until she touched his arm. Her eyes were wide and as frantic as the man's voice. Her hand went to her mouth when Nicholas promised no police and begged to know where his daughter was. "She's in 30 River Street, Hyde Park," he said and hung up.

Nicholas managed to tell Ina, "Kate's in Hyde Park." He rose from his seat and had to help Ina stand. In the car, he started the engine before he realized he didn't know where to drive. It was difficult to remember how to get to 93 South, never mind where to go after. He wrote the address into the GPS and the computerized voice rose from the silence.

Nicholas would remember the haunting streets of Somerville and the highway with its stray cars that brought the notion that the drivers were complicit in teenage runaways because they had to have been mindful of the terror in the car they passed and yet they carried on. Nicholas would dream of the journey often, and when he dreamt of this night, he would wake gasping for air. He would reach for Ina, needing her more than he did while they were moving towards Kate, because he had to survive those nightmares. But while he was living it, he did not think of surviving. If something happened to his daughter, it would be the end of him too. He would stop living. It couldn't be any other way. So, he could not reach for Ina's hand, though he smelled her fear

He knew he smelled the same, that the thick, heavy atmosphere of the car was from their bodies.

He followed the directions off the highway and merged onto Granite Ave.

Turn left onto Milton St. It was so quiet — no cars, no pedestrians — a scene from a horror movie. These thoughts came to his head and he didn't know how to stop them. *Turn left onto Adams St.* He wanted to know what Ina was thinking. But he couldn't look at her, never mind speak. *Continue onto Washington St.*

Turn left onto River St. Your destination is on the right.

He would never understand why they paused in their seats. After all the time waiting for Kate, their restless hours pacing, they did not jump to her straight away. He was numb during those seconds, until he saw a figure receding in his review mirror, and he thought, *Kate*, and felt as if he'd just woken.

He had the door open, while Ina grew flustered trying to open hers.

Nicholas was out of the car looking for that man and seeing nothing but that emptiness again, those lonely streets, and a light in the house before him. The front door was open. The path was narrow, bordered by overgrown weeds. The house was a blue two-story building. Ina was beside him. Her hand grazed his, but found nothing to hold. He was moving towards the light the man had run from. He had been standing, waiting for them to arrive, and then he'd run away and left the door open, inviting them in. There were never such burdened steps. That short journey to the door took so long. Ina was behind him when he stepped into the hall. The building had two apartments. A ground floor door was open. He pushed it in to see Kate curled up on the bed.

She was watching them with a wariness that made the shabbiness of the room seem harsher. Nicholas wanted to pull her out of there, but he had to go slow. He sat beside her, and when he touched her hand, she started to cry. He didn't know what she was crying for and he was scared that it was the man's departure, because, though she let him hold her, there was no tension, no clinging hands of a person who had prayed to be found.

She lay against his chest. The computer was

off. He wondered if she had checked her mail, or if she had resisted the temptation, seeing it as a means to lure her back. There was a counter separating the kitchen and bedroom. He saw no chairs. On the surface, an opened package of bread leaned downwards. He always asked Kate to close the bread tightly, otherwise the slices would harden. She never complied; such a simple thing that showed her age. How could that man not see that she was barely fourteen with one look at her face?

Ina's hand was on Kate's head, roaming her scalp and neck, as if she were blind and this was the only way she could be sure of Kate's presence. They had not said anything. Nicholas wanted to take pleasure in his daughter's safety, to bring her home and manage to sleep through the night, but he didn't think it would be so easy. This room would haunt him, as would the possibility of Kate's return to this house. He sensed her reluctance to leave, and knew she wanted to believe in Colin's love. It would be too hard to admit that it was a lie.

Nicholas knew all this, but it didn't make it any easier when she pulled away and asked, "Where's Colin?"

"Kate," Ina said.

"Where did he go?" she asked again. She

scrambled off the bed. She was wearing a Boston Bruins t-shirt that went down to her knees.

"What happened to your cheek?" Ina asked, and Nicholas couldn't get over her strength. She was managing to look past this place and Kate's bare legs. Nicholas saw Kate touch her cheek and the flash of recognition from the tender skin and he realized she'd been hit. The bruise under her eye had turned a yellow color, and it was all he could do not to pull her to him, or tear the place asunder. The dread and worry he'd been feeling had turned into a restless rage that he had to control. It would be so easy to push Kate further from him. She must have seen something on his face though, because her hand had dropped, and she was staring at him defiant.

"It wasn't his fault. I lied about my age. He thought I was eighteen until he found my ID. He was scared for the two of us." Her voice was rising, but he heard the tremble and how close she was to breaking down. "It wasn't about him, it was about US!"

She shouted the word us, although her adamancy had lessened with, "He loves me."

"No," Nicholas said. Kate glared at him, but her ferocity had dimmed from being in this place.

She said, "What would you know about it?" She put her arms around her waist, as if suddenly conscious of her clothing.

"Mom didn't have a wedding ring." Kate's voice left Nicholas speechless. She sounded old and hurt. "You never married her."

"You knew that," Nicholas said. She had studied the photos enough, and besides, he'd never pretended otherwise.

"I don't know if I did," she replied. After a moment she said, "What's her full name? It's not Giovanni, is it?"

"I'll tell you when you come home," he said.

"Why should I believe you?" Kate asked.

"Because I don't want you to run away again, and you will if we don't bring you to her." Kate's face fell. Ina was beside her, though Kate didn't seem to notice. She was trying hard not to cry.

"Where is she?" Kate asked. Above them, there was a thump on the floor and a shuffle of steps.

"We need to leave," Ina said.

"Where is she?" Kate repeated.

Nicholas said, "I won't tell you here."

"Please, Kate," Ina said. "We will bring you to her, I promise." The footsteps stopped, as if the upstairs neighbor was struck by the lingering quiet as Kate watched Ina pick up the jeans that had been tossed at the end of the bed.

"You know where she is." Her voice tore at Nicholas's heart.

It must have been the same for Ina, but she didn't

show it. Her face stayed neutral as she handed Kate the jeans. "If you want to see her, you need to go now," Ina said.

Kate seemed reluctant to take her clothing, as if the jeans were evidence of what went on here, and not the crumpled sheets, her bruised skin, and the musty scent. But finally, she took them and dressed. With shoes and socks on, she retrieved her hair brush from under the bed. Her clothes were folded on the floor. She put them in her bag. The toilet flushed upstairs and Nicholas heard a cough. The shuffling of feet must have followed, but all he was aware of was Kate leaving the room, and the anxiety turning his stomach once she was out of sight.

Kate was standing at the end of the driveway. Her features were soft in the light. She was not gone, like the sickness that Nicholas would continue to experience whenever Kate was out of view. He felt as if she were a baby again, when the world had suddenly become filled with dangers and disaster. Only he couldn't save her from Kathleen.

The journey home was quiet. Morning had started to lighten the blackness to a bleak grey. Ina's shoulders were slumped. She threw glances towards Nicholas, but he knew she was unable to say anything. Nicholas kept his eyes ahead, and hardly noticed if a car passed until its noise reached his ears. Kate had her bag on her knees, her chin rested on it. Nicholas felt as if the backseat were packed. There was more than one slight girl. There were all those other Kates: the five-year-old who had nearly died, the nine-year-old who had started to fight back, the suspicious teenager, and Kate, the woman, was there, too. She had started to rise in a shabby room in Hyde Park, and Nicholas was frightened that the meeting with her mother would bring that woman into focus and define her.

On Summer Street, the neighboring houses were coming alive. Lights were turned on and shadows moved behind windows. In the living room, Kate asked, "Where is she?" There was nothing Nicholas could do now, but give her the name of St. John's State Hospital. The fall of Kate's face was instant. He saw the surprise in her parted lips. She said, "A hospital?"

"Yes," Ina said, because Nicholas hadn't been able to answer. Hurt had dimmed Kate's eyes, which were beyond crying. He saw the new paleness of her skin.

"Is she a patient?" Kate's voice came out as a whisper.

Nicholas nodded. He waited for her to ask her mother's name. He would tell her. There could be no more holding back, even if it meant losing her. There would be no reason for Kate to stay once she knew everything. Maybe this was why she chose not to probe, because she didn't have the energy to leave that night and trek the miles to Hyde Park. But, more than likely, the word *hospital* was all she could bear. She didn't ask why Kathleen was there or what had happened. There were too many questions to start now. She walked past them to her room and her distance stretched in miles. Once her door closed, Ina said, "I should leave."

Nicholas said, "No, Ina. No more leaving."

If Kate was surprised to see Ina at the kitchen table early the next morning, she didn't show it. Nicholas couldn't remember a time when Ina had had breakfast with them, but Kate had other things on her mind. She stood at the door. Her red hair was tied back in a ponytail and her eyes were tired. She looked as if she hadn't slept at all.

"What's my mother's name?" she asked. Nicholas had the impression that she wasn't seeing the two people before her. All she saw now was her mother's face. There was more than a little fear in her voice.

"Her name's Kathleen Lehanne," Nicholas said. Kate nodded.

"Do you want to know why she's in hospital?" Nicholas asked.

"Not from you," she told him.

She had a right to say that after all these years, but it still hurt. It took a few moments before he said, "We'll need to phone the hospital and arrange a visit."

Kate glanced at his phone laying on the table beside Nicholas's plate of eggs, and asked, "Can I have my phone back?"

Earlier, when Nicholas had woken with the sound of the birds, he'd slipped out of bed to take Kate's phone out of his bureau. He'd turned it on and checked if Colin had called. He wanted to go to the police, but Kate would never make a statement against him, and he'd achieve nothing. The previous night, Nicholas had thought of Colin as the "man who'd waited." He'd been something distant, because Nicholas had to put all his effort on his daughter. Now, he thought of him as Colin. He saw his face, the features as correct as memory would allow, and he knew he'd take that drive to Hyde Park again. There was no way he could let Colin hide.

"Kate, are you hungry?" Ina said. Kate looked up from the phone in her hand. She seemed confused and lost. She needed to sleep and ease back into her normal life, to give herself time to adjust after Colin, but she couldn't take that time. It was obvious there would be no rest until she finally came face to face with her mother. When Nicholas offered to make the call for her and arrange a meeting, Kate said she had to do it. He found the number in the phone book. At one time, he'd known it by heart, but that was a long time ago, and he'd done his best to forget. Kate stood at the living room window and dialed. Ina came as far as the kitchen door; neither she nor Nicholas were acknowledged by Kate, though they knew she didn't want to be alone.

"I'd like to talk to Kathleen Lehanne," she said. The strain in her voice was audible, making it low and shaky. After a pause she said, "Her daughter, Kate Giovanni."

Nicholas and Ina exchange worried glances. Kate gave her phone number, hung up, and turned around to say that the woman she spoke to would ask Kathleen's doctor to phone her. While they waited, Nicholas cooked her eggs and toast, which she hardly touched. She kept glancing at her phone that lay on the table. Nicholas's stomach was turning at the idea of Stein speaking to his daughter.

Ina's hand was on his back. "Are you okay?" she asked. "You've been washing the same dish for ten minutes."

He managed to let the plate go. The wait was shocking. Christine's phone call late in the morning brought some respite. Nicholas had phoned her before Kate rose from bed and told her the news of Kate's return. She sounded relieved but subdued, too.

"Will you talk to her?" Nicholas had asked and she'd said she didn't know, but around ten, she reached out to her friend, and Kate eased in those few moments of phone conversation.

The doctor phoned in the early afternoon. Kate was pacing around the living room when her phone rang. She said hello and then, "Yes, I do," before frowning and saying, "I'm her daughter.

"Okay," she said. She brought the phone to Nicholas in the kitchen. "He wants to talk to you." It was good to see the scowl on his daughter's face. It made her seem less vulnerable.

"Hello," Nicholas said.

"I'm Doctor Boden. I've been Kathleen's doctor for three years. I need to be sure you are aware of your daughter's intentions." The voice was deep. There had been no pause before his greeting and inquiry. Nicholas thought he might have felt relief with not having to deal with Stein, but there was no place for that now.

"Yes," Nicholas said. "I'm aware."

"Does she know what happened?" Boden asked.

Nicholas glanced at his daughter. "Not in detail."

On the other end of the line, Nicholas could hear a door slamming and another voice. "Just a minute," Boden said. Nicholas was sitting at the kitchen table.

"Sorry about that," Boden said. "I'm not sure if it's a good idea; Kathleen has never talked about her daughter. I don't think the meeting will be good for Kate."

"I know," Nicholas said. "But Kate wants to see her mother."

Boden sighed. "I'll have to ask Kathleen if she's willing to see her."

Nicholas looked at Kate, who was staring at him from the door with her arms wrapped around herself. Boden must have said the same thing to her. "I'm her daughter," she'd told him, while Nicholas asked, "Do you think she will?"

"I really don't know," Boden said. "But I'll let you know soon."

"What did he say?" Kate asked, after Nicholas handed back her phone. It was hard to meet his daughter's gaze and see the sadness in her eyes that must have been always there, only she'd kept it back with her anger. He wondered what she would have been like, had her mother been present all her life, if this sorrow he was seeing would have been at the forefront.

"He'll let us know."

Kate didn't ask why her mother would refuse to see her, or why the doctor sounded so unsure, but the questions was written all over her. It took a moment for her to retreat and when she did, the small space of the kitchen bore on Nicholas. Ina had gone home to freshen up and do some work, and he wished she was there now, a glance or a touch from her would have eased him a little. He was still sitting by the table a half hour later when his phone rang. "Kathleen has agreed to see her." There was surprise in the doctor's voice. "Can she come tomorrow?"

Nicholas's stomach turned. "Yes, we can make it tomorrow. What time?"

"Mornings are best." Nicholas didn't want to think of what that meant. "Say, 9:30."

When Nicholas told Kate about her appointment, she sat on the couch and looked as if she might be sick. "Are you okay?" Ina asked. After a while, she nodded, the gesture made her look like a rag doll. Nicholas wondered how she would get through the next hours. Luckily, Christine arrived after school. She smiled at Nicholas, but there was hesitation on her journey to Kate's bedroom. Kate opened the door, and Nicholas saw the pale hand that reached out for her friend.

Christine came out hours later and closed the door behind her. Nicholas was stirring white sauce for lasagna. "She's really nervous," Christine said. He was glad Ina wasn't there to hear Christine ask, "Is it true what Manuel said? Did her mother hurt her?"

With Ina present, he wouldn't have been able to counter with, "Do you think she remembers?"

Christine took in what he said, and he could see

the sorrow in the drop of her mouth. She said, "I don't know, but I thought she'd be more excited to see her mom."

Nicholas turned down the heat under the saucepan. The wooden spoon left a mess on the cooker. He said, "Her mother is in a state psychiatric hospital. I wouldn't call it exciting." He started to grate cheese into the sauce.

Christine told him, "I'm going to stay with her tonight. And she wants me to go tomorrow."

He'd been expecting this, and so had Ina. They both agreed that he had to say no. When he told Christine, she said, "What if she decides to run away again? You know what she's like when she's angry."

The front door opened. Ina said hello. He was facing Christine now. Cheese bits fell from the grater to the floor. He said, "If she wants to do this, it has to be with me."

Nicholas woke early with Ina asleep beside him. Each morning he woke to her in his bed felt like the first. There was an element of surprise and disbelief that led him to stay still and listen to her soft breathing. He would have to let that settle into the bottom of his stomach before being able to slip away. The room was still dark. A grey stream of light slipped in through the gap in the curtain.

He'd hardly slept from the thought of Kathleen in the hospital, waiting for her daughter. Kate would want to see her alone, and it hurt him to think of how vulnerable she would feel when she gave her jacket and possessions to security before walking the corridor with its white walls and resounding footsteps, that led to the visitor's room, where Nicholas had sat so many years ago. The room had tables and chairs for visitors and patients to sit across from each other, and he remembered the two large windows that looked upon the car park, and how much he'd wanted to be on the other side of them. He was sure Kate would pause at the door of that room. Without her father, she would show her nervousness and look like the child she was. In the car, she probably wouldn't talk to him. She would fold up in her seat and look out the window and refuse to say how scared she was or ask any questions of him, but at the visitor's door she would be a softer version of herself. He imagined that her mother would watch Kate's approach and be struck by her red hair and pale face. Kathleen would probably be frozen in the chair with the surprise of seeing her daughter as a near woman with her graceful walk and shy air.

Kathleen had not spoken to anyone about what had happened. Her doctor said it would be hard on her and Nicholas prayed regret had kept her silent all these years. He prayed that she'd thought about her daughter with sorrow, because soon Kate would look into the grey eyes of her mother, and he hoped she'd see some warmth. What did Kathleen look like now? Nicholas imagined she'd gotten more solid. She would have filled out through the years. Her once slim body would have weight holding it down, and her cheeks would be fuller. Her hair would lack its luster, though it would be easy to see that she'd once been beautiful. She'd see that Kate's blue eyes hadn't darkened to match her father's as they'd once expected, and that her daughter's gaze was frightened and unsure. For a long time, the two of them would look at each other in silence. Their gaze would be like the fingers of children taking in every detail, and Kate's eyes would fall on her mother's sturdy hands that lay on the table, the fingers now thicker and unadorned, the nails bitten, but clean, and the trembling would start inside Kate. She wouldn't be able to lift her gaze until her mother slid her hands out of view and laid them on her knees.

In the kitchen, Nicholas filled the kettle, the light bright above his head. It was not yet light outside. Quietness hung on the street and made every sound he produced seem too loud. Who would speak first? He was sure it would be Kate. Her trembling and fear would irritate her and make her sit straighter, though it would be hard to look her mother in the eye.

"Why are you here?" Kate would ask.

Kathleen would pull back. "Didn't he tell you?" Kate would shake her head and see the onslaught of the truth in her mother's eyes.

"I had a breakdown because your father took my pills. First, he stopped giving them to me, and then he took them." So many questions would flow then. *What pills?* Kate might ask, and Kathleen would tell her about the medication that stopped her delusions.

"What delusions?" Kathleen wouldn't answer this. She'd shake her head and explain that Nicholas took the medication because he wanted her to go.

Kate would want to argue against the fear she was feeling. She might have an urge to flee or she might feel a sad resignation, just as she used to as a child when she was told to go to her room, but Kate would resist and rebel. She would sound accusatory when she said, "He could have told you to leave."

"I had nowhere to go," Kathleen would tell her. Her grey eyes would stay fixed on her daughter, and the sorrow on her mother's face would keep Kate rooted to the spot.

He imagined Kathleen's voice shaking when she said, "He told me to do it. He shouted at me, 'Go on, do it then, if that's what you want,' and all of a sudden, I couldn't see you."

There might be a pause then, a moment where Kate couldn't breathe, as if memory were working its way through, and she would notice the lines around her mother's eyes and across her forehead, as well as the dryness of her cheeks. "I did what he said and then he hit me," Kathleen would say.

Nicholas heard his daughter rising, and loosened his grip on the mug. He remembered Kathleen waiting for him that morning with the pillow in her hand. On his way to Kate's room, she'd pulled at him, begging him to listen, telling him that he couldn't leave her alone with Kate. She said she'd stood for hours over Kate's bed, that she saw her mother inside Kate. Her mother, who had let Kathleen down again and again, had been on the bed, and Kathleen had stood over the form, and she'd hated it. She'd done this before. It was not the first morning he'd come back to her angry and upset, but this time he'd pushed Kathleen from him, and she'd stumbled by Kate. His decision had been quick, a slip in time that he fell through and never recovered from.

He'd said, "Go on, do it, if that's what you want. Do it." He'd shouted, and he'd seen the pillow lower before he screamed.

Nine years later and soon Kate would walk into the visitor's room and sit before her mother with her thickening skin and sad grey eyes. He decided her mother would be shaky and unsure. Years ago, he'd grabbed her hand at that visitor's table and said, "You hurt her. It was your fault," and the terror in Kathleen's eyes showed she believed it.

So now, she would wait for Kate to ask what happened and she'd shake her head and say, "I didn't mean to hurt you."

The silence would come between them, not strained or heavy with the want of things to say, but sad and disillusioned. After a time, Kathleen might tell a story about one of the patients in the hospital, because she never liked sitting in silence. Kate would sit back and listen, and on the journey home she might relay this tale to Nicholas. There would have to be more ease between them once Kate wasn't overshadowed by her mother. To think otherwise scared Nicholas too much. He heard Kate's slow saunter to the bathroom, and he wondered after the visit what would she tell him first.

Acknowledgments

Over the years I had so much help with this book, it was tempting not to write an acknowledgment, but that would mean not thanking Christy for sitting me down after reading one of the many drafts and asking me, "What is this book about? What do you want to say?"

A question which has helped everything I've written since.

To my classmates and teachers in Emerson who helped me realize how this story needed to start.

To Kate-who has always believed in my writing and was so convinced I should go to Emerson, she made me apply.

To Sharon and Bernie, Sonya, who read the draft when it was 'Distance Between Lovers."

To Ryan, who reads everything and always has a way to make my stories better.

To Kim, who has eyes like a hawk and the patience of a saint.

My mother and sisters for listening to me talk about writing and not locking me out of the house.

My in-laws here for their unerring encouragement — Davor and Noelia, and Gloria, my number one supporter.

Of course, Matias, my partner in crime, who knows how to make me laugh when I need it, and our daughters Leyla, Amelie, and Cameron, for keeping me on toes.

To my brother William, who left us twenty years ago, but not without teaching me that it's possible to follow your dream.

And Marc and Donna for saying yes and putting up with my excitement and many emails.

Thank you!

More Novels from Fomite

Writing a review on Amazon, Good Reads, Shelfari, Library Thing or other social media sites for readers will help the progress of independent publishing. To submit a review, go to the book page on any of the sites and follow the links for reviews. Books from independent presses rely on reader-to-reader communications.

For more information or to order any of our books, visit:
http://www.fomitepress.com/our-books.html